MW01221654

Shadow's End
Light and Shadow, Book III

By Moira Katson

Cover art by Zezhou Chen

Discover other books by Moira Katson:

The Light & Shadow Trilogy:
Book I: Shadowborn
Book II: Shadowforged

The Yeshuhain Chronicles:
Mahalia
Inheritance
Origins

For drabbles, sneak peaks of upcoming
works, and more, visit Moira's website!

http://moiraktaston.com

Thank you to my friends and family,
whose support, encouragement, and feedback
have helped me to take this leap!

Cast of Characters

The Duke's Household

Catwin – servant to the Duke, Miriel's Shadow
Donnett – a member Palace Guard, who fought with
      the Duke at the Battle of Voltur
Eral Celys – Duke of Voltur
Emmeline DeVere – younger sister of the Duke,
      mother of Miriel
Miriel DeVere – niece of the Duke, daughter of
      Emmeline and Roger DeVere
Temar – servant to the Duke, the Duke's Shadow
Roger DeVere – father of Miriel (*deceased*)
Roine – a healing woman, foster mother to Catwin

Members of the Royal Family: Heddred

Anne Warden Conradine – sister of Henry, aunt of
      Garad; Duchess of Everry
Arman Dulgurokov – brother of Isra
Cintia Conradine – daughter of Anne and Gerald
      Conradine
Elizabeth Warden de la Marque – cousin of Henry,
      mother of Marie
Henry Warden– father of Garad, former King of
      Heddred (*deceased*)
Garad Warden – former King of Heddred (*deceased*)
Gerald Conradine – husband of Anne; Duke of Everry
Guy de la Marque – husband of Elizabeth Warden,
      father of Marie; Royal Guardian to Garad
Marie de la Marque Conradine – wife of Wilhelm;
      Queen of Heddred
Isra Dulgurokov Warden – mother to Garad, widow of
      Henry; the former Dowager Queen
Wilhelm Conradine – King of Heddred

William Warden – former King of Heddred, Garad's
uncle, Henry's older brother (*deceased*)

MEMBERS OF THE ROYAL FAMILY: ISMIR

Dragan Kraal – brother of Dusan, father of Kasimir
(*deceased*)
Dusan Kraal – King of Ismir
Jovana Vesely Kraal - Queen of Ismir
Kasimir Kraal – nephew to Dusan
Marjeta Kraal Jelinek – daughter of Dusan and Jovana
Pavle Kraal – younger brother of Kasimir
Vaclav Kraal – son of Dusan and Jovana (*deceased*)

HEDDRIAN PEERAGE

Edward DeVere – courtier; Duke of Derrion
Efan of Lapland - courtier
Elias Nilson – son to Piter; betrothed to Evelyn
DeVere
Elizabeth Cessor – daughter of Henry and Mary
Cessor
Evelyn DeVere – daughter of Edward, betrothed to
Elias Nilson
Henri Nilson – brother of Piter
Henry Cessor – courtier, father of Elizabeth
Henry DeVere – courtier, younger brother to Edward
Linnea Torstensson – a young maiden at Court;
daughter of Nils
Maeve d'Orleans – a young maiden at Court
Piter Nilson – Earl of Mavol
Roger DeVere – father of Miriel DeVere (*deceased*)

THE REBELLION

Aron – a servant of the Merchant; member of the rebellion

The High Priest (Jacces) – head of the Church in Heddred; leader of a populist rebellion in the Norstrung Provinces

Jeram – a member of the rebellion

The Merchant – a member of the rebellion

Chapter 1

On the first night, wrapped in our warmest furs and still shivering violently against the cold winds of the plains, Miriel and I confronted the fact that there was no going back. We had not stopped for hours, desperate to get as far as possible before our guards knew that we had gone. They would follow us—they would have to, they would be desperate to find us before the Duke ever found out that we had slipped through their fingers. Whether we wanted to go to Penekket or not was of no concern to them, and I had no illusions about my skills at combat: if it came to a fight between me and a score of guardsmen, they would likely win. So we pushed the horses as far as they would go and then sought shelter in a stand of trees, vainly listening for the sound of pursuit even as the howl of the wind blocked out any noise but itself.

"Catwin, do you know how to get to the Norstrung Provinces?" Miriel asked, finally, after we had sat in silence for an hour or so. For some reason, the question struck me as incredibly funny, and I laughed so hard, and for so long, that I could not catch my breath. When I looked up, I saw that Miriel was laughing, too, stifling her much-practiced giggle behind a perfectly manicured hand, and holding her side as she shook with mirth. We laughed in disbelief at our own recklessness until at last we had exhausted ourselves, and then Miriel leaned back against a tree and asked simply,

"What have we done?"

The last vestiges of humor disappeared at once. I looked at her and saw her not as she was to me—ally, friend—but as she was to the world: the betrothed of the last King, a young woman of uncertain birth, wearing a priceless gown and cloak and sitting in the middle of a field on an early spring night. A runaway. A woman who could be everything if she chose to work her magic on the new king, or nothing at all if her uncle wished to punish her for her actions.

"We ran away," I said wonderingly. *We ran away.* I felt the shape of the words in my mouth and, oddly light-headed, wondered if this was a dream. For a moment, I drifted, until the realization that all of this was real slammed down, and I felt a wave of nausea and pure terror. I wondered, wildly, if there was any lie we could tell to go back to the warm, well-fed, half-safety of the palace and the Duke's patronage. I was ashamed of myself even for wondering, but I was terrified. I was taunted by my own mind, the little voice that said, mockingly, *you said you wanted this*.

And there was no going back. The nausea grew stronger, and from the look on Miriel's face, she had come to the same realization: this was nothing we could deny or explain away, it was an irrevocable breach with the Duke. We could not pretend that we had done this in his best interests. We had said that we did not want to lie and dissemble anymore, and here we were: honest at last. And filled with fear.

This was a terrible, terrible mistake.

"Oh, Gods," Miriel said, biting her lip. "We ran *away*." I only nodded, numbly, and she rubbed her face, then sighed and looked up, "So what do we do now?" The golden light of dawn gleamed in her hair and gilded her face, and I realized that it had been growing steadily lighter. Exhaustion counted for nothing; our rest was over.

"We keep riding," I said, and with the first decision, my confidence began to return. "We're not far out of Penekket, so we should start veering south now. We need to stay off the road. And you should change." I had procured a serving girl's spare gown for Miriel, but we had left so quickly that she has not yet changed. She was sitting on a pile of bracken, wrapped in her warm velvet cloak and wearing silk and jewels.

"We're still going south?" Miriel asked, wide-eyed. Even now, with no one to see us, she used her beautiful, practiced mannerisms. She had made her mask so well and so completely that she might never strip it all away. I could not have said how I felt about that—even in our disgust at how our masks and our true faces had become intertwined, at how the twisted darkness had crept into our very hearts, I would have lied if I said that Miriel's mask was not exquisitely beautiful. It was so finely crafted that it would almost be a shame to see it broken down and destroyed.

"We have to go," I said, judging by her fear that I should not say, *and there is no other choice*. I understood her fear; I could not revile it. "You're going to be a great leader for the rebellion, after all." I was trying to coax her away from her terror, and her face warmed at the thought, though she looked pained.

8

"I feel a fool," she admitted, as she took the rough, homespun dress from one of our packs and shook it out.

"Why?" I looked at her curiously, and she took a moment and chose her words carefully.

"Because I'm doing this for Wilhelm." She saw my face and hastened to explain. "I know it's useless. I don't hope to win him back." She swallowed and curled her hands into fists, so tightly the knuckles went white. "I shouldn't have to. He should have waited for me. I know I should be angry and forget him. But when I try to be angry, and cut him out of my heart, I...can't." She swallowed and blinked away tears. "I think: I told him that he must do whatever he could, risk everything he had, for the rebellion. I told him I'd do the same. And so even if I think he's betrayed me...this is to keep faith with him. Even if he's turned from me, I have to believe that he's still true to this, or I won't survive. So I am true to it, as well."

I did not respond; I had no words to speak of hope, they would have choked me with jealousy. Miriel could still believe that Wilhelm kept true to their cause, and I...

If you meddle again, you will die. Bad luck to adore the man who had turned me into a Shadow, and worse luck that my love had not disappeared when he became an enemy. When I thought of him now, it was not only with hatred and fear and the sense of a coming fight—it was to wonder what his kisses might be like, it was to think of the body that I knew, after years of sparring, almost as well as my own. My heart betrayed me every day, and it was bitter indeed to have none of the comfort that Miriel took from her hope.

I had the thought, so overwhelming that bile came to my throat, that the prophecy had spoken of betrayal—and who could betray me in this world more completely than could Temar?

"Please tell me you don't think it's—what are you *doing*?" Miriel's voice rose to a shriek and she clapped her hands over her mouth. I held my braid out in my hand and shrugged. Distracted by my misery, I had not hesitated, only sawed the hair away with one of my daggers; I could feel the rest drifting, ragged, around my head like so much honey-colored silk.

"Better to seem like a girl and a boy than two girls," I said. "In case anyone sees us." I had been staring down at my hair, and now I looked up and my voice trailed off. "Gods be good," I whispered.

"What?" Miriel looked down at her dress, checking for stains.

"You look..." *Beautiful.* I should have known better than to expect that clothing alone could make Miriel less noteworthy. The rough cloth only set off her beauty all the more. In fine gowns and jewels, her looks were only a piece of a perfectly-polished puzzle, but now they were jarring. Her hair seemed darker, her eyes bluer. "Don't let anyone see you up close," I advised, trying not to let my envy show. But she saw it anyway, and smiled.

"Beauty hasn't done me any favors," she pointed out. "I'm not Queen, everyone hates me but you, and the man I love..." She swallowed. "And anyway, do you really think *you* can pass for a boy?"

"You'd be surprised," I said drily, thinking of the dozens who called me, "lad," or, "boy," every day, their eyes seeing no further than my britches and tabard, their gaze moving on before they saw the hint of curves under my clothes. I knew for a fact that no one had ever noticed me at all, for the Court was so mad for rumors of Miriel that if anyone had ever noticed me, it would have been all over that the Lady Miriel was accompanied by a girl dressed as a boy. But their eyes had only ever slid over me; another servant in livery. "Are you ready to go?"

"One moment." Miriel picked her way over the frozen ground and took my dagger. She pointed to the pile of bracken. "Sit."

"We don't have time."

"We have a moment." She stared at me until I sat, reluctantly, and then she took the locks of my hair in her hands and began to trim the chopped mess of it. Her hands were gentle as they cut it all to evenness, so that my hair no longer stuck out from my head but smoothed itself into a neat, golden cap. She ran her fingers through it, nodded decisively at her handiwork, and then she flipped the dagger about and presented it to me, haft first.

"Thank you," I said, awkwardly, rising up. I checked her saddle, and then lifted her up and guided my horse to a nearby boulder so that I could jump up myself. I surveyed the road in both directions, then sighted our direction from the sun. I wished that I had a map, but hoped that I could remember well enough where we were that we would not run into any major towns.

Then, seeing our way clear, I urged my horse out of the trees and led the way southeast, away from the road.

We rode until noon, checking over our shoulders frequently, but we never saw any signs of pursuit. We had gotten away cleanly, and I dared to hope that it had been fully light out before the guards realized that we were missing. I tried to tell myself that even if the men rode their horses to exhaustion, they would never think to veer off the road as we had—but still, I craned my neck to look behind us so much that I developed a crick in my neck.

As the first day drew to a close, we began to search for another copse of trees. Soon, we would sweep south into the fertile marshes and forests of south Heddred, but for now our horses were still picking their way over dormant, half-frozen fields, and cover was rare. At last, we found a few trees on the side of a hill, and I set about gathering wood for a fire. Donnett, whatever he thought of my chances in a fight, had taken it upon himself to teach me survival skills for living in the wild, remarking more than once that if my archery did not improve, I would need all the help I could get.

As I began to build up the fire, a thought came to me, unbidden: Roine, her hair plaited for sleep, her dark eyes worried, embracing me and telling me not to fear my exile. *I'll see you soon*, she had told me, and I had agreed. But Miriel and I had been so terrified of facing the Duke and the Court, so preoccupied with the fact of running away, that I had not thought of Roine until now.

"We have to tell Roine," I blurted out, and Miriel looked over at me. Regretfully, she shook her head, and when I opened my mouth to protest, she held up a hand to quell me.

"We can't," she explained gently. "There's no way to get a messenger to her. My uncle be having her watched. I closed my mouth and looked down, and Miriel added, "And who's the first one he'll question when he knows we've gone?"

"He'll question her?" My voice came out in a squeak. Panic closed in, and rational thought fled. I could not bear the thought of Roine being questioned for my sake. "We have to go back. Right now."

"No!" Miriel laid her hand on my arm. "We can't go back. And he won't be angry with her, what could she know? He's smart, Catwin, he'll see that. And she wasn't born yesterday, you know—she'll be alright."

I swallowed. Miriel was entirely correct. I could picture it clearly if I set my fear aside: the Duke, furious, and Roine sitting calmly, asserting in her low, clear voice that she did not know where I was, she had not known I was missing until the Duke came to speak to her. In the corner would be Temar, watching. I had to believe that he—and the Duke—would see the truth of Roine's words. And I must believe, or go mad, that the Duke would not think to use Roine against me.

Miriel was right: the best thing for Roine would be to know nothing. Ignorance would be her shield. No messages would arrive for Temar to intercept, no knowledge would show in her eyes. But she would think that I cared for her so little as to go without even telling her; she might not know how it had been, that we had made our plan in less than a day, and had no chance to get word to her. She would not even know that we were safe.

"You know…they may think we were kidnapped," I said, struck by the thought, and Miriel nodded.

"They won't think so for long, but it could buy us time before Temar figures out where we've gone." Her face twisted, as it always did when she spoke of Temar. Not for the first time, I wondered just why it was that they hated each other so instinctively, each of them ready to believe that the other might ruin everything. I was trying to find a joke to make about it when Miriel said,

"He's dangerous, Catwin. Have you ever thought…." Her voice trailed off as she saw my face. She knew this was not something I wanted to hear. As much as I could, I had resolutely refused to think of Temar in our months at the Winter Castle, and I did not want to think of him now. Worse, feeling disloyal, I admitted to myself that I did not want Miriel to speak badly of him. But we did not have that luxury.

"What?" I tried to keep my voice even, to speak reasonably instead of walk away. I knew I did not want to hear whatever she had to say. But Temar *was* our enemy; I never forgot it.

"I used to think he was just loyal to my uncle," Miriel said, "but I don't think so anymore."

"He's loyal. He'd kill either of us in a moment if the Duke wanted." That was the fact I always chose to remind myself of where Temar's loyalties lay, because it was the fact that hurt the most. I reminded myself of it whenever I could not help thinking of him—I hoped that the pain of it might break me free of my foolish infatuation.

"I think he's playing his own game," Miriel posited. She did not tell me to think on it. She knew that, now that the theory was out, I would not be able to rest until I found the truth. For a moment, I hated her for knowing me so well. "Good night," she said, knowing as well that I would not welcome any further conversation, and she wrapped her cloak around herself and curled up.

"Good night," I said moodily. I lay back and stared up at the star through the bare branches of the trees. Exhausted as I was, I knew it would be a very long time until I would be able to sleep.

Chapter 2

The next day dawned bright and clear, but clouds gathered as we rode, and the weeks that followed saw the onset of spring rains. Miriel and I rode hunched over, huddled into our cloaks, increasingly sodden and miserable. The ground thawed and cracked, and ice gave way to fields of mud that slowed our progress to a crawl. In any other season, the countryside would have been beautiful: verdant fields, or acres of ripened grain, the brilliant riot of fall colors or the sparse, white-on-white beauty of snow. But now it was mud—mud, and bare-branched trees, and rain.

There was no staying dry, and there was no staying warm. I spent an hour each evening constructing some sort of shelter for us and for the horses, and equally as much time trying to coax sodden branches into some sort of fire. I coddled Miriel as well as I could, but with the constant damp and persistent chill, both of us soon developed racking coughs, and the horses grew thinner, miserable, and prone to staring at me as if I was a willing architect of their misery.

Miriel, thankfully, showed no signs of fever, but I watched her as carefully as I might a priceless jewel that had been entrusted to my care. I had the sense in those few weeks, inexplicable, that all our fates hinged on Miriel. She was not only my friend, the other half of myself—she was something of infinite value to us all, and I was entrusted to keep her safe from harm, that she might fulfill her purpose. I wondered if this was only foolish fancy, the wanderings of a mind worn down with constant fear and endless cold, determined to make something worthwhile of my suffering, and I knew that there was no way to be sure; I only wondered, and wondered, as well, at the strength of my belief.

It was better for me to wonder on that than to let my mind wander, for the moment I relaxed my vigilance, my thoughts always came back to the puzzle of Temar. Miriel's words rang truer than I would have wished. I had known for years that Temar hated the Duke; and yet, undeniably, he served the Duke without question. I had thought it a puzzle, but never thought that he might be playing his own game. More the fool I, I thought now—how many clues were there, now that I thought to look back and search for answers? His words that I was meddling in things he said were too great for me to understand, meddling in his plans—not the Duke's plans, but Temar's own. There was the rift between him and the Duke, their tension over how Miriel and I might be best handled. There was the sadness behind Temar's eyes that never seemed to go away, and the words he had spoken to me when we had first met, when he had told me that he knew I was fate-touched, for those who were fate-touched called to each other.

Above all, there was the way that neither I, nor anyone else, seemed to know the first thing about Temar's life before he became a Shadow, and the way no one seemed to think to ask; even I had only wondered once or twice. He might well *be* a Shadow, in very truth; I wondered if he was even human, and a wave of melancholy swept through me at the thought. Who should know better than I what it meant to be a Shadow, to have come from nowhere? If I died, there would be no web of family to mourn me. I could count on my fingers the number of people who would ever miss me if I was gone. I had come from my village and then disappeared, like a breath of mist on a cold day, and I might as well have come from the land of faerie. I was a nothing child, an ill luck child, an ice child—completely forgotten by my kin.

When I thought such things, reminding myself of Temar and the Duke seemed almost a relief. I thought often on the night that I had come upon the two of them in the tunnels beneath the palace. They had spoken of a vow, Temar's vow, and of the Duke's choice of his Shadow. I remembered Temar's anger, and the Duke's humor at it. The Duke, who was so relentlessly driven, who trusted no one—no one, except Temar. The Duke saw Temar's anger, and even his hatred, and yet he still trusted the man. And the Duke was no fool.

I realized that if I suspected Temar of playing his own game, and not the Duke's, I must first know what vow they had made together—I must know what it was the Duke sought. I remembered his words well: *I wanted the power of the throne for myself, not that brat.* Was that it, truly? Was that all? Or were there layers beneath it, shifting? What did I know of the Duke's life? Shockingly little. For all I knew, he had emerged fully-formed from the skull of a God on the day before he had led the Heddrian army to victory.

Thinking of it was maddening, for I had the sense, when I did so, that I could see a vast pattern, beyond the Duke and Temar and Jacces and Garad, stretching across the whole of the earth and all of time. I had always scorned fate and those who believed in it, and yet here we were—and for some reason, when I thought on that, I did not think we were simply on a cold, muddy field. I had the sense that we were following a path, some direction we could not quite see. It was far beyond my knowledge as yet, but I knew some of the shape of it. Miriel and I were learning what questions to ask, that we might realize what it was we saw.

So, as Temar had taught me to do, I laid out my questions in my head: Who is Temar? What vow did he make to the Duke? How did the Duke choose him? Why has the Duke, who sought to guide the mistress of the king, never married and gotten children of his own to marry to the royals? The last was a question I had wondered and discarded, thinking it was too small, the whim of a rich man, nothing more. Now I wondered, and kept the question close. Nothing was irrelevant now. To understand Temar, I knew that I must first understand the Duke.

"What do you know of your uncle's life before he became...well, the Duke?" I asked Miriel one night. She was shivering, wrapped in a blanket and looking at her piece of bread and dried meat as if she would rather not eat it. She might be free of illness, but the journey had been hard on her: she was thinner, the gown hanging loose and her cheekbones standing out. Her eyes seemed overlarge in her pale face as she frowned, trying to remember.

"You mean before the war? Not very much. My mother once said that he had no right to reproach her for bringing shame to the family, for he had been no good to them, either. She said that when they had needed him, he had been gone. But she wouldn't explain it, and no one else would speak of it." She shrugged. "You know how Voltur was." I nodded; I did know. The guardsmen of Voltur worshipped the Duke, and everyone else was plainly terrified of him; even the Lady's sullen dislike did not overcome her fear. No one would have told a story that he did not want told. Miriel tilted her head to the side. "Why do you ask?"

"I feel like he's the root of everything with Temar," I explained. I held up a hand to stave off her question. "I don't know why. Well, I do. Temar is bound to the Duke, like I am to you, and he'll obey him in everything…I think. But you know it's not for love. He hates the Duke, and still he obeys. Why?"

"Is he religious?" Miriel asked. "That might be it, he made the vow and he thinks the Gods will hold him to it."

"No, I don't think—wait." I thought back to Temar's exclamation as we had fought in the palace, all those months ago. He had been trying to uncover Miriel's misstep, and I had been trying to keep it hidden. I remembered that he had been furious, driven by energy I could not understand—something entirely beyond loyalty. And he had said…what was it he had said? "He did say something once," I murmured. "He mentioned a God I had never heard of, or a saint: Nuada." I raised my eyebrows at Miriel, who shook her head.

"I've never heard that name before."

I sighed. "I'll keep thinking. I just don't think…I don't think we'll ever know."

"If anyone can get it out of him, you can," Miriel said. After a moment, I decided to take that as a mark of confidence. She sighed and stared into the acrid, smoking fire. Each night, I dreamed of starting a proper fire, with crackling flames and dry wood, but this mess was all we could ever accomplish in the constant rain. "Do you dream of him?" she asked, her voice strangely yearning.

"Yes," I said shortly. I knew better than to dissemble with her about this, but I did not want to speak of it. The silence stretched until I realized that she was not going to ask anything more, and then I found myself unbearably curious. "Why?"

"I dream of Wilhelm," Miriel admitted, after a moment. "And I hate it. I wish I didn't. But it keeps me true. I keep thinking that maybe when we are there, working for the rebellion, the dreams will end." She paused, and then said, very softly, "I hope I never see him again."

She looked over at me as if she was worried that I would think her mad, but I did not; of all people in the world, I knew what she felt. More than anything, I wanted to see Temar and share a silent joke, know the companionship of the only other Shadow in the world, revel in his smile. But that could never be; Temar and I would share caution and mutual mistrust instead of laughter, if ever we saw each other again. Worse, I feared that if I ever saw him again, it would be death for one of us, or both.

With this fear fresh in my mind, I did not admit to myself that I *knew* beyond doubt I would see him again. I told myself that we would never return to Penekket, that my fate would catch me before he ever could, that the Duke would never think to look for me and Miriel in the heart of the rebellion. It was impossible that Temar and I should meet again. I told myself that I believed him to be no more than a dream to me, now. He was a face in my dreams; he had no form, no voice. He was an echo.

Only, without fail, I did the exercises that he had taught me every night. I practiced my tumbling, I threw knives, I used the stands of trees to practice moving silently. I ran through all the poisons and antidotes I knew in my head, and during the long days of silence, I recited everything I had ever been taught: the Kings of Heddred, the religious tenets of the old faiths, lists of the Saints, historical alliances of each noble family. I was no longer a creature of the Court, but I kept myself honed for it, ready for a fight, ready for the endless intrigues of nobles. All of it, I did with a blank mind; I never questioned why, and I never admitted that it would be useful only for scheming and Court battles.

After the first, panicked day, Miriel and I had not spoken of returning. Unlike me, Miriel seemed to have set aside her constant practice; her beautiful mannerisms might remain, but she no longer cultivated them. For a great many evenings, she sat quietly by the fire and watched me as I ran through my exercises, the only sound being the hollow rasp of her cough. This, after her days and days of prayer at Voltur; Garad's death had knocked something out of her, and I could not say yet what it had been.

"Why don't you practice anymore?" I asked her one night, and she smiled at me bitterly.

"Why, what do I have to practice?" she asked, and I saw that her silence had been masking fear. "I don't think the soldiers of the rebellion will care much if I can dance or sing. I have nothing to give them. We've been thinking we'll be heroes, buts..."

"Don't say that." I sheathed my daggers and went to sit by her side. "You've got your mind. It's...what Garad loved about you." I had not spoken his name to her since the night he died and Miriel stiffened slightly. Finally, she nodded, and I pressed on. "You've read all of Jacces' letters, and you have your own thoughts. You know how government works, and the Court, and even military theory. I bet you have a plan, for how to become a leader of the rebellion—don't you?" I was truly curious. Miriel was beautiful, effervescent, charming—but what did such things mean to farmers, struggling for their rights? How could Miriel ever earn their trust? But she nodded in response to my question. Miriel always had a way forward, toward her goal.

"I'll offer them a leader who will take action," she said promptly. "A leader who will do what the High Priest does not dare to do." There was anger in her voice, so long suppressed that even now, in the wilderness, she whispered the words. "He stirred up this rebellion, but he gives them no direction, no resources—and this from a man with the wealth of the Church at his fingertips!"

"They don't know that."

"No, but they know that they've had soldiers coming into their towns, searching their houses and interrogating their wives and their children, looking for Jacces. If they haven't already begun to wonder what good Jacces has really done them, it won't take much to make them ask."

"Miriel..." My voice trailed off. The High Priest, bound to Penekket as he was, was a powerful man. He had roused thousands of hearts to his cause, he had a network of messengers to deliver his letters—I could only think that he must have spies as well. And this was a man who had sent assassins before. He was ruthless, he would make a terrifying enemy. At Miriel's knowing look, I saw that she had thought the same thing.

"We need to gain their trust, we need to lead them," she said simply. "You know that as well as I do, there's no way for us but to act quickly. The longer we wait, the longer the Court has to find us, and the longer the Council has to try to change Wilhelm's mind about the rebellion." She was determined. "Who will help him there? Jacces? Or will he wait, to choose his time?"

"We'll make an enemy," I warned her. I could not refute her words. I knew as well as she did that we needed allies, and we needed to move quickly. But I must caution her. "He'll have spies, he'll hear what you say—he'll know it's you."

"Oh, we won't say anything directly," Miriel assured me. "No, we'll just offer them what they want, we'll make them think it's their idea. If Jacces wanted to control this, he shouldn't have started a movement of the people. It's their movement—and if they want to push for change, I will help them."

"What if they don't want to push for change?"

"If they didn't want to push for change, they wouldn't be forming mobs," Miriel said, logical to the last. "And how can they be content?" I shrugged, and piled more wood onto the fire. Sometimes, I found it amusing that of the two of us it was Miriel, the high-born one, who was the revolutionary; sometimes, when I reminded myself that I had sworn to serve such a woman, I thought that I was putting my own head in the noose. Miriel must have seen the look on my face, for when I sat back and looked over at her, her face had gone grave.

"Will it be enough?" she asked me. There was real fear behind the words. Miriel, who had always looked forward, who had so trusted in her wit and her charm, had learned the hard lesson that chance could overwhelm carefully-laid plans in only a moment. She had learned that enemies were everywhere, and that she was never, ever, safe. Now she had realized that she was not evading danger, only riding into greater uncertainty.

"Of course it will," I said bracingly. We had chosen our course—any of my teachers would have told me not to let our plans be shaken by fear. *Choose your escape, and go*, Donnett said. *Never look behind ye—it only slows ye down.* So I smiled at Miriel, hoping that she could not see the echo of her fear in my own eyes.

"We survived the Court, didn't we?" I coaxed her. "And these are true allies. Better than the Duke." *Better than Temar.* And, in a burst of spite: *Better than Wilhelm.* Miriel, who blessedly could not hear my thoughts, who had forgotten Wilhelm for the moment, smiled at me.

"At last. You know, for the first time in my life that I'm traveling somewhere, I don't feel trapped. I'm afraid, but I feel happy, too—we're going somewhere we chose, to people who are our allies." Her temper and her brilliant charm alike were stripped away. She was only a young woman, happy and at peace with her life. "I wonder what it'll be like," she said thoughtfully, "not to have to look over our shoulders."

"Get some sleep," I said, hiding my face from her. I did not have the heart to tell her that her words had touched off a wave of superstitious fear, so strong that it was all I could do to speak calmly. "We're getting close. We might arrive tomorrow." I curled under my own blankets and wrapped my arms around myself, and told myself that it was time to cast away these superstitions: that Miriel and I were part of a pattern, that Temar was some strange, half-human creature, that I could know the future and that it was dark. But when my dreams came, they were nightmares, and I knew that the fear still lay in wait, in the back of my mind.

Chapter 3

"I don't see *why*," Miriel protested, for the eighth time in as many minutes. I frowned at her as I pulled on my other suit. It was marginally cleaner, but still covered in dust. I smelled, and I wrinkled my nose at that. Baths were one thing I missed, whole-heartedly, about the Court. Baths and good food; with so many kitchens, there had always been a tray of rolls or a meat pie left unattended. Here, food was scarce, and carefully watched.

"You do know why," I told Miriel sternly.

"Alright, yes. I do." She waved her hand as if it were irrelevant. "But I'm so tired of being shut up in this room! Can't I just—"

"No." When we had arrived in the tiny town of Norvelt, I had hidden Miriel in a barn and sought out the Inn, oddly named the Widow's Tears. I told the innkeeper's wife that I had spirited my sister away from her lecherous master, and I must hide her and work for our keep. The woman had nodded sagely and offered to keep Miriel safe as long as she was hidden, not wanting lovesick swains banging on her doors at all hours of the night.

The woman was right to worry—a girl like Miriel would draw attention anywhere, and most especially here. An unmarried woman, beautiful, with fine clothes to wear—all of it painted her as a whore. Even I was already receiving invitations crude enough to render me speechless, and I seemed only to be an exceptionally pretty boy. There was no way that I would be able to keep Miriel safe and seek our rebel sympathizers at the same time, and so Miriel needed to stay hidden, however bored she might be. Whatever her brilliant plans for taking control of the rebellion, they would only lead to disaster if I could not find trustworthy allies first.

"Just stay here," I pleaded. "I have someone to meet tonight—we could be gone tomorrow. It's not for much longer." Miriel only slumped back onto the bed, crossed her arms, and looked away. Her petulance was so childish that I left the room before I could laugh in her face.

As I hurried towards the bar, I rotated my arms in their sockets and twisted my back, trying to stretch away the hours of work I had done. I had spent the past week helping out at the Widow's Tears, doing everything from tilling the garden to restocking the wine cellar. The work was exhausting, but I did anything and everything I could. I would sleep from dinner until late in the evening, then creep downstairs to the taproom to nurse a mug of ale and listen. Above all, I never—ever—asked questions.

The men were uneasy around me, a strange lad with city clothes, an accent they could not place, and yet with calluses on his hands. I had sat over by myself, never trying to make it into their circle, only trying to hear what I could over the din, but the men watched me even so. They were farmers, blacksmiths, butchers—all of them with arms as big around as my head, it seemed, and I was too afraid to open conversation on my own account. Finally, earlier in the day, the Innkeeper himself had taken me aside.

"What's yer game?" he asked me gruffly. "Don't you lie. We've seen a dozen like you from the city. But yer the strangest of 'em."

"A dozen like me?"

"Spies," he said flatly. "Sent by the King to see how we think and what we say. And a week after they go there're soldiers and arrests and men who never come home to their families." I said nothing, only looked down at my feet. "But yer the only one as worked fer their lodging, and yer the only one as won't ask questions. So what's yer game, lad?" I had been waiting for this question for days, and I had half-expected it to be accompanied by a dagger between the ribs—I was so relieved now that I did not speak for a moment.

"I'm not a spy," I said, as blunt as he was. "You know about my sister, I'd expect."

"I hear she doesn't look much like you," he said, narrow-eyed. I shrugged.

"She's my half-sister. From a whore, if you want to know." I apologized silently to Miriel. "We ran away to the city and I was going to be a priest, only it was worse there. Her master wanted her, see, and I..." I hunched my shoulders. "I'd read a book," I said, my voice low. "And then the letters. I was a fool, I thought I could talk to my teachers of it. But one night another student told me the City Guard was coming for me. So my sister and I ran away." I prayed he was a sympathizer; I still was not sure when he said,

"A letter." His eyes were narrowed ever so slightly.

"If you don't want my kind here, I'll move on," I said quickly. "I won't make trouble for the town. Just let us leave. Please."

"Your kind?" I had become certain, over the past week, that these men were sympathizers, and yet now, in the face of this interrogation, I felt my confidence flag. I let him see me trembling. It was not all an act; I was terrified.

"Sympathizer. Sir."

"Are ye then, really?" He looked at me and shook his head. "Ye know, I think ye may not be lying. But Jeram's the one ye'll have to convince. Tonight, I'll have ye meet him."

"Jeram?"

"Never ye mind. Come down to the taproom after dinner."

And so here I was, dressed as smartly as I could be, my hair washed with water from the pump in the yard, my clothing brushed free of dust, and my heart in my throat. I had limbered up, half-afraid that this Jeram, whoever he was, would think it better just to knife me and have done with it all. I told myself that I was prepared for anything, but as I rounded the staircase, I realized that I had been wrong. Every man in the taproom was waiting for me, their chairs turned to the stairs, their faces set and cold. I had been so absorbed in my fear that I had not noticed the unusual quiet. At the bar, the innkeeper nodded to me. His manner was not greatly encouraging, but I tried to take comfort from it. Surely if they wanted to kill me, they'd just rush me, or throw a knife.

One of the men, who I recognized the village blacksmith, stood slowly from his table, and looked me over. His eyes narrowed as he stared at me, taking in the fairness of my skin, the close-cropped hair, the black suit; I looked back, the work-roughened hands, the dirt under his fingernails, the air of authority he held. So this was Jeram. I had seen him before, but not known his name.

"We hear you're a rebel sympathizer." He had worked to strip the country drawl from his voice, and when I looked at him again, more closely, I saw past the brawny arms and soot stains; his eyes were unsettling, more intelligent than those of most priests, colder than those of most courtiers. I swallowed and nodded.

"I am, sir."

"Prove it," he said. I froze. Prove it? How could I possibly prove it?

"How?" I asked at length, and they laughed. I saw my death in their eyes. "Anyone could have read the letters," I said desperately. "How can I prove to you what's in my heart?"

"Try," Jeram said, merciless. And I did—I tried to think of anything Miriel had told me about the letters, I tried to think of philosophy and pretty words. I tried to think of the tenets of their cause, and how I might make these men believe that I held to those tenets. What came out of my mouth, however, was something else entirely.

"I was born in the village at the base of the Winter Castle," I said. "In Voltur." It was like a dream; the words came forth entirely without my volition. "My mother nearly died birthing me, and the healing woman for the Duke took me in. I grew up there, without a family. When I was twelve, I was sent to Penekket to serve at the Court." I tried to stop myself, choose my words, but my voice continued without a pause. "I had heard of the rebellion, but I thought it was foolish. I thought that anyone who sympathized signed his own death warrant." They stirred, and I flinched. Still I heard my voice go on. "Then I saw what the Court was doing to me, and to my…sister. We had started to go dark. We were surrounded by lies and…" I shook my head. "Everyone wanted to use us. She was the one who turned me to the rebellion with her own belief. A month ago, we decided to run away. We just took our clothes and went. We didn't have a plan, we just came here, looking for the rebellion. We didn't know where to go or what to do, but having a roof over our head and fine clothes…it wasn't worth it anymore. We were being…twisted."

They watched me, silent and unforgiving, and I saw that they doubted me. It was not the story they had expected, but how could they believe it? I had been able to hold back only one thing, our identities, but like a wild animal close to danger, they could sense it. I closed my eyes and tried to think of anything that might stave off the attack, and then I heard a rustle behind me and a collective indrawn breath. I knew without looking that Miriel stood behind me, in all her beauty. I looked at her, and she smiled at me.

"Catwin is telling the truth," she said simply. She stood on the stairs above me, her head held high, her chin tilted proudly. Her beauty shone like a jewel, she was stunning. The men at the tables gaped, and Miriel smiled out at them. But her gaze did not waver from Jeram. Under her bright scrutiny, he cleared his throat and made an admirable attempt to remain focused.

"And who are you?" He was trying to be brusque.

"My name," Miriel said, "is Miriel DeVere. I am the niece of the Duke of Voltur. Before the death of King Garad, the Gods protect his soul, I was to be Queen." The rising tide of murmurs was cut off in a moment when she held up her hand for silence. "Gods willing, in time I would have turned Garad from your enemy into your friend. I believed that such was my calling in life."

"Yer really th'Duke's niece, then?" one of the men called, and I shot him a veiled look, marking his face. Behind him sat another man, in finer clothes, his eyes narrowed at Miriel. I resolved to ask the Innkeeper about that one, if Miriel and I survived the night.

"Yes." A faint smile touched Miriel's lips. "But you should know that my uncle is no ally to me. It was I who argued against his plan to send soldiers here. He would let me die without a moment of regret, if it would serve his cause—and if I die here, he *will* use it to persuade the council to use force against the rebellion."

"Is that a threat?" Jeram demanded, and Miriel smiled at him as if it were a great joke; despite himself, the man smiled back.

"Not a threat," Miriel said, the gurgle of a laugh in her voice. "Call it a concise summation of the reasons no one should kidnap or kill me." Jeram could not help himself, he chuckled. He was serious again in a moment.

"So what do you suggest we do?" he asked, and I saw that he was still alert for signs of betrayal. She was the one who could be the most convincing city spy sent so far, dazzling his men and turning their heads. I smiled despite myself; Jeram was so worried about Miriel that he had forgotten entirely about me, the one he had come here to interrogate. Standing at the base of the stairs, in full view of a dozen men, I marveled at the fact that I had become completely invisible; not a single man remembered that I was present.

I stole a glance at Miriel and saw the same mix of emotions I was feeling, reflected in her demeanor. Miriel had been made to be bright and shining, just as I had been made to be quiet and unseen. She reveled in drawing a crowd like a beacon, and I preferred to melt into the shadows. But for one of us to become wholly Light, and the other Shadow, had been the Duke's dream— not our own. We lived as two sides of a coin because we knew no other way.

And we lived this way because it worked, beautifully. The men did not, could not look away from Miriel as she outlined the plan to them. They had never seen the work that went into every gesture, the careful crafting of the tableau; they accepted her act as her true self. They watched her, and I watched them, marking who watched her like a fool, and who had a gleam in his eye.

"Hide me from my uncle," Miriel said bluntly to Jeram. "He *will* send spies. Shelter me, and Catwin, and I will teach you all I know of how to outwit the Council and its army for long enough to draw up a treaty, a law, and sign it with the King."

"We need an army," Jeram objected. "Not words on paper."

"No," Miriel contradicted coolly. In a moment, she had turned to ice. "I can teach your men proper formations, and Catwin can train them on the uses of weapons, but it is extraordinarily unlikely that you could meet the King's army in an open battle and win." For a moment, she was truly her uncle's heir: a woman well-versed in military history, with a keen grasp of army formations and a calculating mind. Her eyes swept around the room, marking the men Jeram would have as soldiers.

"And if you defeat them, what then? The great lords will regroup, and we will face generations of civil war as the common people struggle with the nobles. Is that what you wish for Heddred?" She dared them all to say yes, seeking to hold their gaze; only Jeram would meet her eyes, and he did not speak.

"Just so," Miriel said simply. "What we need, as a nation, is an understanding that the people should, and will, have a voice in their lives. What we need is to establish the mechanism by which the people have such a voice. What we *need*, is a treaty. A treaty for the King to sign, and thus show the Council that they no longer rule all. A treaty that promises that the rights of the people shall be enshrined in law." There was a murmur, but this time it was Jeram who held up his hand for silence.

"Useless," he said flatly. "The King would never sign it."

"Garad would not have done so," Miriel agreed. "But Wilhelm will." I heard the hope in her voice, and wished with all my heart that Wilhelm would prove to be our ally. It would break Miriel's heart if he were not. And, of course, our new allies would most likely kill us. It occurred me to that we had not greatly improved our position in the world. We were still bargaining, still living on the knife's edge.

"How can you be sure?" Jeram was no fool. I saw him cast an annoyed glance at the men who had nodded to her words without a thought. He was a common man, who had always known the simple fact that the laws protected the lawmakers. He had no confidence, as Miriel did, in the sanctity of words on paper.

"I know Wilhelm to be a sympathizer," Miriel said, with great dignity. "You forget, I was at the Court with him before he was King. He and I spoke of the rebellion. And I tell you truly that Jacces, also, knows Wilhelm to be a sympathizer." There was a murmur of interest, and Jeram's eyes narrowed. I marveled at Miriel's daring, but knew the necessity of it—she was nothing to these men, an outsider. But if she was a woman who knew their fabled leader…

"How do you know this?" Jeram demanded. Jacces was the leader who might never have existed, the man that no one—even his own adherents—could find.

"While at court, I maintained a correspondence with him." Miriel stood calmly under Jeram's scrutiny. She never wavered. Her confidence was palpable.

"You know his identity?"

"I have a guess." Miriel lied without hesitation. "But for that person's safety, I will not speak it."

"You must tell us," Jeram said, and she shook her head; she had marked, as I had, the true desperation in Jeram's voice. He might be the leader of the rebellion in Norvelt, but even he had no knowledge of Jacces himself. And here, again, lay the difference between me, and Miriel: I only marked the fact, and looked about to see what the other rebels might think, but Miriel noted it, and played it for what it was worth, turning the minds of her listeners back to her purpose.

"No. Does it matter? What we must do, whoever he might be, is be true to his vision. This is a movement of the people, not one man. Jacces knows that." I rather thought that the High Priest might have something to say about that, but the men nodded readily enough, and at length even Jeram conceded the point.

"Very well. We will shelter you." He held up a finger, cautionary, when he saw her satisfied smile. "You have half a year," he said bluntly. "In that time, you will help us draw up a treaty that all of us agree to, and you will get the King to sign it. Your servant will train our men in the use of weapons and in troop formations. If you cannot persuade the King to sign *our* treaty by then..." He had the agreement of his men. They nodded, gruffly, and for a moment the spell was broken; but Miriel was dauntless in the face of his mistrust.

"I can do it," she said. "We will draw up the treaty together, all of us." As Jeram had done, she included the rest of the men; her brilliant smile warmed them, and I could see them smiling back at her. "We will be a force for good in this nation, Jeram—all of us together."

He inclined his head—the gesture of one player to another, and she only smiled back, as if she were not striving to replace him in the hearts of his men, as if she had not played this game day in and day out, against rivals far more sophisticated than he was. He had lost, and he simply did not know it yet. I wondered, with the detachment of a courtier, when Miriel's chance would come—what moment, what opportunity would present itself for her to cement her triumph.

We bid them goodnight, Miriel curtsying prettily to their cheers, and returned to our room. Jeram had promised us lodging with the baker. This would be our last night on the lumpy cots of the inn, and I was glad of it.

"We're lying again," I said glumly, and Miriel tried to mask her discomfort with one of her elegant shrugs.

"The only lie we told was that we didn't know who Jacces was." Her voice was pitched low to make sure no one could eavesdrop. "And do you have a better plan?"

"It was all a...performance." The distaste was thick in my mouth.

"It's always a performance for me," Miriel said simply. "You're in the shadows, you pretend by being unseen. But I'm in the light, so I perform." Her face softened. "And we'll give them everything we promised. It's a performance, but not a lie, Catwin. This isn't like it was with Garad." I swallowed down the wave of guilt that rushed over me when I heard his name, and nodded.

"But aren't you afraid that he might not sign?" I asked, and Miriel looked down rather than meet my eyes.

"I cannot think of that," she said. "I never think of it."

She went to bed at once, but I could not sleep. Miriel had announced her presence here, and who might have slipped off to tell the Duke where we were? I no longer underestimated Temar's spy network; it would have been very like him to send someone to wait for us in the southern cities. If we stayed in one place for long enough, I knew, he would find us.

I lay awake, watching the door fearfully, but I must have drifted to sleep at last, for in the dead of night, we were awakened by someone scratching at the door. When I approached it cautiously, I heard the voice of the innkeeper's wife.

"It's Allena," she whispered. "Jeram sent me to take you to your lodgings tonight. He wants you hidden away before the lady's uncle finds her." I opened the door and peered out at her, and saw only frightened honesty in her eyes, and so we packed our things as quietly as we could in the dark, and followed her out into the spring night.

"Why did he want us to move tonight?" I asked, as we picked our way over a frozen field. "And where are we going?"

"There's a merchant in town who'll keep you," Allena said. "And Jeram trusts no one—there's a reward out for finding the both of you, did you know? No? Well, there is. And there's no saying who might think it's worth more than the rebellion is." I remembered the sly gleam in one man's eyes, and thought that Jeram was right to be cautious.

"Why does he trust you, then?" Miriel asked. I stiffened at the blunt words, but Allena was not offended.

"I am his twin," she said. "I am the only one Jeram trusts. He knows that even blood is not always enough." In the dim light, she looked over at the two of us. "So you're not really brother and sister, then," she guessed. "I told my husband I thought as much. You don't look much alike." I hesitated, but Miriel reached over and took my hand. She shook her head at the woman.

"We're twins, too," she said easily.

Chapter 4

We were greeted by the Merchant, master of the house himself, wrapped in a brocade robe and surrounded by his riches. He was courteous to a fault, clasping our hands warmly in his own and offering any amenity his house might provide. Nothing, he assured us, was too dear for the saviors of the rebellion. I, having been raised as an overlooked servant, found such titles patently ridiculous, but Miriel, who had spent the past years either showering such praise on the favorites of the court, or being feted as one herself, accepted his flowery language with her best court manners.

"You do us too much credit," she said warmly, to cover my snort of disbelief. As he gestured towards his study, she did not precede him, but threaded her arm through his own, smiling sweetly up at him as he guided us.

"Oh, no, my Lady," he assured her, shaking his head at her demurral. "The rebellion has long needed one like you." He ushered her to a couch and settled himself into his own great, carved chair. After a moment, entirely forgotten, I sat on the edge of the couch as well. The Merchant did not mind; he was staring off into space, looking troubled.

"The rebellion is...divided," he said finally. "I understand that politics makes for strange bedfellows, that I do, but I tell you truly, many of the men who flock to the rebellion are nothing more than savages, looking to avenge the wrongs of their station. I think that where I have failed to caution them, you may succeed."

"Are you the leader of the uprising in this town, then?" Miriel asked. She was probing for the fault lines of the rebellion, disconcerted by the Merchant's talk of infighting. Jeram had presented the movement as one force, and now, seeing cracks in the show of unity, she must know at once how deep the division ran. The Merchant's face darkened; she had found the first sign of resentment.

"No. I might say that it should be, for I am a learned man, but my wealth—although honestly gotten—makes me an outsider among the rebels. I send my servant in my stead, to speak for me." He gestured to a man at a nearby desk, a clerk who was busy at work on ledgers, and took a breath to steady himself. "No, the leader of the rebellion in Norvelt is Jeram. A good man, to be sure, honest. Devoted. Uneducated...but they listen to him." His tone was bitter.

"Often, a leader is no more than a figurehead," Miriel observed. "While it is the rest who are the of the truest benefit to the cause." The Merchant nodded, his ruffled feathers soothed, and I thought for the thousandth time that it was far better for Miriel to be the Light, than me. Her pleasant smile, her Court smile, had not once wavered in the face of this man's petulance. She brightened. "You will have heard that we are drawing up a treaty for the King to sign, yes? Tomorrow, you must tell me your thoughts."

"Oh, I will," he assured her. "My Lady, let me say again how glad I am that you have come to us. The men will surely calm themselves for love of you. But now, you must rest! Such a long journey, and I hear you were sleeping in an inn! Ah, not a life for one such as you. My servant will show you to your rooms. Aron?"

I looked over at the desk, and as the man raised his head I stifled an exclamation. There was the same sly gleam in his eye as I had seen at the meeting, the careful flick of his eyes over my clothing, lingering on my boot to see if I carried a dagger there. It was all gone in an instant; he made a bow to Miriel and gestured to the door.

"My Lady, if you will follow me."

We walked quietly through hallways of rich carpets and priceless works of art, and when we were alone in our room, Miriel frowned at me.

"What was that? Your face, just then."

"I don't trust him," I said shortly. I expected her to brush it off with a laugh, and tell me that we were amongst friends, the allies she had spoken of so confidently during our escape, but she only nodded. The Merchant's words, Jeram's insistence on an army—those had worried her. She was no longer the calm, self-assured girl she had been. Her confidence had disappeared in a moment.

"Good," she said shortly. "Don't trust anyone." She began to peel off her homespun gown and wrinkled her nose. "Another thing..."

"Yes?" I frowned.

"Tomorrow, we both need baths."

On the morrow, after a thorough scrubbing in a big copper tub, we set to work in earnest. The Merchant was quick to send for anything we might need for our work, and eager to suggest things that would make our stay more comfortable. He slyly murmured to me that a young man might enjoy the company of one Kerelle, a young lady of the town, if I knew what he meant, and I—having decided that life would be simpler if the rebels continued to think I was a young man—tried not to blush, and thanked him with as much good cheer as I could muster.

"Yes," Miriel said wickedly, when I told her. "We should see you married, Catwin. A nice country girl, who you can trust to raise your children with strong populist values." She grinned up at me from where she was writing a list of supplies for the rebel army, and when I shot her a glare, she bit back a laugh and went back to her work. There was no saying who might be listening in this warren of a house, and so we communicated as we had in the palace: with eyebrow raises, glares, and the occasional grin.

It became clear that we would see each other very little during the days; I had fretted at that, but Miriel was insistent that we were amongst friends, and she did not need constant protection. When I reminded her that she herself had told me to trust no one, she only shrugged helplessly.

"What else can we do? We cannot be always together if you are training the men and I am helping to draw up the treaty. We're safe for half a year. Until then, no one will want to attract notice, not when they know the Council is distracted. What with the Ismiri...." Her chin trembled a bit, and I reached out awkwardly to pat her shoulder.

The unrest that had swirled around us as we left Voltur had only grown more pronounced. We had known that matters were grave when half of the soldiers that had arrived with our travel party had stayed to guard the Winter Castle; they had brought supplies, well-used weapons, and royal orders. The raids had attracted notice in Penekket, and it was not only the Duke who worried; the King was fortifying the border, and as we had ridden away from the Winter Castle, the Warden standard had been flying above the battlements.

Even in the Norstrung Provinces, far from the Ismiri and the constant wariness of the mountains, the men in the taverns spoke of war, and said that Garad's treaties were crumbling. The Peacemaker himself was dead, and a young Warlord in his place, facing down a war-hungry Council on the one hand, and Kasimir on the other. We heard tell that Dusan's health was failing, and he no longer attempted to curb his heir. They said he had given his own troops into Kasimir's command. Men whispered that the raids were not militia now, but the Ismiri army itself, and how long could it be until Wilhelm tired of it and sent troops for an invasion, to crush the Ismiri forever?

The unrest might mean that the Council was blessedly distracted from the rebellion, that a large detachment of soldiers would not be sent to the Norstrung Provinces, but Miriel could take little pleasure in that. I knew that despite her relief at being free of the Court, she yearned to be in Penekket, advising Wilhelm on renewing the peace treaties. She passionately resented the fact that it was Marie de la Marque sitting at Wilhelm's right hand, offering opinions and sharing his trials.

And worst of all, the unrest meant that Miriel's mother, and her homeland, would be the first to fall when the attack came. It had been one thing to be in Voltur ourselves, seeing the guards bruised and bloodied, hearing the sounds of weaponry and the war cries, but then we had been in shock, the two of us. We faced the border raids not with fear, but dull acceptance; we had seen our king slain, and our world turned dark and uncertain. It was now, in the relative safety of the southern summer, that the horror of the war seemed so much sharper.

I could only give thanks, silently, that Roine, and Temar, and Donnett were safe in the capital, but when I thought of the peasants living in the village of my birth, my blood ran cold. Both Miriel and I had read the histories—we knew what happened to the common people when war broke out.

And so we were both glad enough to lose ourselves in our work. Miriel spent hours hunched over scraps of paper, scratching out phrases, writing in the margins, arguing late into the night with Jeram and the others. She had always been passionate about the rebellion, and that passion was her shelter now. When I saw the stacks of notes she had written, I wondered if her philosophical tract, abandoned in our rooms at Penekket, had been the early drafts of just such a treaty.

I, having less genuine conviction about the rebellion itself, was at least easily convinced that this work was far nobler than anything I had done at Court. The men had been contemptuous of me at first, noting—in loud whispers—my thin arms and my city hands. But after some bouts of sparring, not only bare-fisted but with spears and short swords and daggers, the men had learned a

34

grudging respect. They laughed and called me the Weasel, but they listened when I spoke, and bought me rounds of ale after our days of work. They were eager to learn, these country men who had never held weapons of their own, how a spear or blade might be wielded properly.

We drilled each day with weapons, the men coming in shifts so that the work on their farms and in their shops would not cease. Every day, there were a few new faces. To my disquiet, news of Miriel had spread far. Men arrived from other towns, claiming that they had heard a real uprising was afoot at last, led by an angel, and they would be part of it. My only comfort was that each of them withstood Jeram's questioning. I heard of one or two, "city men" who had gone to the inn for a meeting with Jeram and never emerged, and I applauded his relentless suspicion even as it chilled me to the bone.

The first few weeks passed easily, but I dreaded teaching these men the mechanics of troop warfare, and I delayed as long as I could. The truth was that with every few men who arrived to complement the crowd in the Merchant's courtyard, the more I realized how paltry our little army was. I had known Miriel's words for truth, when she told Jeram that his men could never defeat the royal forces, but it was another thing entirely to see it. This ragtag group was fully inadequate to the task of standing against the Royal Army, not only by size but also by training. I could teach these men basic troop formations and drill them every day for the next half year, but even I, who had never seen a battle, knew that it was far different to lower spears into formation in a courtyard than withstand the charge of a thousand horsemen.

I spoke openly of these troubles only to Jeram, confiding in him that we could not expect to mount an invasion on the city of Penekket itself. The best we could hope for would be to repel an invading army, and even then, we had best resort to less direct tactics: cutting supply lines, spoiling food stores, picking off the men a few at a time. But however logical the man might be, however practical, he had set his sights on winning a battle with the army, and nothing would do for him but that his men be trained. In the face of his cold-eyed stare, knowing this to be the last refuge for Miriel and myself, I bit my tongue on further arguments and kept at work, hoping that Miriel might have more luck with the treaty than I was having with the men, and that my own discouragement would not discourage her.

I did not need to worry—Miriel, determinedly ignoring news of the war, grew more confident in her treaty by the day. Her early uncertainty, spurred by the divisions within the movement, had been restored by her own research, by the simple act of moving forward. When she questioned Jeram as to what guidance he received from Jacces, he had only stared at her blankly. The High Priest, it seemed, had continued to be only an inspirational leader; he had sparked the rebellion with his letters, but he hung back, offering no guidance as to how the movement might come to fruition, and Miriel took this as a very good sign, indeed—with no lines of communication between the leaders in the towns, and the High Priest himself, we might well accomplish something before he learned of it, and took exception.

I marveled at all of it: the men, drilling each day in the courtyard, lending their thoughts for the treaty, leaving their families and devoting their lives to this. The rebellion had been begun by the wealthy, the educated—those with much wealth and much time to waste, as I had once cynically thought—but it was now carried on the backs of the poor, men who worked hard from sunup to sundown and then gathered in taverns to speak of rights and injustices.

"What do they know of philosophy?" I asked Miriel skeptically, and she shook her head.

"Philosophy is nothing but a mask," she said, surprising me. "It's only pretty words for grand concepts. But at its core, it's no more than yearning for justice. You don't have to be educated to understand that—these men feel injustice as much as any priest or scholar."

Odd as it was to hear her, of all people, dismiss philosophy, I believed her. She had spent the first weeks of our stay listening to the Merchant and to Jeram for hours, and calling the men in from the tavern so that she could hear to their opinions as well; she would sit silently, hardly moving, marking everything they said, learning their hopes and their anger alike. While Jeram thought that she was merely learning what they would accept for a treaty, and I had first thought that she was only drawing out their thoughts to gain their trust, I now knew that her reasons ran deeper: Miriel was busy learning the undercurrents of the rebellion, searching out the points that could fracture it all.

Before we arrived, there had been no plans for a treaty—the men had been bound together only by their dislike of nobles and kings. Now, Miriel must forge a treaty pleasing to a group that had, as it happened, wildly disparate beliefs as to how the kingdom *should* be run.

She had told the Merchant that there was a great difference between being useful, and being a figurehead, but Miriel was determined to be both. I raised my eyebrows when the men called Miriel the Lady of the People, or an angel, or a goddess; I shrank from such notoriety, and would have cautioned her against seeking herself, but Miriel told me seriously that such things were to be sought, and courted. She knew what it meant for a leader to be half-myth—men would give their hearts to her cause whole-heartedly, not mistrusting her motives as they might if she were only another of them. Miriel must strive to be more than human, so that the rebels would forget she was a noble herself.

Once, we would have planned such things openly between us, secure in the privacy of our rooms, but here, we were afraid to speak of such things out loud—for once or twice, I had heard the Merchant's sly-eyed servant listening at our door—Miriel took to writing notes on scraps of paper, burned at once when I had read them. When the man came to deliver us our dinner, we were always hard at work, myself with diagrams and lists of weaponry, and Miriel with her drafts of the treaty.

They cannot seem to agree on anything, Miriel wrote. Jeram says that all the children of Heddred must be given an education so that they can read the teachings of the church, but he wishes the rich to give their money for this, and the Merchant will not agree. Jeram believes that the Merchant only wants to be a noble, and strives for equality because he cannot stand being lesser—and that if the Merchant could become noble, he would betray the cause.

Is he right to think so? I wrote back, having burned her note in the fireplace and stirred the ashes about with a poker.

Yes, Miriel wrote. But I think it can be changed—is it not true that both Jeram and the Merchant believe in the rebellion because they know they are equal to the nobles, but held back by laws? Surely a compromise can be forged.

I only nodded. Miriel's belief was as much a puzzle as an inspiration to me; even in her notes to me, she never admitted that this enterprise might fail. She trusted against all odds that a fractured rebellion of men with little wealth and no power could rise up and be granted rights by their King. I could not bring myself to tell her that I believed the rebellion was too weak to survive, doomed to be obliterated as soon as the Council was not distracted by the rumble of war from the east. I could not admit that I feared, having heard no proclamations from the throne, that Wilhelm had turned away from the revolution when he had turned from Miriel. Instead, I kept my mouth shut; where in anyone else, this illogical persistence would have annoyed me, but in Miriel it seemed like something precious, a tiny flame that must be sheltered at all costs.

Chapter 5

To my surprise, and relief, Miriel and I adapted well enough to life in Norvelt. I was reminded of the first months spent at the palace, of the strange ease with which I had slipped into a rhythm that was completely different from the familiar. We were plunged into such a strange new world that there was nothing to do save move forward on instinct alone, and both of us were too exhausted, by the end of the day, to spend our time paralyzed with fear or indecision.

By the second month of our stay, I had stopped looking over my shoulder, freezing into the stillness of a Shadow when I saw an unfamiliar face. In Jeram's eagerness for action, in his constant curiosity at Jacce's identity, I began to believe that perhaps the High Priest had no spy here at all. Jeram swore that each man was known to him, and had been for years, and when I looked at these honest, straightforward country men, I did not think that the High Priest would have been able to offer them anything that could secure their loyalty to him over one of their own. If he had tried to use one as a spy, Jeram would know.

Aron was the only one I suspected, and I continued to watch him. His smile always sent a crawling sensation up my spine; he, of all of them, seemed the sort to grasp for something beyond the rebellion—secrets, riches, power. The Merchant swore that Aron had served him for years, but still I watched him. The one thing I felt sure of was that he was not Temar's spy; Temar would never choose someone he knew I would see at once.

That left the question of who Temar would choose, and when they would join our ranks. I could hardly doubt that Temar *would* send a spy here to search for us—of everyone, he would know where it was that we had gone, just as he would be the most likely to know that we had left of our own volition. Whatever Temar felt for me, he hated Miriel, and he suspected both of us. But with each new recruit I saw, I became more and more sure that I would know Temar's spy when I saw him. Whatever his reasons, Temar had not sent anyone yet.

Indeed, none of the new men seemed to care about me or my past at all, beyond what I could teach them. Though I must pretend to be a boy—difficult enough for these men to accept being taught by a citydweller, let alone a girl—I found that despite myself, I was at ease in their company. If I thought their manners crude and their idealism uninformed, well, I had learned at the Court that a well-taught noble could be as great a fool as a peasant. I kept my head down and only blushed at some of the stories they told, and they roared with laughter to see my face, and told me I had much to learn about the world.

For a few hours each day, I could forget that Miriel continued to struggle with politics and rival factions, and forget the dire news from the east as well. I lost myself in the pleasant exhaustion of hard work. My muscles, which had atrophied in the tedium of life at the Winter Castle, grew accustomed to combat once more. I dropped into bed each night with scrapes and bruises, and the pain and tiredness, the pure feeling of hard work. Doubt that had plagued my waking hours since Miriel and I had left Penekket—only exhaustion could drive the fear away during the day.

But sleep brought no true respite: I dreamed of Roine, sad dreams where she told me that she missed me, and that she feared for me. I saw her worry that she did not know where I laid my head at night, and that she did not know if I had been kidnapped, and was in danger, or if I had chosen to leave her without saying goodbye. I would wake curled into a ball, tears wet on my cheeks, knowing that, for another day, I would know that she feared for me, and yet I would not send word.

Worse, I dreamed of Temar, and I awoke feeling a loneliness I had never experienced before. I felt like the otherworldly creatures in the fairy tales Roine had once told me, doomed to wander the earth without ever seeing another of my own kind. Miriel might be my other half, my only true friend, but she was not a companion in the darkness and shadow, just as I could not be her companion in the glare of the Court. We both dreamed, I saw, and we both woke with a sadness in our hearts, pulling us back to the place that had so twisted us. My sparring could not banish those feelings, but it was enough to distract me for a time, and I welcomed that, just as Miriel threw herself into her work on the treaty.

And then, in the second month, the game changed. Jeram himself came to the field where I was teaching spear work, and called me away from the drills, insisting that I come at once. I left the men to practice in pairs, and hurried along in Jeram's wake, afraid to ask what his scowl might mean. When we entered the

Merchant's study, I found the Merchant examining a scroll, and Miriel pacing worriedly.

"We've received a message from the King," Jeram said to me. "The Lady insisted that you should be present for our deliberations." I blinked; the Lady was a woman with golden hair and hard eyes, red-painted lips, a face scored by disappointment—she was not Miriel, with kindness in her gaze and the hope of a better world. But Jeram would not know that. He was scowling at including another person in their deliberations. He might appreciate the way Miriel could work the Merchant around to the ideals of the common men, but Jeram hated to open decision making to others.

"What does it say?" I asked Miriel, and she cast a look at the scroll.

"It's an invitation. We're to go to Penekket and meet with Wil—with the King."

"An invitation to us? How was it delivered?" I felt as if I had been doused in ice water. If Wilhelm could find us, then Temar might—no, this message would not even be from Wilhelm at all. This was Temar's doing.

"It's an invitation to Jacces," Miriel said. "It was posted in the town square."

"Oh," I said softly. We exchanged a look, she and I, and I knew that she feared the same thing I did: that this message could be from anybody, King or Council, the Duke, or some enemy we did not yet know. "So why the meeting?" I asked, and the Merchant frowned.

"We're receiving reports that it was posted in other towns as well," he said. "But not all. The King may not know where we are yet, but he seems close. This suggests that our activity...has been noticed."

"Perhaps it is time to cease open operations, and have the men practice their weaponry in their own homes while we finish the treaty," Miriel suggested. Jeram's eyes flashed.

"My Lady, need I remind you that the training of my men was a condition of your continued safety here?"

"And need I remind you," Miriel said, her good temper faltering at last, "that of all of us in this room, I best understand the workings of the Council, the King's spy network, and the mechanics of government?"

"You are a noble!" Jeram burst out, his anger sparked by her own. "You think that words and treaties protect the people. You believe that laws ensure justice. You know nothing."

"I know that your band of two hundred cannot hope to stand against the Royal Army!" Miriel flared. "And I know that if a letter has been sent, spies have been sent with it. Perhaps they are from the King, and perhaps they were sent by his lords, but spies there are. And our military operations put us in far more danger than they are worth."

The Merchant stood, cutting off Jeram's retort by holding up his hand.

"My Lady," he said, placatory, "please—tell us, do you believe this invitation to be a sincere offer of friendship from the King?"

There was a silence as Miriel looked away. Her face was composed, but in her complete stillness I saw her doubt. In her ceaseless work, in her constant conversation and activity, Miriel had tried to bury her own misgivings about Wilhelm. But the thoughts had gone on, however deep they might be hidden. As I dreamed of Roine, of Temar, Miriel dreamed of Wilhelm. In this moment, at least, she knew what I had once tried to tell her: that a King was not a man like any other. Others strove relentlessly upwards, to the throne, in the unpredictable currents of power; a King was trapped in his place by those same currents. More, he was shaped by them. And now Wilhelm, a man who had once been passionately in favor of this uprising, had held his throne for months and not once reached out to these men. Miriel must, at last, ask herself why.

"I believe the message from the King to be a sincere offer of outreach," Miriel said finally. "I believe him still to be true to the rebellion. When I left court, the Council was hard at work to persuade the King to send soldiers. The Earl of Mavol was insisting upon it. In order for Wilhelm to resist this, even in the face of war, he must still be true to our ideals." I said nothing. I might doubt, but the absence of soldiers was compelling proof, indeed, and I could not trust my own judgment. Just as Miriel could be blinded by hope, so, too, could I be blinded by my own hope on her behalf.

"You think it wise to accept the King's offer?" Even the Merchant was skeptical, and Jeram shot him a look, nodding at his caution. But Miriel shook her head.

"No, I cannot say that. Wilhelm is new to the throne, and..."
She bit her lip. "I cannot say that he could hold the Council in line,
on a short enough leash to make this meeting safe. If the letter is
public, then the members of the Council will know of it through
their own spy networks, if nothing else."

"And so..." The Merchant cleared his throat awkwardly.
"What do you suggest, my Lady?" Miriel had been gazing off into
space, lost in thought; now she looked around at us as if she had
thought herself alone.

"We must continue our work," she said. Her voice was so
low that I could barely hear it. "We must continue our work,
continue to hide, and pray that the Gods favor us so that we may
continue our mission here before the Council decides to obliterate
us." She ducked her head and left the room, but when I made to
follow her, Jeram put a hand on my arm.

"Can she be trusted?" he asked bluntly. I would have flared
up, just as she had done. I would have told him that Miriel had
lived her whole life as a pawn, and she deserved better than to be
regarded only for what she could bring to the rebellion. But I
knew better than to think that Jeram would care.

"She has been betrayed by nearly all those she loved," I
said simply. "To ask her who can be trusted...it makes her think
on her betrayal."

"Can she be trusted?" he repeated. He did not think more
kindly on her in light of her trials. He wished only to hear that she
could not fail, whatever the cause—and in that, I remembered the
Duke's uncaring insistence on perfection. Miriel was now, as she
had been at Court, only a stepping stone, a weapon. I bristled.

"She can be trusted," I said shortly. "She has favored the
rebellion above good sense, above even her own life. And before
you next fight with her, remember that more than anything else in
her life, she wishes for this rebellion to succeed. She would
sacrifice anyone she loves for it. It is not that she does not wish
you to go against the Duke's forces for his sake, but for your own."
Jeram nodded, quite unrepentant.

"Anyone could betray us," he said flatly. "I trust no one,
especially nobles." I was in no mood to have this fight. I tried to
jerk my arm out of his grasp.

"Can I go now?"

"No." When I would have protested, he held out a fold of
parchment. "This arrived today. For you." I looked from it, to him.

43

If it were poisoned, I reasoned, he would already be showing the ill effects. I opened it and smoothed it out, and, without shame, Jeram and the Merchant both moved close to read.

> Catwin—
> I have told the messenger to seek you
> wherever he can find rebels. He can be trusted.
> I wish only to know that you are well.

"Who is it from?" Jeram asked. There was no signature, but I knew the writing well enough—I had seen it on the labels of medicine bottles, in the notebooks she kept in her study, in her lists of herbs and materials. I stared at it, shaking.

"It's…my mother."

"Your mother?" Both men stared at me.

"In a way. She took me in when I was born," I explained. "My own mother nearly died, and Roine was the healing woman, she took me in. I should tell her that I am well. Is the messenger still here?"

"Can he be trusted? Can she be trusted?"

The answer sprang to my lips, and I had to try to slow myself, think carefully. At length, I nodded. "Yes. She holds for the rebellion's values, I think she always has."

"Are you sure this isn't a trick?" the Merchant asked, worriedly. "Could the Duke have forced her to write this?" I thought of Roine and her cool disdain for the Duke, and grinned; my first humor in days.

"No," I said. "The Duke could never make her do that. He'd have to torture her, and then she wouldn't be able to write—" At that thought, the humor disappeared, and I thought I might be sick. I fought the urge to vomit on the Merchant's fine rugs.

"Do you think he *has* tortured her?" Jeram asked. He had no time for my sickness.

"No." I shook my head and straightened up, reminded myself of Miriel's assurances as we rode through the wilderness together. "He would have questioned her, but we didn't tell her where we were going. She didn't know anything. He would have seen that."

"I don't like it," Jeram said, and the Merchant murmured an agreement. "Even if she can be trusted, too many things could

---

go wrong. The messenger might be killed—or bribed. Someone might see her receive the message. We can't risk it."

"Please," I whispered. The word was out before I could stop myself, and the men stared at me. "Please, just let me tell the messenger that I am well. We need not tell her anything else. I can tell her that any lie you wish, but please let me tell her that I am safe. That I have not been kidnapped, or killed." The men wavered, and I saw their indecision. "Please, this is a woman who has been my protector, all my life. She saved me when I was a baby, she saved my mother, and she raised me herself. She took me in without a word of complaint. Please?"

It was Jeram, to my surprise, who broke first. "You swear she is a sympathizer?" I smiled weakly, still afraid.

"Yes, she's been talking of the excesses of nobles and the inequalities of government since I was a little child. I just didn't know what any of it meant until I was older." The men looked at each other, and at last nodded.

"Go get the messenger," the Merchant said to one of his guards, and the man went out into the hall. The Merchant looked back at me. "He said if you were here, he must see you to know that it was you. Then he would go."

"He'll bear no messages from you," Jeram said. "Risky enough that she knows you're here." I swallowed down my anger and nodded, reminding myself that it was Jeram's caution that had kept court spies away from us for so long.

"Thank you." I waited as the Guards pushed the door back open and dragged in a young man, barely a boy, really, that I recognized as one of the Palace pages. He looked at me uncertainly.

"It's me," I said.

"She said you had a mark," he said, "on your right arm."

"I do." I pushed my sleeve up to show the scar I had gotten. I remembered it well enough: a hot iron, four years old, howling at the top of my lungs for Roine. The boy only nodded, wide-eyed, and, with a nod to Jeram and the Merchant, I pushed past him and went to go find Miriel. I could feel relief coursing through my veins, but also a new urgency—there had been a message, a proclamation. The attention of the Council had returned. We must move quickly, or we would be caught here.

Chapter 6

From that day on, Miriel was more driven than I had ever seen her. She did not dwell on her memories of betrayal, but devoted herself entirely to her work. At Court, I had seen her stay awake long into the night, struggling to keep sleep at bay as she studied theology, cards, poetry, dancing, even laughing—anything to remain the best, the wittiest, the most charming and learned. In those days, she would fall into a sleep as deep as death itself, exhausted by her constant charade.

I watched her carefully for signs of the exhaustion that had consumed her in her days at Court, but now, as she spent her days shaping the future of Heddred, she hardly slept at all. She was still working each night when I fell into bed, and she woke before I did in the mornings, and shook me awake as the sun peeked over the horizon. When she had approached her betrothal with Garad she had been fearful, drained by the need to weave a fantastical illusion, but as she worked on the treaty she seemed driven by something quite beyond herself. Her eyes were shadowed, but her shoulders were unbowed, and she never failed to greet me with a smile. Her belief, that I had once wanted to shelter as a tiny spark, had become a roaring flame.

As I watched her belief guide her, I found that I began to believe, myself. It was not the burning sense of injustice that drove Jeram and his men, or the intellectual passion in which Miriel reveled. It was quieter, softer: first, the sense I had found at the start, that I at last had the chance to do something that might be truly Good. Then, later, I started to believe that this was what I needed, to heal myself from the darkness of the Court.

I had always understood Miriel's belief, and known that she was right: nobles were no better at heart than the common-born. It was riches and books that separated the two, and no more, and I believed Jeram when he said that a commoner with an education might have as fine a mind as a noble. I had simply never been driven to right those wrongs; now, I believed that I could, and, strangely, that I wanted to do so.

I did not tell Miriel, but most of all, I believed in the rebellion because it gave a purpose to the alliance she and I had made. When we had sworn loyalty to each other, we had been bound by nothing more than a common set of enemies, our fear, and worst of all, our hopes for vengeance. This was something greater entirely—she was leading the nation to a new age, and I was guarding her, so that she might be what she was fated to be. And if that belief made me question, uncomfortably, what my own fate might be, I was too busy to spend much time wondering over that.

And even if we were both fearful, we never had a need to admit the true reason. Fear of prophecies, of lost love, was nothing to those who worked in the shadow of the scaffold. We watched, always, for the distress signal that troops were on the march, heading for the rebel stronghold—alerted, at last, to the arming of the common people. They had established an impressive network of signals, this shadowy rebellion. There were beacons and messenger birds, tradesmen and wandering priests; they dealt in whispers, and spread hope to the despairing, and caution to the boastful.

For weeks, there was nothing—so long that we began to relax, thinking that perhaps the King's offer had come to nothing. No city-bred newcomers had arrived in the town, and even Jeram had lost the grim look in his eyes. Then a rider arrived at a dead gallop, gasping that he was only hours ahead of a Royal Messenger. He fell out of the saddle and was carried to the Merchant's study as Jeram was summoned from the smithy, and we crowded around the messenger as he sipped some water and rasped out his tale: the raids on the border had escalated until the King, Gods protect him, had sent a large contingent west and fortified the Winter Castle. And that must have been Kasimir's plan, for once the Royal Army was ensconced in the mountains, the Ismiri had rushed south, over the foothills that lay in the north of the Bone Wastes, and now they swept across the southern farmland, towards Penekket itself.

The messenger told us that as he had left the city, the King was withdrawing his family and the Council into Penekket Fortress, and his father was preparing the Royal Army to march westward, and meet the Ismiri forces head on. We gaped at this news, all of us, unable to take it in, and Miriel and I exchanged an anguished glance. We had hoped night and day, and I knew she had prayed, that Voltur would be safe; now it was, but we could take no joy in when we knew that there were other citizens bearing the brunt of the attack.

"We have to help them," Miriel said, breaking the silence. I nodded, but the Merchant and Jeram looked at her, aghast.

"No," Jeram said at once. "This is not our war."

"Of course it is." Miriel shook her head in confusion. "This is an invasion—the farmers whose fields are being burned, the shepherdesses whose flocks are being slaughtered, those are our brothers and sisters. We must help the Army to stand against Kasimir." She was incredulous. Eloquent and passionate, Miriel had never had trouble persuading others to join her cause; even I, cautious to a fault, had agreed from the start. But Jeram would have none of it.

"Join the Army?" He stared at her as if she had gone mad.

"You would not have to join it," I offered. "Your men are trained, now, to disrupt a march. They can break the Ismiri supply chains, spoil rations, set horses free. We could have them pick off soldiers as they march—anything could give the Royal Army the advantage that tips the balance."

"I'm not risking them for this," he said flatly. "What have they done, that they should pay for the sins of the nobles?"

"It's not just the nobles—" Miriel began, but the Merchant cut her off.

"My Lady, I must agree with Jeram." His tone was regretful, and he held up a hand to stop her protests. "You are a kind girl," he said, "with a gentle heart. A caring, woman's heart." Miriel's eyes flashed at this, but the man did not notice. "It is bitter to leave the farmers to stand alone against the Ismiri, yes. But we must safeguard our own men."

"For what?" Miriel cried. "What greater cause could there be than this?"

"I must give them a fighting chance against the Royal Army." Jeram leaned against the hearth and crossed his arms. "Let those soldiers deplete their strength against Dusan's forces—then we may be in a position to meet them in open battle."

"No," Miriel said, bewildered. "Those men are not your enemies now."

"They could be. We will not fight them if we do not have to do so—but neither will we aid them." He spoke as if she was a fool, as if her worry was weakness, and I felt my own anger awaken. This was not an echo of Miriel's passion, it was the burning coil of resentment that had gone unspoken for so many weeks, here in the heart of the rebellion.

"You're leaving your countrymen to die." My pulse was roaring in my ears. "Families. Children. We could move quickly enough to save some of them. You would be the saviors of the nation, the Council would be beholden to you."

"The Lords would never give us that credit." Jeram's face twisted. "They'd hang us as soon as look at us, and savor the peace we earned for them while we rotted in our graves."

"Wilhelm—" Miriel began heatedly, but she was cut off.

"Wilhelm is a King. A *King*. He is a Warlord. He is no friend to the people—and you, My Lady—" Jeram broke off, breathing hard, and continued in a voice that reminded me eerily of the Duke. "*You* must decide whether it is the rebellion you support, or the nobles. We'll waste no time on traitors."

"Perhaps it would be better if we discussed this in the morning." The Merchant was between them, placatory, but Miriel pushed past him.

"No," she said tightly. "We end this now."

"You don't want that," Jeram warned, and the Merchant put up his hands just as I reached for the dagger in my boot.

"In the morning," he repeated. "We will make decisions in the morning. My Lady, I believe you and your servant should retire for the night. Aron will escort you." I cast Miriel a look, but there was nothing to be done—aside from bolting, we had no choice. Reluctant to break the only outside alliance we had left, we followed his man up to our rooms, and my cheeks burned to see his smirk at our misfortune. As he closed the door behind us, I saw him smile, and my blood ran cold. I knew that smile. That was a killer's smile.

The key turned in the lock, and I looked over to Miriel, who stood frozen with fear. She had seen his smile. She knew it as well. It was Kasimir's smile, Gerald Conradine's smile. It was the smile Guy de la Marque had worn during the few short weeks that Miriel was a Queen-in-waiting. It was a smile that promised us that death stalked us, and that it would wait for its moment.

"They're going to kill us," Miriel said, panic rising in her voice. I did not want to spark her fear by agreeing, but I did not have the words to contradict her. Instead, I went to the window and peered out. Men were patrolling around the house, and as I watched, a detachment of the men I had been training took up position, practicing their sword work as they faced the house. From his vantage point atop one of the nearby statue pedestals,

Jeram waved and gave me a mocking bow, and I slammed the shutters closed.

I went hot, and then cold. *Think, think.* The Merchant would forbid Jeram to kill us, he would assure Jeram that we could be trusted. Jeram would, in time, agree. He knew that his men were better trained now than they would be without me. He even knew, deep down, that Miriel's treaty offered them a better chance of survival than their suicidal siege plan—surely, he must know that. But what of the others? What of later, when Miriel's fight with Jeram was reported to the men at the tavern? Who might decide that they were better without the noble then?

And so, we should be ready to escape in an instant. Silently, I pointed to my spare suit, and then to Miriel. Her eyes widened, but she did not argue. She had run away in a gown before, gasping as the ribs of a corset bit into her, holding her skirts out of her way; she put no stock in vanity now. She pulled the suit on and rolled up the pants and the sleeves, looking delicate and striking, her black hair gleaming darker, truer even than my black suit, her skin standing out, creamy.

There was nothing for us to do, and so when Aron arrived to bring us our dinner, Miriel was already in bed, the covers pulled over her shoulders and her dark curls spread across her pillow. I saw Aron's eyes flick around the room, resting on her briefly, before he shoved the food into my hands and slammed the door once again.

I wanted to laugh, or cry. Giving two imprisoned girls food. The Merchant would not know what had happened to us before, he would have no way of knowing that poisoned food had been sent to us—and that that one incident had been the what bound us together as allies. In truth, I doubted that The Merchant would ever poison us. He was a soft man, softer than he believed Miriel to be—he could not wield a knife or order a young woman's death. Still, I laid the tray on the table, the food untouched, and went to bed myself.

It was past midnight when the key turned in the lock, and I felt no rush of fear, only a calm acceptance that I had been right. I reached up, silently, and wrapped my hand around the haft of the dagger I had laid by my pillow. The door opened with barely a whisper of sound, and the figure slipped inside, shadowy. Aron. My eyes were accustomed to the dark, and I knew his walk; I had watched him out of the corner of my eye since the first day we had lived in this house.

I did not hesitate—only flipped the blade into my fingers, sat up, and threw. He gave a choked cry, and I heard Miriel wake, saw her scramble towards the window. I gestured to her not to jump. I did not know if she saw, and I had no time to check; I was hurtling across the room to Aron's side, wrapping my hand around the dagger where it protruded from his chest, my other arm across his windpipe.

"Who sent you? Who sent you to kill us?"

"Not—both." His teeth were stained with blood, but he was laughing. "Just you."

"What?"

"They said—necessary." He gave a shudder of pain.

"Who? Who said it?" He looked over at me and smiled, terribly, and then he wrapped his fingers over mine and jerked the dagger out of his chest. His blood flowed out over my fingers, and his head lolled back.

"Catwin!" Miriel was at my side, her fingers twining in mine, an arm around my waist. "Catwin, are you okay? Are you hurt?"

"Did you hear him?" I demanded. I could feel shock setting in: I felt that I was floating. I could feel her arm around me and nothing else. Then reality slammed down, and Miriel's fingers and my own were slippery with blood. I held a dead man in my lap, his weight was pressing down on me. I could smell copper and death. I shoved the body off my lap, pushed away from Miriel, and was sick on the floor.

"Catwin?" Miriel reached out for my shoulder.

"That doesn't—" My stomach twisted, and I gasped and spit up bile. "It doesn't get any easier." I saw Miriel look over her shoulder at the man on the ground, then back to me. She clasped my shoulder and knelt by my side, heedless of the mess.

"Are you okay?" Her face was very close, her eyes worried. "Catwin?"

"I'm…" I felt tears coming to my eyes, and realized that I had never cried in front of Miriel before. In front of Roine, in front of Donnett, once or twice during practice with Temar. Never in front of Miriel. I tried to hold the sobs back but I felt my throat ache with them and bent my head to hide my face. To my surprise, Miriel tugged gently on my arm and let me lay my head on her shoulder. I felt her arms around me, and the comfort of having her close.

"You survived," she said tentatively, and I shook my head.

"He came for *me*," I said thickly. "Not you and me, just me."

"I should have saved you," she whispered. "Like the time the man came for me, and you saved me. I should have saved you this time. I'm sorry."

I sat up and wiped my eyes angrily on my sleeve. "Sometimes I wish my father had listened to my mother," I said. "She said it would be kinder to kill me than let me live only to be betrayed."

"Don't say that!" Miriel was genuinely shocked, and I swallowed and looked down. I had not even thought before speaking the words.

"It's eating away at me," I whispered my voice hoarse. It was true, but I realized that I had never admitted this, even to myself. "I thought perhaps it was over when we came here, but what if it follows me all my life?"

"Betrayal?" Miriel whispered, and I nodded. She frowned, and then she reached out and squeezed my hand. "I'll protect you," she said seriously. "The next one, I'll kill." I laughed at the thought, and she shook her head stubbornly. "I mean it, Catwin. You've saved us both, time and again. You protect me. I need to protect you, too."

"You don't." I shook my head, choking on my words, trying to find a way to show her that she did not owe me this. Miriel had gone still for a moment, thinking. Now she twined her fingers with mine once more and tilted her head to look into my eyes.

"Are you well enough to walk?"

"Where are we going?" I was not sure I had the energy to escape once more.

"We're going to the tavern," Miriel said simply. "I've had enough of their cowardice. I won't stay like this, with you in danger here, and the country in danger in the west. We're going to secure their help."

"They might try to kill us." My muscles were shaky; I was not sure if I could stand, let alone protect both of us. Miriel shook her head.

"Someone already tried," she pointed out. When I smiled weakly, she added, "I don't think the Merchant wants us dead, or Jeram. I don't think most of the men want us dead, either. We'll be safe enough, maybe even safer than here." I nodded after a moment, accepting the grim logic, and looked around myself for a pitcher and a towel.

"I should wash."

"No, we'll go as we are. And here." Miriel leaned over and pried the dagger out of Aron's lifeless fingers. "Take this. Someone will recognize it. What are you looking at?" Slowly, I stood and went to the window, pried back the shutters so that the moonlight spilled over the object in my hand. A heavy blade, a pitted handle carved with interlocking circles. The blade, finely crafted, and the ripples of the metal.

"I've seen this dagger before," I said softly. "The captain of the men who killed Garad—he carried its twin." We stared at each other across the expanse of the room, unable to process the enormity of what we faced. Aron, and the men who had killed Garad. Either—

No. I could not think of it.

"Hide that," Miriel said, suddenly superstitious. "Don't let it see the light. Hide it." Her jaw set, and she turned for the door.

"Where are you going?" I called after her, and she turned to look over her shoulder.

"The tavern, still. I don't know what—that—means. But those men owe Heddred, and I am going to call in the debt."

Chapter 7

It was hardly a struggle to escape the house. Jeram had stationed men outside the window, and they patrolled with purpose. Inside, however, the Merchant's servants had long since gone to bed, thinking Miriel and me to be asleep. We crept down the hallways, ran quickly through the great entrance hall, and escaped out a side door, having only one patrol to avoid. I made a mental note that if we survived this, I would teach the men how to avoid multiple patrols. I even began to plan the lessons out, as well as I could—anything, to keep from thinking of what had just happened.

But as we picked our way through the darkness to the tavern, the thoughts began to creep into my mind without my volition. It took long minutes of silence until I could untangle the mess of anguish and understand what lay beneath: betrayal, but not of the human sort. I had thought, however foolishly, that when I came here I had outrun my fate, or that it was finally done with me. I was no longer a spy to a ruthless noble; I had begun to do something good, I had begun to believe in something that gave a purpose to my life.

I had believed betrayal somehow could not follow me here; I had left my life behind, the Court and its intrigues seemed a lifetime away. But someone had come for me. They had sent an assassin here, to find me as I tried to build another life. And now I had nothing: no hope that I could have a life untainted by fear, no hope that I could turn myself back from an assassin to a girl. When the first false belief crashed down, all of the others came with it.

I walked in a daze, the darkness closing around me like a loving caress, shadows calling to a shadow. Now I could see myself drawing closer to them. I had tried to stop the tide of darkness within myself, but it had been too late. I was slipping away. I had deluded myself into thinking that I could yet be a person like any other. I had killed, twice; I had killed without hesitation. No work for the rebellion, no good deeds, could reverse that. All my life, I would live with this, and it would eat at my heart until nothing was left, and I was a shadow, indeed. Was that what had happened to Temar? Was that why he always had such sadness behind his gaze?

Ahead of me, Miriel strode purposefully, her bloodstained hands clenched, her back straight. She was muttering to herself, as she had once been wont to do when she walked through the Palace tunnels to meet the King; she was rehearsing. In my mind's eye, she had gone as bright and hard as steel, brittle and unbending. The change she had tried to push away was pressing back, insistent; it was consuming her. She was becoming light untempered by shadow, unsoftened by darkness. Beautiful, and entirely inhuman.

Across the windy fields, the lights of the town glittered in the darkness. It seemed so welcoming, I thought, that I was overwhelmed by a wave of homesickness. I was not homesick for any place I had ever known, but for a home I did not have, would not have. We had run away, only to find that we could not settle here. We could not settle until we could outrun what stalked us— and there was no outrunning fate. I would never walk across the fields, seeing lights in the distance and knowing them for my house, knowing that my family waited there. I would never roam the earth and know that there was always a place for me to return to. I would spend my life as I always had: a stranger, a cuckoo's child.

I followed Miriel and wondered how she could still believe in the rebellion now—now that we had seen what had followed us here. I wondered if I should slip away, leave her to lead the rebellion as she should do, and take myself and my fate away from her. Anyone who betrayed me, now betrayed the cause I held dear. I looked at Miriel's profile, and could not bring myself to tell her; I held the pain close inside, and walked in silence.

Jeram always stationed men outside the tavern, men in filthy clothes who looked like sots and drunks, but who could fight as well as any, and sound an alarm. Tonight's sentries straightened up as they saw us coming, and banded together to block our path, but they did not raise their cudgels. They knew that we had been imprisoned, and we should not be here—but we were not running away. We were coming to them, covered in blood, and they did not know what to do. They stared at us, sidelong, and at each other. I would have hung back, but Miriel only stopped when she was right in front of them, her chin lifted, her jaw set.

"Come with me," she ordered. "Come inside. All of you will hear what I have to say." She was shining so brightly, to me, that I fancied even they could see it. They followed her as if in a daze, trailing in our wake as we strode into the barroom. The men there, shouting to each other about armies and victory, quieted at once when they saw us. I saw shock on Jeram's face, but I could not have said if it was shock that we had been attacked, or shock that we had survived. He stood to face us.

"Not a word." Miriel's voice cracked across the room like a whiplash. To my surprise, Jeram sat. He did not command his men to kill Miriel as a traitor, nor did he throw his own knife. He only sat, and watched Miriel as she looked around herself, then stepped onto a bench and from there onto one of the tables. The men craned to watch her as she looked around at them, beautiful and disheveled, blood-smeared, furious.

"Who knew of this?" Miriel demanded. "Who knew there was a man coming to kill us tonight?" The men stared at her, open-mouthed and afraid. I scanned the room, and my heart sank: not one face was cloaked, not a single man was smiling, or frustrated. Aron had not acted alone, he had been sent—but not by anyone here. By whom, then? Miriel did not even seem to care. "Which of you helped him?" She pointed to the Merchant, who was sitting awkwardly in the corner. "Was it you? Aron was your servant."

"It was Aron?" The Merchant seemed incredulous. "I told him to guard you, my Lady, no more. I swear it. It could not have been him."

"His body is lying in my rooms," Miriel spat. "Go see for yourself if you do not believe me." She turned away from his shock and swept her gaze over the men; they hunched their shoulders under her scrutiny. "Is this what we've come to, then?" she asked them all. "Assassinations?" She gestured to me. "Gods help us, we thought when we joined the rebellion that we had found truer allies than this."

"We did not know—" Jeram began, and Miriel shot him a furious glare.

"You didn't know? Your own men planning to kill one of our number, and you did not know? You've interrogated every man in this room, and you did not know that one of them was a murderer?" Jeram's eyes narrowed, but Miriel was equal to it. She had faced down the Duke in his rages—this man did not frighten her. "This ends now," she said. "This cowardice, this sneaking around, turning on each other like a pack of dogs. It ends. Now."

"And what does that mean?"

"It means," Miriel said coldly, "that we are going to help our countrymen. We no longer stand apart. We no longer watch as our kin die at the hands of an invading force. You want to rule this nation?" She looked at the crowd, challenging each of them to meet her eyes. "Do you want that?" Slowly, they began to nod. "Then you *defend* it. If you think you're so much better for the people of Heddred, you keep them safe. You protect them from those who would see them dead, or you're no different from the nobles you say care only for riches. If you sit and watch, letting your people die so that you can turn on the army that defended them, you're nothing but cowards."

The men gaped. These were strong men, men who had defied the soldiers and the spies sent to frighten them, the nobles determined to rule them. They had left their families and their homes to come here and join the rebel forces. They had been called rabble, traitors, scum—but never, never had they been called cowards, and certainly not by a young girl.

"It is not cowardly to choose your battle," Jeram said, the only one who would dare defy her. Miriel looked over at him, cold as ice.

"If it were your children who stood in the path of the army, how would you call those who could help you, but would not?" He had no answer, and she knew it. "Could any of you look those mothers in the face, women who saw their sons murdered and their daughters raped, farmers who saw their fields burned, and tell them that you did what was right? Any of you?" The men looked down, aside, afraid to meet her eyes. Miriel waited for a moment, then held out her hands, pleading. "But that's not how it has to be," she said. "We can help. Catwin has taught you how to fight hand to hand and with weapons, you can disarm their sentries, spoil their rations. You can stop this force and aid Heddred.

"I ask that you do this freely," Miriel called out, "for love of your country and your people. Jeram has told us that any decision of the rebellion must be unanimous, and so it shall be. Those of you who would sit out this battle, who would hide on your farms and hope that Kasimir's army is stopped by those braver and stronger than you are—you may go. No one here will stop you. Go home. You have your chance, now. Those who stay—you are with me. You pledge that you will do what is best for the people you hope to govern."

There was a silence. It stretched until I began to doubt, terrified, that Miriel had swayed a single mind. All of these men would go home to their wives and their children, the rebellion would live on in the hearts of bitter men who hated Miriel, and resented her hope for a treaty. I cast a look over my shoulder. *Push the tall one aside, grab Miriel, get her out the door. You can move quickly enough that they won't catch you. Cut the tether on the black horse outside, and the roan, and ride.* And then, unmistakable, I heard the creak as the men rose to their feet.

"I'll go with you," said one of the farmers.

"And I." His son, barely a man, stood proudly at his side.

"And I." I looked over to the bar and saw the innkeeper hoist a tankard to Miriel.

"And I." The men rose to their feet, raising their mugs and clapping; their words swelled to a chorus, a dozen voices, men slapping each other on the back, others cheering, and Miriel smiled before holding her hands up to the throng to silence them.

"That is not all," she called. "I will not forsake my mission. Before we march, we will agree on a treaty, and I will have it signed for you. I will make sure that the King himself grants you the rights you seek, and that they are enshrined forever more in the laws of Heddred. Your children, and your children's children, will live in the world you have pledged to build today."

They yelled their approval, they stamped their feet and whistled, blinded by her beauty, swayed by her words, hearing and believing in the conviction that shone in her face. I looked up at her and smiled, forgetting that I was a woman marked for betrayal, forgetting that what awaited us now was battle and the threat of the Court. For a moment, everything melted away and I saw only Miriel, her face radiant.

She turned and held out her hand to Jeram, that he might climb up beside her and receive their applause as well, and he, silent at her triumph, accepted her hand and raised it into the air. He had a wry smile on his face, he was a man who knows that he has been overruled. And yet, despite himself, his mistrust was fading. He helped her down from the table and the three of us huddled together.

"A man—he truly came to kill you?" I looked into his face, and saw fear. He did not like the thought of assassins in the fold.

His concern was genuine, none of the telltales of lies in his demeanor. I deemed him innocent of our attempted murder, at least.

"Yes," I said shortly. I remembered Aron's words, and shuddered. *Just you,* he had said.

"And you killed him?" He eyed me sidelong, and when I frowned at him, he shrugged. "You know weapons, lad, but I'd never have figured you for a killer."

"Well, I am," I said shortly. Any good humor I might have felt had disappeared; gone in the memory of blood spilling over my hands, Aron's last breath hot on my face. "I've killed before, another man who came for her. And I'll kill anyone else who tries, too."

"We should go," Miriel said, diplomatically, breaking in before Jeram could comment on my threat. "There is much to prepare, and we will all need our sleep. Jeram, I would like you to come with me, to confirm that it was indeed Aron who attacked us. And the Merchant will need some comfort, I think." As we walked back across the fields, the promise of summer warm in the air, Miriel, drew me aside.

"Are you alright?" she asked, so soft, so normal that I blinked at it.

"No." Miriel only nodded.

"I've been thinking," she said slowly. "I wonder: when the rebellion has triumphed, when this is all over—is that the ending, the balance that tips?"

"What if it is?" I was too weary, and too defeated, to care.

"It would mean that your betrayal would end then," Miriel said simply. "Whoever it is, whatever it is that has you marked—that might be the end of it." I stopped and looked over at her, caught between happiness and fear.

"You think so?"

"I do." Miriel held out her hand and we started walking again. "And I did mean what I said earlier. I'm going to kill whatever this is that's hunting you."

"You can't kill anyone," I said, and she looked sharply at me. "I don't mean that way. Well, a little bit. Do you even know how to kill someone?"

"Knives are sharp," Miriel said drily. "I think I could figure it out."

"And then what?" I looked at her. "I promise you, you don't want to do that. You don't want that on your conscience."

"I want you to be free," Miriel said stubbornly, and I sighed.

"Let's see if we can manage that without you killing anyone."

When we finally crawled into makeshift beds by the kitchen fire, too exhausted to be frightened any longer, I gave myself up to sleep gladly. I wanted to sleep before the memories returned, before the horror of what I had done set in. But that night, as I had hoped against hope they would not, the dreams returned.

My mother, for the first time in my memory, did not look frightened. She was not a woman close to death, speaking with the voice of the Gods. She looked like a mother, indeed, weary, but offering comfort. She patted the edge of the bed and I came to sit, hesitantly, fearing what she might say. I smiled when she did, but there was pity in her eyes, and she reached out to touch my cheek. I was looking into her eyes, as grey as my own, like winter storm clouds, when she said,

"I would have spared you this. But you will not need to fear for much longer, my daughter. It will be done with soon."

Chapter 8

We made ready to march in three days. On the face of it, it was an insane proposition, but one to which we grimly devoted ourselves. Any small comfort the men might take with them was put aside; there was no time to pack anything beyond what was absolutely necessary, no time to organize a great wagon train to carry supplies. The plain facts were that our chances of stopping the Ismiri army were laughably small, and they grew smaller each day.

I worked myself to the bone, falling into bed so exhausted that I woke just as I had gone to bed, and remembered nothing of the night before save winter winds and the echoes of my mother's voice. I worked half in hope that Miriel might be right, and that this final charge might end the betrayals I faced, and half in despair, sure that nothing I might do might free me from this fate. I had thought, once, that perhaps Miriel was right, but that the betrayals would be ended by my own death—and I had prayed that my death came not as a dagger between the ribs, or poison in my food, but instead as a fair fight. When I realized that that was my prayer, and not that I survive, I had escaped into the darkest of the Merchant's wine cellars, hidden behind one of the great casks of wine, and sobbed so hard that I thought my throat might bleed.

I had never told Miriel of these thoughts, but I sometimes saw her watching me, and I thought that she suspected. She was kind to me, stopping the sharp retorts that came so easily to her lips. She was careful to make sure that I ate; she brought me food herself, and I noticed that she stayed until I had eaten it. Even as she herself grew pale, and the skin under her eyes became darker and darker with fatigue, she looked after me, and I had no words to thank her for it. If I acknowledged it, I acknowledged the fear that lay, always, at the back of my mind.

That fear was easy enough to forget when I could keep my mind focused on the march, on the strain of the men, on the fear of the invasion. As we outfitted men and prepared rations, we all kept an ear cocked for the sound of a galloping horse, we all cast an eye to the road to see the telltale cloud of dust. We received new reports of the Ismiri army every day, the network of spies sending information whenever they had it. There was always a messenger taking his rest and a meal, it seemed, ready to take a horse and ride back to the capital for more news.

The news was only ever grim. The King had been warned by one hard-riding scout, but by the time that man had seen the Ismiri army, they had been leagues into Heddred. Now they were traveling as if the hounds of hell were at their heels, and each day the news trickled in: first they were close to Castle Derrion, the DeVere family seat, and then past it. When our own scout had seen them, they had cut north, making for the road that would lead them to Penekket—and that had been two weeks ago.

Late in the evening before we were to march, a small group of us clustered around the Merchant's great map, studying the markers that showed the army's progress. I, who had spent more time with the men than the commanders of our group, was frowning at the map and wishing that I had paid more attention in my history lessons.

"We're planning to sweep south around Penekket, and approach them from the marshes," the Merchant said. There were shadows under his eyes, and new lines around his mouth. As Miriel had predicted, he had grieved heavily for Aron, the servant he had trusted for years. To my surprise, he had channeled his grief and his pain into activity, sending for supplies to be sent to our forces as they marched, paying for all the weapons and food he could lay his hands on. He was outfitting the army as if he had no need of a fine house or rich furnishings, and I rather thought that the man did not expect to return home. He reminded me of an animal who knows that its time has come, who will disappear into the wilderness without a goodbye.

"What's that?" I pointed to a strange trail behind the main front.

"The foot soldiers," Jeram said. "It's only a guess, but at the speed they're driving the horses, the men won't be able to keep up. The last scout reported that the army stretches farther than it should."

"What purpose does that serve?"

"None," Miriel said. She was smiling. "Kasimir is driving them so hard that they'll be exhausted when they reach the city."

"But why?"

"Ah, that I don't know." She tapped her mouth with one finger. "At this rate, the men will have to stop and rest before they make their final approach on Penekket. But you saw him at the village—he's not subtle, and he's not patient. And that's an advantage to us." The men exchanged one look. They forgot sometimes that we had been at Court, that we had spent time with royalty; first they had forgotten that I had done so, an easy enough task, but then, gradually, they had even forgotten that dainty, perfectly elegant Miriel had been a noble lady of the Court. When we reminded them, the men tended to be overawed and uncomfortable.

"Why doesn't Dusan put a stop to it?" I tried to remember Dusan as he had been at the Meeting of the Peacemakers: older, now, in the twilight of his years, but still sharp-eyed, clear-minded. And weary of war. Willing to take a chance on an untried boy, for the possibility of a lasting peace. I could hardly believe that he would hold with Kasimir's invasion plans, and most of all with this relentless march.

"We're beginning to think Dusan isn't there at all," Miriel said, biting her lip as she looked at the map. She cast me one look, meaningful, and I gaped back at her. I knew from her sardonic smile that there was more to this than Dusan's absence.

"You think..." I could not even put it into words. Treachery in one court—why not both? And yet, we had heard nothing. If Dusan were dead, surely we would know. The world, for a moment, seemed vast and terrible, frightening. At my silence, the Merchant spoke.

"No statement has been made," he observed. "There has been no declaration of war. Dusan is of the old line of Kings, very formal. He's honorable to a fault, that man. Whatever the advantage, he would never have moved without first trying negotiations."

"We don't know that." Jeram raised his eyebrows at my dour mutter, and the Merchant fell silent. Miriel gave me an exasperated look. "I apologize," I muttered.

"Catwin is...overcautious," Miriel said sweetly, laying her hand on the Merchant's arm. She looked over at me. "I think our host is correct," she said firmly to me. "If Dusan were betraying us, I think he would believe strongly enough to lead his own army. It is considered a duty of a King, he would hold to that. And..." Her eyes got a faraway look. "Even if he wanted to conquer us, he's a cautious man. He'd rather a surrender than a battle. He's practical. He'd have sent assassins rather than an army."

"He sent his assassins first," Jeram objected, and Miriel and I exchanged a quick look. We had never spoken of Garad's death with these men, being more concerned with the present King and his army, and so we had never voiced our doubts about the assassins' origins. Neither had we shared that Aron carried the twin blade to that held by the commander of Garad's killers. We had simply accepted, the two of us, as we always did, that things were likely not as they seemed. There were plots, so many and so confused that we might never know who had caused Garad's death; of all things, we were the surest that Kasimir, the one implicated, was the least likely to be guilty. Clearly, however, the citizens of Heddred had had no such doubts.

Jeram and the Merchant saw the look that passed between me and Miriel, and misinterpreted it. "You think it was the Conradines!" Jeram said eagerly. Miriel flushed, and this time it was I who shot her a quelling glance. I responded myself, to keep her from speaking.

"The King's father, perhaps, might have done such a thing. We've come to doubt that it was the Ismiri, though we have no accusations in mind." Indeed, we worked very hard to keep such accusations out of our thoughts. Neither of us wanted to wonder, and neither of us wanted to know.

"Why do you doubt?" The Merchant was more measured than Jeram. "Sit, tell us." He saw my hesitation. "If we are going to where the King is, it is only right that we should know where enemies and traitors might wait." I nodded, and we sat, all of us leaning together as I outlined my suspicions.

"Kasimir first." I held up one finger. "The men carried orders, supposedly signed by Kasimir. But why would he be so foolish? I thought it was possible that he might try to tempt us to invade. Eight wars, in our history, and never has the invading country won. If he could have tempted us to come over the mountains...but now we see that was not his plan. Not only that, he's exhausting his men. It's a poor plan, unless he has some trick up his sleeve. And even more—who would choose the Warlords for an enemy, when they could have had Guy de la Marque instead? He's a commander, surely, but not as skilled as the Duke, not as skilled as Gerald Conradine." The Merchant and Jeram were both nodding, thoughtfully.

"And Dusan," I said. "He's smart, like Miriel said. He's practical. Why would he go to the trouble of sending men and infiltrating the palace, only to kill Garad and no one else? Yes, the men were ambushed, but he would have planned for that, I think. He would have sent a man, or a group, for any living person who could claim Warden or Conradine blood. If he wanted to invade, he would want the country in disarray—he would not have left any clear heirs." Let alone two, who could marry and thus make the lineage of House Warden whole once more—but I would not say that in front of Miriel.

"So that leaves the Conradines," Jeram insisted. "Who else stood to benefit?" I saw Miriel's head rise, as both of us stared at Jeram and the Merchant. In their eyes, we saw only incomprehension, and honest confusion. I felt myself let out a slow breath, relieved. Even as I had known that the men of the rebellion had no knowledge of Jacces, I had still doubted—all the more so since Aron's attempt at murder.

But, as they had not known of Aron's treachery, it seemed that these men, also, did not know anything of Garad's murder. I felt the slow creep of wonder. Was it all from the rebellion, or was it someone else entirely: Gerald Conradine, Isra Dulgurokov, Guy de la Marque? But the men were waiting for an answer, and I had no heart to sow doubt. I knew without looking that Miriel felt the same.

"Who can say?" she asked lightly, after a pause. "In the Court, grudges span centuries. And it's not always that—they fight for scraps. I can think of a dozen men who would kill, even kill their own kin, if they believed it would bring them closer to the throne." The Merchant was not convinced; his eyes flicked back and forth between me, and Miriel, but she was focused once more on the map, and I could meet his scrutiny with a practiced look of incomprehension.

"Well enough," he said wearily, after a moment. "We should all get some rest. Jeram, you should have a chance to say goodbye to your family." With a start, I remembered that Jeram had a wife, had children. I knew from watching him that he, as well as the Merchant, did not expect to return home again, and my heart twisted as I watched him leave; at my side, Miriel also watched him go, as if she were forcing herself to see this. Her hands were clenched, her back rigid, and she watched the door long after he had left. It was only at my tentative touch on her arm that she shook herself and bid the Merchant goodnight, starting up the stairs to bed and leaving him staring into the fire.

"Do you really think that Kasimir led a coup?" I asked Miriel as we walked. "Or did he just take the army and go?" Miriel was silent, thinking, as we climbed the Merchant's great marble staircase. She held her skirts up, daintily, and the pretty turn of her feet made me wonder if she would ever forget what it was to be a court lady.

"We really don't know," she said at last. "I'll be glad, at least, to know what information the army has." As we padded down the rich carpets of the hallway, she asked, tentatively, "Are you scared?"

I looked over at her, confused. I had faced down assassins, the Duke, the enmity of a dozen nobles with deep pockets and no conscience. Unlike the men who marched with us tomorrow, Miriel and I would not be harrying supply lines, or going up against the Ismiri horsemen. We would not see the armies charge. We would be with the Court, trying to persuade Wilhelm to sign Miriel's treaty. It meant lies, it meant sneaking about—but that had been my life, for years. That fear was nothing. When she saw my confusion, Miriel's face changed; there was pity in her eyes.

"To see Temar," she said, almost gently. "Are you scared to see Temar again?" It was the first time I had ever heard her say his name without anger, but I hardly noticed. The bottom had dropped out of my stomach when she spoke.

Temar. I had kept him so far from my mind in the past days that I had not even admitted to myself that I was afraid to think of him. When I woke in the mornings, I had enough tasks to lose myself in, that it was easy to forget the dreams of the past night. I did not think of him in my free moments because there were none—there was always another man to outfit, a problem with the supply lines, horses to be shod and plans to be conveyed. I had contrived to forget where it was that Miriel and I would be going: to the court, to face everyone we had left.

And Miriel had been right to ask, because I was scared. I was terrified at the thought of coming face to face with any of them again, and most of all Him. How could a man with whom I shared such an easy friendship, tell me outright that he would kill me if I stood in his way? And how could I believe that I would do the same to him? For I knew, now, that I would do so, and so I held no real grudge. I had not told Miriel, knowing that she would not understand; sometimes, I did not even understand it myself.

Temar and I had lied to each other, hidden things from each other, fought each other, and yet we understood. We knew why.

That did not mean that I wanted to face him. I would be watching him to see what he suspected, and I knew that his eyes would flick over me, looking at my face, my shoulders, my neck, where the pulse beat. He would look for lies, he would try to strip away any deception and see my soul bare. He would watch me as if I were a courtier: a collection of desires and ambitions, motivations to be puzzled out.

And if anyone could understand why Miriel and I had come back, it would be Temar. He would never believe any story we told about our disappearance. Whatever others might have thought, he would have known this was a plan of ours. He would have spent these months torn between the surety that we were playing our own game, and worrying, despite himself, that we had been taken against our will. When he saw us alive and well, he would hate us both for the worry he had felt.

And then, for just a moment, I saw Temar's face in my mind's eye: his smile, the dark eyes, the way his hair fell; I felt my face flush, and I caught my breath strangely. I missed Temar—whatever else, whatever fear I held in my heart, I missed him. If I thought only of him like this, the little moments of humor and friendship, I could forget everything else.

I came back to myself, feeling the flush on my skin, and looked over to see Miriel watching me; she was very still, very quiet. Once, she would have given me a fierce lecture on propriety, on knowing my enemies. Now, she watched me as if even she did not know how to play this, or even what to think, having seen me catch my breath at the thought of our enemy. She was so still, in her fear, that I found myself disquieted.

"What?" I asked, trying to smile, trying to make a joke of it. I was inviting one of her speeches on being careful. I found that I wanted her to tell me to stop mooning after Temar. But she only shook her head and dropped her gaze away from mine.

"Nothing. Sleep well." She undressed in silence and slipped under the covers, and as we lay together in the dark, it occurred to me to ask the question she must have wanted: if she was terrified to face Wilhelm. She had asked, hoping that she might speak of her own fear, so I could tell her that it was unwarranted, and instead of assuring her that Wilhelm remained her ally, I had only sparked doubt in her mind about myself.

"Miriel?" I whispered into the dark. I wanted to tell her not to be afraid, that I still believed that Wilhelm loved her, whatever he had done. I did not think him capable of turning his back on the rebellion. I waited, propped up on my elbow, for several long minutes. But, although Miriel's breathing was not the slow, deep breaths of sleep, she did not respond. Eventually, I lay back down, but I stared into the darkness for a very long time before sleep came.

I remembered Miriel telling me that Wilhelm would wait; even then, I thought, she had known he would not, could not. A King could not remain unmarried, not in the wake of such upheaval—he must secure allies, and fast. Miriel would have brought him nothing, and she knew it. But even then, when a logical mind should have told her that Marie was a good choice, she had not suspected it. Emotion had clouded her reason, and still did: it was beyond belief to her that Wilhelm had married her chief rival.

And while Miriel clung to the rebellion as the last link between her and the man she loved, Wilhelm had sent only one message, as much an invitation to murder as a true offer of friendship, and there had been no proclamations on the rights of his citizens, no effort to establish the principles of the rebellion in law. What would Miriel think that the thought of seeing him, of showing him the treaty she had written? Once, she could have been sure that he would sign it—now, for I knew her, she would be terrified not only that he had turned his back on his people, but, in a very human way, that she would look a fool. She would be afraid that he would laugh in her face, and tell her that he had never cared for the rebellion, or for her. And then where would she be? Where would any of us be?

Chapter 9

We set out early in the morning, bleary-eyed from lack of sleep and fearful dreams. Miriel and I avoided each other's eyes as if to deny that we had ever doubted our mission, or each other, and packed our meager possessions into the saddlebags. After a few moments of indecision, I lifted Miriel's mattress and pulled out Aron's dagger. I wrapped it in a scrap of linen and shoved it into my saddlebag, trying not to look at it. I did not want to see it, did not want to think on what it meant—but I knew, also, that if I left it here, I would always wonder if the twin daggers had been a flight of fancy, a trick of my mind. I must bring Aron's dagger back to Penekket, and hope that my possessions had been carried back without me, so that I could see the two daggers side by side.

As I carried the packs out to where the men waited, Miriel changed into the gown we had chosen for her—rough linen, and dirty. She had been worn pale and thin by her work, and could pass for a woman who had been held captive; but we were taking no chances. We knew that the Duke would never believe our ploy, and so Miriel was doing what she did best: painting a tableau so appealing, so scandalous, that the Court would believe it and the Duke would be forced to play along.

The air was deceptively sweet with birdsong, the day already warming as the first rays of the sun illuminated the eastern sky. The Merchant and Jeram had both insisted that all goodbyes must be said the night before, and so there were no tearful embraces now. There were only the men themselves, some sullen, some hungover, and some with the wide eyes and pale faces of men who have realized that they have signed their lives away. They had spent so many nights sitting in the taverns, shouting that they knew how the country must be governed—now, they were marching to war in defense of the citizens they called their brothers and sisters, and these rebels knew that they might never come back to their fields and their families. If they fell on the battlefield, their bodies would be left and forgotten, far from home.

Jeram would not let us leave so forlornly, and he gave a speech, his voice strong, the pain in his eyes covered, for a moment, by his passion. At Jeram's call, the men gave a cheer, half-hearted at first, but growing stronger as they drew courage from each other, and spurred their horses to a trot. For a moment, as the flag with the circle billowed out, I felt my own heart lift. Miriel had been right, and this was right. The rebellion hoped to break down the very framework of Heddred, and if they hoped to bring a better country into being in its place, they must give their own courage to defend the people from invaders. The men believed it as well. As we trotted along country roads toward the town, a few men called out cheers, and the others responded with roars of approval.

Their attempt at good humor might have held, and been forged, by fear and necessity and patriotism, into determination, but for what we saw in the town. There was no bustle of morning activity, no sweet scent of bread baking, no calls of the vendors. Instead, the people lined the streets in utter silence, women and children, the old, the lame, all watching us with shadowed eyes. They held their hands up for us in farewell, and they marked our faces.

With a shudder, I realized that they were grieving. No matter what I had known of war, no matter what fear I had seen in the men's faces in the past days, I had not understood it until I saw my own death written in the eyes of these townspeople. And, to pair with the fear that now chilled me, named amongst the dead, I felt an overwhelming wave of guilt. The blacksmiths, the farmers, the cobblers and bakers and millers: all of them were coming with us, at our insistence, and there would be a town bereft of fathers and brothers and sons.

And the guilt only deepened, for this—this—was what Garad had fought so hard to prevent. As Miriel railed at him for his stupidity and his short-sightedness, as we both believed that his Golden Age was more a childish dream than a reality, and that he should devote himself to the rebellion Miriel held so dear, Garad had been devoting himself to peace. Somehow, he must have known this grief in his heart, understood the cost in lives. He had been cruel, and short-sighted, indeed, and yet we had never given him his due.

I looked over to my lady, and saw her looking down at her hands on the reins, biting her lip. Miriel was not the confident beauty she had been even a few moments before, radiant in the sunshine and riding to her glory. She, too, felt the weight of guilt, and—I remembered our whispered conversation from the night before—she was terribly afraid, now, that she had led these people on a suicide march for nothing. She was afraid that they would lay down their lives and be granted no rights in return.

It was a miserable day. The men rode through the pristine, blooming countryside as if they were dead already; no one spoke, and there were no smiles, and no cheers. I edged my horse close to Miriel's, to ride at her right hand in case she should need anything from me, and smiled half-heartedly at the memory of learning to do this four years ago as we first rode to Penekket, struggling to control my horse and hating Miriel, knowing nothing of what the future held for me.

And there had been no way to know. Even if I had not been so willfully blind, even if Temar had told me everything that he knew, I would have been just as ignorant of what was to come. For who could have known that the world would go topsy-turvy, that my greatest enemy in the world would now ride at my side as my only ally? Who could have foreseen that I would have run away to join an uprising, and that at the behest of a noblewoman?

Darker than that, who could have known that a peasant woman's mutterings were a true prophecy, and that I would be betrayed time and again? Miriel's words, her true belief that my fate was tied to more than my own self, had awoken both hope and fear in my heart. Hope—that this might have a greater, better purpose. Fear—that this was somehow beyond me entirely, on another scale from my life, part of a greater pattern.

For what could be more terrifying than believing that the Gods had a purpose for me? Those whom the Gods had chosen had a hard road to walk, everyone knew that. And it did not matter how often I had wondered these things myself in the darkness, or been told them by Roine. She was always talking of the old ways, of honoring fate and the Gods, and I—I was just another human, with fears and thoughts, and nightmares that disturbed my sleep. Miriel's calm acceptance of the prophecy was another thing; this was not dreamy words in the dark, but the clear-eyed belief of a young woman who had seen death, and betrayal of her own. Miriel, so quick, so bright, so relentlessly logical, believed the prophecy my mother had made. I was afraid of that.

I was surprised to see her grow more confident as the roads widened and we approached the outlying towns. When, before, we had traveled to Penekket, or the mountains, or the Meeting of the Peacemakers, Miriel had seemed to curl inside herself. She had disappeared behind her mask, and her eyes had gone blank. I could not understand the sense of purpose I saw in her eyes until I realized that now, at last, Miriel was riding back to Court of her own free will, to fulfill her own purpose. She was no longer in a cage.

Even purpose and free will could not stave off fear, of course, but Miriel bore it well. She was attentive to the rebel soldiers, visiting each campfire at night with Jeram and the Merchant, offering kind assurances to the men and taking the time to converse with any who might wish to speak with her. She was proud to sleep in a tent, on a bedroll, as they did; at last, I understood that when I had hated her, on our first journey together, for the luxury of her wagon and her warm bed, she had known. She had seen derision in the eyes of the guards who rode with her, she had known envy and malice from us all. And so she made no complaint of the aches and pains she had in the morning, smiling cheerfully and drinking the awful camp tea we made without a grimace.

"You know that the men would be pleased enough to coddle you," I said to her one day. The misery of the march had eased a bit, and now there were a few murmured conversations between the men. It was enough to cover our own words, but I was glad enough simply to have noise. In grim silence, it was difficult to keep my mind away from its dark thoughts.

Miriel looked over at me, one eyebrow raised, and I smiled at her. "You're a figurehead," I explained to her. At her instant denial, I shook my head. "No, not just that. You wrote their treaty, they know that. But you're pretty, and nobly-born, and gently-spoken. They're glad to know you're on their side. They want to hold you up." For a moment, the calm mask slipped away.

"They're going to die because of something I said," Miriel said bleakly. "While I'm going to the palace." The love of the soldiers gave her no comfort.

"They made their choice just like you did," I said bracingly. It was the only thought that had kept me from going mad, in the first few days of the march. Any one of these men had had the chance to walk away.

"They're in more danger than I am," she said stubbornly.

"They know who their enemies are," I countered, after a pause. "If you want me to teach you to cut horses loose and ruin grain stores, I can do that, but if it's guilt you're feeling, you must know that you are going into danger, too. Do you think Guy de la Marque will be pleased to see you, or Gerald Conradine? Do you think that your uncle will accept us back without asking questions?" When she hesitated, I added, "And you're the only one who can get Wilhelm to sign this. We have to go back to Court, or they'll lay down their lives and no one will ever know of the treaty. True?"

"True," she said finally. And, with a flash of humor, "Maybe we can ride out with the army, afterwards."

"A fine sight you'd make with a broadsword." I was laughing. "Donnett showed me one once, and it was taller than you are." She giggled, and relaxed a bit, looking out over the fields of wheat and barley that lined the roads.

"Do you think it will work?" she asked at length. "Really, Catwin." I paused. I had tried very hard not to give myself time to doubt; I had tried to learn from Miriel's unflagging hope.

"You said that maybe my fate was larger than just me," I said finally. "That it was tied to the rebellion. Think about what we've done together—we found the leader of the rebellion, when no one else could. You would have turned the King into our ally, if he had lived." I swallowed down guilt and went on. "And then we ran away—we're two girls, we were only surviving before, but we made something more of it. Jacces only ever wrote letters; *you* inspired these men to ask for something more for themselves, not just sit in taverns and drink and complain."

"And so?" Her brow was furrowed.

"And so I can't believe we've come so far, just to fail now."

"That would certainly be unfortunate," she said drily. She saw my frown and shrugged. "Yes, I see what you mean. I'm just..."

"Afraid?" I suggested, and she nodded, wordlessly, and she smiled, but I could see tears trembling on her lashes.

"I know it doesn't help," she admitted, wiping her eyes.

"It lets you know you're not insane."

"Catwin, we're going back to Court. We're crazy." At last, I laughed, and she smiled. "And so are the courtiers, if they think we're telling the truth," she added.

"It's not a bad story," I protested. I was proud of it, our great ploy: we had been captured, to be used as surety if the King tried to send troops against the rebels. I had freed Miriel, and the two of us had escaped, making our way north to the city, where we would be properly shocked to learn that the rumors of an

Ismiri invasion were true. We had prepared and practiced answers to all of the questions we were sure the Duke would ask us: Why did they not send a ransom note? What town were you kept in? What were the names of your captors? Did they hurt you? Are you sure you're not lying, Catwin?

"It's suspicious," Miriel said.

"But plausible."

"But plausible," she agreed. She drew a deep breath. "We should split off tomorrow. Are you ready?"

"I am."

Chapter 10

"You have everything you need?" the Merchant asked solicitously. He reached over to tuck Miriel's cloak around her shoulders, and she smiled courteously at the gesture. The morning was cold, mist rising off a nearby lake, and she had been shivering.

"We must look as if we barely escaped with the clothes on our back," she said kindly. "It is to our benefit not to have saddlebags. And in any case, we can buy supplies. It is the men who will have more difficulty staying fed."

The Merchant nodded, and Jeram gave an affirmative grunt. When the men had set off, they had been the heroes of the rebellion, marching through the land where their ideals were held in high regard. For the first few nights, they had been sure of a welcome in any town, camping on the village green, feted in the taverns, but as they had left the well-known landscape of the Norstrung Provinces, they had seen suspicious glares from the townsfolk. Now they proclaimed themselves a group of men marching to join the Royal Army, determined to show that the people of Norstrung were loyal to the King. Still, as they drew closer still to the capital, they often tried to escape notice entirely, bypassing towns where they might have procured fresh food.

"And you? You have everything you need?" Miriel asked them. "No last words to put in the treaty?" It was a poor joke, over the fuss that had been made for every word in the document, but Jeram smiled at it.

"Be true to us," he said simply, and Miriel did not flare up, as she might have done. She inclined her head and met his eyes.

"I will. Thank your men every day, from me, and know that I will be praying for their safety. I hope to advise the King so that the war may be won quickly, by soldiers, and your men may go home to their families."

"I hope so, too," Jeram said, but I knew that he did not expect it. "Go, the two of you. And the Gods speed your way."

And so we set out in silence, two figures on horseback, plodding carefully through the early morning mist, spurring our horses to a trot, and at last to a gallop, casting a last smile at each other before letting our faces settle into the pallor of fear. We were to look desperate, afraid, exhausted, frantic—and as we approached Penekket, we would need to feign nothing.

We rode for two days, skirting towns and sleeping under trees: a young lad and a girl with the hood of her cloak pulled up in the unseasonably warm weather. This had been a piece of the plan devised by Miriel, who knew her uncle to have spies placed all over the land. If we did not find soldiers, she reasoned, the Duke would find us. I agreed with her, and yet I kept my right hand free of the reins, to snatch at one of my daggers in case the men the Duke sent had been ordered to take us as captives and not family.

In the end, it was so easy that I almost feared it to be a trap for us and not for the soldiers. We came upon a detachment in a little town only a few leagues south of Penekket, and spurred our horses to meet them on the road, as I waved my arms to call their attention. They pulled up, several men reaching for their swords, and I swung down from my horse, so as not to spur an attack.

"Please," I called, "you are soldiers of the Royal Army?"

"Aye," one of them called back. "And who're you? And who is that?" He jabbed a finger at Miriel, and I saw one of the bowmen poised to shoot. I held up my hands.

"I am a servant of the Duke of Voltur. You'll have heard that his niece disappeared some months ago?" They raised their eyebrows.

"I heard of it," one of them offered. "She was t'marry the Queen's nephew, and then she was gone on the road, and the Duke never found her. Probably dead, lad."

"Fool," the leader retorted. He pointed to Miriel, and looked at me. I nodded.

"She's not dead," I said, and I gestured to Miriel, who drew back her hood. His men stared, open-mouthed, lowering their swords.

"Gods be good," their leader murmured. "You swear that's the Lady?"

"Yes," Miriel said softly. She made an exquisitely tragic figure, her eyes wide and her skin pale. "I am the Lady Miriel DeVere. Please, good sirs, will you give us safe passage to the city?"

"Quickly," I added, hoping that I looked urgent and not duplicitous. "We have men after us, sir. We only just escaped, and

I don't know how far behind us they are. They'll know we're making for the city." We had him, I knew it—the wheels were turning in this man's head, I could see his thoughts of a glorious rescue, of the reward he was certain awaited him for finding us.

"Form up!" he called to his men, and he crooked a finger at me. "You, lad, you ride with me and tell me what happened. The men'll keep the Lady safe."

"Yes, sir." I swung up into the saddle once more as the men wheeled their horses about, and as we set off at a brisk trot, I launched into the story Miriel and I had concocted. "We were taken at an inn not far out of the mountains. There were four of them. A man recognized the Lady, and they came into our room; I tried to fight them, but...I failed." I hung my head.

"And who're you, then, if you were in her rooms?" the captain asked, skeptically. "You can't tell me the Lady travels with a manservant." He cast a look over his shoulder at Miriel, and then back at me. "Even one so...well, begging my pardon."

"I..." I cleared my throat. "I'm a girl." The man's eyes widened. I saw him take in my face, the set of my eyes, my mouth, my throat and my hands.

"Well, I'll be." He whistled. "So you are." He guffawed. "And you tried to fight off the kidnappers! That must have given them a good laugh." I swallowed down my retort that I could probably have won against four attackers, and only blushed.

"I did the best I could to keep her safe, sir."

"I'm sure you did, lad—lass." He shook his head and chuckled. "The Duke's niece, and a girl dressed as a boy! Where'd you get the pants, then?" I gritted my teeth and refrained from rolling my eyes.

"I'm sure the Duke will be most appreciative for your help, sir," I said, as sweetly as I could. "Please, might I ride with my lady? She's been so frightened."

"Of course." He waved me away, then changed his mind. "Wait. Come back. Have you heard the news?"

"News?" I frowned at him. "You mean, the rumors? We couldn't believe it was true..."

"Oh, it's true," he said grimly. "The Ismiri army is marching on Penekket now, and word is, they're making good time. If you want to get into the Palace, we'll need to travel quick. The royal court's in the fortress already, and word is, no one gets in or out." He cast another glance at Miriel. "I think she might be able to—but only if we get there soon." I nodded, as gravely as I could, and trotted back to Miriel.

"The rumors are true," I said urgently to her, and she turned a properly shocked face to me. I tried not to laugh at her feigned amazement.

"No! How did they get over the mountains? Are they at the city?" Miriel looked around herself at the soldiers. "There is truly an invasion?"

"Don't you worry, my Lady," one of the soldiers said. "Their army's a good few weeks away from the city, yet, and ours'll be out to meet 'em soon."

"We'll be riding hard," I told her. "The sooner we can get inside the fortress, the better." Miriel nodded, looking frightened. I knew that it was not entirely an act; I myself could hardly think of an army marching on the city without feeling fear rise up in my chest. We were children of peace, she and I. This was beyond us.

The days passed in a daze: fear, the relentless heat of the summer sunshine, and the pain of riding horseback for so many hours. True to the captain's word, we went quickly, keeping the horses to a brisk pace, claiming replacements at each aid station, and I could not have said if I was pleased to be going so quickly, to be meeting our final challenge at last, or terrified, wishing desperately to stretch the journey as much as possible.

On the last night, having reached another station after darkness fell, the captain courteously asked Miriel if she would like to rest. He was reassured with her sweetest smile and a shake of her head. Miriel could not bear to draw this out further. She had barely been able to eat for days, as Fortress loomed ever closer on the horizon. In the past nights, we had both laid awake, fear beating a rhythm in our blood, and as we drew closer to the city, it coursed through our veins all the more quickly. Miriel, for all her lies, spoke nothing more than the truth when she told the captain that she had no wish to rest. Rest brought drifting thoughts, and thinking brought fear. Better to ride onwards to the inevitable confrontation, than hang back.

"Oh, thank you, but I don't think I could sleep," she said, her pale lips curving in a smile, her shadowed eyes still bright, still flirtatious.

"We'll ride on, then," the Captain had said, doubtful but relieved. "We'll go first to the Palace. Only the Royal Guard's allowed into the Fortress now. They'll escort you."

"Thank you," Miriel said calmly, her pleasant smile belied by the frantic beating of her pulse, and the fear I could see in her eyes. In the flickering of the torches, she looked barely human, her eyes gone as black as midnight, her hair gleaming. As we rode through the darkness, she looked over at me and murmured, "I find it best to think of nothing."

"You have nothing to fear," I told her, my voice very low. The men were riding loosely in packs, talking amongst themselves, but we could not be too careful. "We know everything your uncle might ask us, and we know what to say. We need only to be allowed to approach the King. That is all." She nodded and took a deep breath to steady herself. She was reminding herself, I knew, that she knew herself capable of this. She had been the most consummate of liars in the Court, creating so many illusions that even I, who knew her best, had not always known what was Miriel and what was her mask.

And therein lay the fear: we had escaped the Court and tried to outrun the shadows that followed us. Now, as we returned, we could not help but fear what would happen to us. We had no way out, after all—for we had been so consumed by our need to get the treaty to Wilhelm that we had not formulated any plan for another escape. In truth, where was there to go? If we succeeded, the rebellion would no longer be secret meetings and passwords, it would be open, lawful. Our desire to hide from the eyes of the court would be suspicious, then.

But we must find somewhere to go. We could not stay. If— when, I reminded myself—Wilhelm signed the treaty, the Duke would see Miriel's hand in it. Whatever his plans, whatever Temar's, I did not think either would welcome this. And so Miriel and I would be known to be liars, and enemies, and if we had no way to escape… No. If I thought on it, I would be sick. I forced my mind away, and focused on my breath, as Miriel had suggested. Seeing my pale face, she gave me a tentative smile and then returned to her own meditations.

Dawn broke as we rode, and we stopped for a quick breakfast: army rations that were nonetheless fresher than the food we had eaten in our escape. We pressed on, the tower rising ever higher on the horizon, and it was barely noon when we approached the gates at last. True to the captain's word, the walls were bristling with guards, and we were met with a bellow of, "halt!" The captain swung down, and held out his hand to Miriel, that she might walk with him. I heard the gasps and murmurs of the guards on the wall; Miriel's face was known to them, there had been ballads sung about her beauty. The Palace Guard, fiercely loyal to the Duke, had been loyal as well to his beautiful niece, thinking it a fine compliment to the Duke's loyalty and bravery that his bloodline should sit upon the throne.

"Is that truly the Lady Miriel?" a man called, and Miriel smiled up at him.

"It is I!" She called back. "I am safe now, and well—but I should like to be reunited with my kin!" There was a cheer from the men, and the grinding of the portcullis as it was raised. Miriel was lifted back onto her horse, and our little party rode back into the palace itself. As we rode, I looked up at the fortress and, as ever, felt the inevitable stab of foreboding. I had never liked the fortress, and I had never known why; it would seem that I was going to find out sooner rather than later.

A runner was sent, racing down the alleyways to the fortress, and we were ushered through side doors and down covered streets, still on horseback, the Royal Guard giving sidelong glances at Miriel. She rode, now, with her head up and her hair flowing down over her shoulders. She was not the driven rebel leader, nor the frightened girl who had sparked the sympathy of the soldiers. She was the King's betrothed, the most beautiful and charming maiden of the court, a lost beauty returning home. Her confidence did not even flicker when we rode into the courtyard at the base of the fortress and saw what awaited us: her uncle, and Temar standing, impassive, at his side.

My gaze was drawn, at once, to Temar: the sheen of his black hair, the dark eyes with all their secrets, the shape of his mouth. I found myself awed to discover that he had substance. After nights spent dreaming of his face, after the memories that came to me at the strangest times—eating sweet rolls, like the ones he and I would take from the kitchens for breakfast; reading maps; working out a bruise or a sprain—I had almost forgotten that Temar was real. I looked at him, and felt my heart sink when he would not look at me. His eyes were fixed on Miriel, but I knew that Temar could just as easily have looked at me for the signs of deception; he was not looking at me because he would not. He did not wish to see my face.

"Well, well," the Duke said, his voice a reminder of deepest winter, and my attention was jerked back to him; my heart began to beat frantically, like a rabbit caught in a snare. "My niece has returned home at last."

Chapter 11

Miriel gave a tremulous smile at her uncle, at Temar, at me—and then burst into tears. She hunched over, one hand cupped over her mouth, as Temar walked over to help her down from her horse. His courtly manners and blank face belied the flash of hatred I saw in his eyes; no, Temar had not believed for a single moment that Miriel and I had been rescued. He was watching her now as he always had, with the utmost suspicion. I saw a spasm cross his face as Miriel leaned into him, sobbing, and let him escort her to her uncle. There, he watched as Miriel held out her arms and, under the gaze of the Royal Guard, her uncle was forced to embrace her as if he was, in any way, glad to see her. As if they were a happy family indeed, to be reunited.

Unwatched, forgotten, I swung down from my horse and stood to one side. I did not know what I should do. I was miserable; the emotion, unexpected, had welled up and there was no denying it now. I looked over at Miriel and the Duke, studying each other with delighted expressions that concealed loathing and mistrust, and then to Temar, whose blank face concealed thoughts I was not sure I would ever know. The last thing I had expected, in this reunion of enemies, was to feel lonely—I knew this happiness was unfeigned—but still I felt out of place, with no one, not even an enemy, to greet me.

I looked to the guardsmen, who seemed pleased with this tableau of apparent happiness, and knew at once that what I wanted more than anything was a hug from Roine, the chance to explain why I had gone, and the assurance that there was someplace in the world that I was valued. I had been so focused on surviving this first encounter with the Duke that I had not even considered when I might be able to slip away, but now I took my courage in my hands and approached Temar. He did not look over at me, but I knew he was aware that I was at his side.

"Is Roine in the fortress?" I asked him quietly.

"She is." He did not look at me. "She is with the healers."

"I would like to go see her," I said. "Please." The corner of his mouth twitched slightly; not a smile, for his eyes were cold.

"Do what you wish," he said simply, and I stepped away from him, trying to make my face blank. He could have said nothing more hurtful. After all of this time away, in the midst of all the suspicion I knew he held for me, he dismissed me as if I was nothing—neither friend, nor even a worthy foe. I turned and left, blindly, slipping past him and the Duke alike, leaving Miriel and running into the cool dark of the Fortress itself.

For a while, I entirely forgot the fact that I had always disliked this place. I forgot that in the pale light of mornings, the beautiful lines and carvings in the marble looked as if they were carved from bone, and I forgot the way that I had always shivered when I looked up and saw the shadow of the Fortress falling across the Palace grounds. This spire was a reminder to the people of Penekket that peace was fleeting; I, a child of the mountains, born to the blood-soaked ground of Voltur, had never seen war, but had never needed the reminder, and had resented it.

But the Fortress, inside, was no more than another great building, with flickering torches lighting surprisingly clean passageways. I slipped down corridors and made my way up flights of stairs, periodically stopping to ask directions, and pausing to peer out the arrow slits in the alcoves of outer hallways. Far below, I could see the pretty sprawl of the royal enclave, the golden dome of the Palace proper shining brightly in the afternoon light, and, as I rounded the Fortress, the stately buildings of the Academies and, beyond them, the riot of color from the market in the city.

I was beginning to pant somewhat by the time I reached the healers' chambers. The doctors and midwives and surgeons— being very useful, but not very good with weapons—were housed on a floor very high up, so that they might not be first killed in the unlikely event that the Fortress was breached. There were two dozen or more in their large chamber, all wearing the plain white robes that marked them as healers, tending to a steady stream of injuries and maladies. Roine was bending down to look into they eyes of a small child, moving her fingers back and forth to see if he could follow them. When I saw her, I broke into a run.

"Roine!" She whirled to look at me, a bowl of ointment clattering out of her hand and onto the wooden floor, and for a moment she only gaped at me.

"*Catwin?*" She was frozen for a moment, and then, slowly, she reached out to touch my face. She was shaking. I knew that look, it was the same confusion with which I had beheld Temar—a dream made flesh. But we were not Shadow and Shadow, and thus enemies, who would look at each other not only to marvel, but to measure weakness. We were mother and child. And so she cried; Roine held me close and cried. "I did not think I would ever see you again," she whispered, and I felt sick with guilt.

"I could not send a messenger," I pleaded, my voice barely a breath, thinking how flimsy an excuse it was. "We could not risk the Duke finding us." And, as she wept, I thought that it would have been worth the risk. How had I been so unfeeling?

"But you came back," Roine said, bewildered. She wiped her eyes. "Why did you come back?" I opened my mouth to tell her, and then hesitated. I did not know who here reported to the Duke, to Gerald Conradine, to the Dowager Queen and her cohort. The knowledge of the treaty, that all-important scroll hidden beneath Miriel's cloak, was too explosive for me to tell anyone— even Roine.

"I can't say," I said wretchedly, and I saw the flash of hurt in her eyes. Still, she drew a deep breath, squared her shoulders, and nodded.

"So you are home," she said, forcedly cheerful. "Miriel will be preparing for her wedding, then?" I froze. Miriel's wedding. Of course. I had forgotten—we had both forgotten. In the aftermath of the assassination attempt, in the panic of the invasion, bearing the treaty that could change the world—we had forgotten. Miriel was to be married.

"I have to go." I headed for the door, as fast as I could, barely pausing at the door. "I'll come back," I called, and then I turned and ran, for the stairs, for the nobles' chambers.

When I presented myself at the doors to the Duke's rooms, I was met with skeptical stares from his guardsmen. I was no longer wearing finely-made livery, with my hair in a neat braid and Miriel at my side, but instead an awkward boy in homespun, my cropped hair brushing my cheekbones. They let me in only reluctantly, one opining that he had seen me before, and I found myself in the middle of an interrogation.

Miriel was standing in the center of the room, her cloak still around her shoulders, her fingers clenched in the rough fabric. For the first time that I had seen, she looked out of place in the finery of the palace: her creamy skin, wide eyes, and gleaming hair would have matched the finery of the Duke's rooms, but for the fact that she wore a rough gown and borrowed boots, that she had bruises under her eyes from fatigue. Her hands and face were dirty, and the days on the road had made her even smaller and thinner.

The Duke was leaning across his desk, intent on Miriel, his eyes wide and staring. He looked almost feverish, he looked unhinged. When I slipped into the room, he swung his head around to look at me, and I tried not to stop dead in my tracks. He did not look like the calculating, terrifying man I had faced, all these years; he was all anger now, anger and ambition. I remembered his tirade when Garad had died, when he realized that his prized playing piece was now no longer the Queen-in-Waiting, when he saw power slipping out of his fingers. He broke off his low-voiced threats and watched me as I went to Miriel's side. I wished that I had some guidance; all I had was Miriel's fear, and the sense that I should continue the charade.

"Are you okay?" I whispered. "I can bring one of the healers to see you." I looked over at the Duke. "Will you be able to find them, my Lord?"

"Find whom?" His voice was so cold that I flinched.

"The men who captured us. They weren't far behind, if you were to ride out—" I broke off when his hand slammed down against the table.

"There *were* no captors! There was no pursuit!"

"What do you mean?" I asked, and his eyes narrowed. On the side of the room, Temar shifted slightly, watching me intently now. I tried to forget his regard, though I felt my heart beat faster.

"What do I *mean*?" the Duke asked dangerously. "I mean that this was all a lie. You thought you could run away, and then when you tired of it all you came back to me with some harebrained story of kidnapping. Why was there no ransom note, Catwin? Why?"

"We told them we could pay them," I said desperately. "They said she was a bargaining chip—but that you'd come to get her back if you knew where she was." I swallowed. "Please, my Lord—Miriel has been mistreated and roughly housed, and I tried to keep her well, but I am afraid she is ill. Please, can she see Roine?"

"My niece is perfectly fine," he said flatly. "Save thinner, which is no use to anyone. How is she to bear a son for the Dulgurokovs when she looks like a child herself? A fine time I'll have persuading them to take her now."

"What?" Miriel had gone white. I reached out for her hand, but she did not notice. She was staring at her uncle, whose mouth curved in his predatory smile.

"Ah, yes. I suppose I had not told you, had I?" His smile widened. "Of course, you were not here. You are to be married, Miriel. To Arman Dulgurokov. The marriage will lift you high." His face twisted. "Higher than you deserve, but it is...necessary." I frowned at him, trying to understand this, but Miriel had stopped thinking entirely at the sound of the name.

"But..." she whispered. "He's...."

"Old?" The Duke smiled. "Young enough to get a son on you, and that's all we need. I've realized, you see—I can't trust you to carry my interests by turning minds. But you don't need to do that now. That's the beauty of this. All you need to do is get with child. You were to be married to Toros, of course," he added negligently, as if he had not seen Miriel's horrified expression, or my own. "Arman's son, Miriel, don't tell me you forgot the Court so quickly? But *he* died in a border skirmish a month ago. Arman was still desirous of the alliance. Of course, he hasn't seen you yet."

There was a pause, and I saw some of the fear lift from Miriel's face. The Duke saw it, too, and smiled, and I realized he had wanted only to see Miriel's hope, that he might crush it. "But he'll take you," he said, smiling cruelly. "He wants to rise as much as I do." Miriel swallowed.

"I thought you wanted me to be the King's mistress," she said. She did not look at the Duke; her eyes were focused on the far wall. "Won't this put rather a dent in your plans?" It was a quiet defiance, something that offered her little enough hope in any case, and I saw the Duke's face flash into anger.

"No," he said shortly. "Not this King. Gerald Conradine would not take kindly to the influence you would have, I think, and then I would have no heir and no alliances. That would do me no good." He took a deep breath to steady himself, and his strange, mad smile returned. "But there is a plan, Miriel. So go bathe and do up your hair; I'll send a servant for your clothes from the Palace. When you see Arman at dinner, you will be charming, and you will be grateful to be marrying such a man." Miriel managed a trembling smile, and a curtsy, and he gave her a curious look. "What has gotten into you?" he asked her.

86

"Only a few days ago, I was in shackles in the cellar of some country house," Miriel said, watching him with quiet dislike. "Now I come back to luxury, to an invasion, to find that I will be marrying a man old enough to be my grandfather. Forgive me, but all of this is a bit sudden." The lie was beautifully executed, and his eyes narrowed.

"Then you had best practice your smiles," he said. He leaned forward, his knuckles braced on the desk, and his eyes bored into Miriel's. "I'll not have this plan, as well, undone by your incompetence."

There was no retort to make. Miriel swept him a curtsy and made for the door to the chambers that would be ours, her back straight but her head bowed. When the door clicked closed behind us, she rounded on me, her eyes blazing. I nodded, and put one finger to my lips. The Duke's rooms were no place for unguarded words. Even now, I was sure that Temar was listening at the door. What we needed was to sow doubt—be angry enough, unbiddable enough, that he did not think we were lying, and yet make him wonder if our story was true. I hoped that Miriel would catch on.

"You *are* okay?" I asked her. "How is your ankle? I can ask Roine for something for it, if he'll let me go." I did not need to worry. Miriel understood at once.

"He doesn't even believe us," she whispered, as if incredulous. "We could have *died*, Catwin. They might have killed us, or caught us escaping, and he—"

"Don't think of it." I bit my lip against a smile, grinning at her and trying to keep my voice grave. "You can't think of it. Tonight you have to be smiling and gay and beautiful."

"I can't marry that man!" Her uncle would hardly believe our story unless Miriel was herself: strong-willed and stubborn. Now she salted the lies with truth, and I reached out to clasp her hand. I hoped that she could see the sympathy in my eyes, for I could see the real panic in hers. I could feel the slow creep of uncertainty. The Duke's smile, his assurances—we were in the middle of a plot, and I did not know the scope of it.

"It's not tonight," I said, a weak comfort. I held up one finger to caution her from believing the next words. "But unless you can find a better alliance, you'll have to marry Arman."

"I can't!" She was trying to believe the assurance she saw in my eyes: that somehow, we would escape this. But the fear was real. Miriel had survived this far, and she was now realizing that when all of this was over, when the treaty was signed, there was nothing more for her. She had no bargaining power, and if we could not escape, she was at her uncle's mercy. If he insisted on her marriage, then married she would be—she would disappear into the life of a noblewoman, and become nothing. She knew as well as I did that the treaty would be a cold comfort then.

"Miriel—we know nothing of him. He could be very kind to you." It was what a sister would say, what a mother would say. *Don't fear, he could be a nice man.* It was the best that I could offer her, and that truth was bitter. I tried to find anything to make it better. "He's an intelligent man, a great man at court. You can still do good for the country. You'll benefit your family. The Duke will be pleased."

"If he didn't care that we were kidnapped, how much can he care whom I marry?" Miriel folded her arms, and I saw that, although she knew she had never been in danger, she was deeply offended that her uncle would care so little. I felt my mood lift at her wounded pride, and stifled a smile. I saw her eyes flash, and then she saw the humor in it; the corner of her mouth quirked.

"Don't talk like that," I soothed her. I heard the faint creak of floorboards as Temar crept away, and I raised my eyebrows at Miriel. "Would you like a bath? And a proper gown? And some jewelry?"

"I don't want to go to dinner," she said, so honest that I stopped on my way to the door and turned back to look at her. "I don't want to see him." Only I would have known that she meant Wilhelm. I bit my lip, then pointed to her side, where the treaty was hidden in its little leather cylinder. Miriel closed her eyes and nodded, and I saw her lips form a silent prayer. I watched her for a moment, and then opened the door and looked about for a page.

"Some water for my lady," I said. "And please send the maid in directly when she returns with the gowns. We will want the white and blue, I think."

Chapter 12

After months of rough, unwashed linen, and scratchy woolen shirts, it was strange indeed to wear my own suit, so soft it felt like a caress, and that over clean skin. The black fabric was unfaded, the Celys crest picked out sharply in black thread. The boots were made for me—I remembered Miriel insisting that I replace them, that they were too old, and I could have laughed at the thought. It seemed a luxury indeed, now, to have boots made just for me, no matter if they had scuffmarks on the heels. I folded a band of black cloth to keep my shorn, freshly-washed hair out of my eyes, and then turned to watch Miriel.

She was resplendent in one of her old gowns, laced tightly so that it still fit her small frame. She was as she always was: beautiful beyond belief. But something had changed, something was not quite right—she no longer glittered quite as brightly, her whole attention was no longer devoted to being the most brilliant, engaging maiden of the Court. As she prepared, she did not turn her head this way and that, practicing her responses, but instead looked into the mirror gravely; she could no longer summon the smile that had been her mask, her shield. Her eyes met mine in the mirror, and she saw my curiosity.

"We didn't come here for this," she said, looking around at me. "We came here for something far greater, something that—" She broke off, and I saw that she was speechless in her anger. "My Gods, there's a *war*," she said, struggling to put words to it. Her voice was tight. "People will die, people are already dying, and we came here for something that could shift the whole world even without the war, and they don't care about any of it! It's still all dancing and banquets and alliances—and for what? What does *any* of it accomplish?"

"Shh." I looked towards the door and she halted her tirade at once, but I could see her struggling to control herself. "We have to do this," I reminded her. *It's not for long.* She understood that, but as she bowed here head and fiddled with her priceless bracelet, the sapphires and diamonds sparkled in the low light, and I understood part of what was causing her so much distress. Before, jewels had not mattered—they were an adornment to wear, or not, to set Miriel apart from the other maidens as the most stylish and sophisticated. Now, Miriel had seen poverty. She knew that a whole village might not create such wealth in a year as she wore on her wrist right now.

I stepped closer and took her hands in my own. "Remember what you are," I said seriously, my voice pitched low. "You have done what even Jacces could not do. You carry the hopes of all the rebels and their families, and you will see their dreams made real. Smile for that, if nothing else. When we have the treaty, we can go, find a way to escape—until then, we must be here." She bit her lip and nodded. "And everything you see, that you dislike—those are the very reasons you are here now."

Miriel smiled and gripped my hands. Some of the tension had gone out of her. "Yes," she said simply. "You are good to remind me. Oh, Catwin, what would have happened if we had not met each other?"

"You would think far too highly of yourself," I promptly, smiling, but I felt a sudden wave of dizziness, and I staggered as darkness rushed in.

"Are you okay?" As my vision cleared, I realized that I was clinging to Miriel to stay upright. The great pattern I had glimpsed once before rushed back to me, I could see it spinning out indefinitely—and then it was gone, in an instant, the details slipping away from me.

"Yes." I rubbed my temples. "Just...it's nothing." I shook my head. "We should go to dinner." I straightened my tunic and took a moment to steady myself. After a moment, watching me worriedly, Miriel bit her lip and nodded. She took a deep breath and straightened her back, dropped her shoulders, lifted her chin—and then we set off through the corridors, walking quickly and trying to ignore the whispers that surrounded us when the courtiers saw Miriel's well-known face.

The change in the Court was visible at once when we entered the banquet hall, it was as if the very flavor of it had changed. Without Isra Dulgurokov ruling the court, fiercely devout, the enforced formality had broken down. Families came to dinner together, or girls, arm in arm with each other, sometimes even a young man and a maiden would arrive together and no one even seemed to notice. The ladies still sat on one side, and the men on the other, even in this cramped banquet hall, but there was a steady stream of young men paying compliments to the maidens, sitting at their table and laughing with them. Instead of

the quiet voices and clinking of cutlery, there was a roar of
laughter and carousing.

On the dais, instead of Isra and the High Priest, the seats
by the King's left hand were occupied by Gerald Conradine and
Anne Warden. To the King's far right, Guy de la Marque and
Elizabeth. I reckoned that I saw a faint, sardonic smile on Guy's
face—he alone, of those at the dais, had clung to his power when
the Court had turned topsy-turvy. Like Isra, he had seen his power
vanish when Garad came to his own; but where Isra had fallen,
where Garad had fallen, Guy de la Marque and his kin remained.

And there, at the center of the dais, a beautiful pair: golden
crowns on golden hair, a handsome king and his lovely wife. He
was leaning to whisper in her ear, she smiling at his words. It was
perfectly beautiful, and I wanted to scream with frustration that it
was not Miriel there at Wilhelm's side. I knew that in Miriel's
truest desires, she did not want to be Queen, most especially a
queen in this Court. But it was one thing to know that, and
another entirely to see Miriel's rival in her place: sitting next to
Wilhelm at dinner, advising him on policy, sleeping in his bed at
night.

Miriel never wavered, she only curtsied deeply to the
throne, gave a grave nod to the gentlemen's table where Arman
Dulgurokov sat, and went to her place. But, as it always had, her
presence caused a stir. I saw that the Duke had not told his fellow
Councilors of Miriel's return; he had waited to see what each of
them might do when she reappeared, and now his eyes were
flicking about the banquet hall, resting on those who looked at
Miriel and whispered to their neighbors.

At last, as I had guessed it would, the Duke's gaze traveled
to the dais. Gerald Conradine's eyes had narrowed, and Guy de la
Marque was smiling openly in triumph as he watched the girl who
had lost the Queenship to his daughter. Marie herself had gone
rigid, staring down the hall at Miriel as if she were seeing a ghost,
and at her side...

Wilhelm appeared not to have noticed Miriel at all. Even
as the whispers rose, as Marie gave a swift look at her mother, as
Gerald Conradine muttered something to his wife, Wilhelm
devoted his attention to his food, to calling for more wine, to
speaking with Marie as if he had not noticed her consternation, as
if he had not noticed the entrance of the woman he had
passionately loved. I watched him, my head tilted to the side, and

wondered at this. He did not have the look of a hound on a tight leash, but instead that of a man who is perfectly content. I could not understand it, and when I looked over to the Duke once more, I saw him staring at Wilhelm as well, wondering.

So, for all his disclaiming, it had been a lie—the Duke would gladly see Miriel back in Wilhelm's arms, if he thought it could be arranged. He would use his niece as a pawn once more, sell her to one man for a bride and another for a mistress. I hoped that Miriel had not noticed, for at the very thought of such a fate, I felt panic closing in on me. And Miriel could not afford to break down, not here.

"At the end of dinner, bring Miriel back to the Duke's rooms," Temar's voice said, very close to my ear, and I jumped. He smiled that he had caught me unawares, and I gritted my teeth at his self-satisfied look.

"Very well." I turned away from him, as if bored, and after a moment, he left.

I did not watch him go. There were few enough hidden alcoves here, no way he could attack me without dozens seeing it; I did not have to watch my back. I could devote my whole attention to the courtiers: their flirtations, their spats, their little alliances. And then after dinner, Miriel and I would hear whatever it was the Duke wanted, we might spar with him, but we would go away in a semblance of obedience—only to wake up the next morning to another day of the same. We had been away for so long, but I was already overwhelmed by the tedium of it all, and it was worse to be in this strange other court—the cramped banquet hall pressed tightly with courtiers, all in their silks and jewels, while the city sweated with fear. When the banquet ended, I was glad to escape with Miriel, and she went willingly, even knowing that the Duke had something planned for us.

"I could hardly stand another moment," she said, through gritted teeth. "After all we've been through, and it's still gowns and dancing and who smiled at whom!"

"They're only silly girls," I said soothingly. "And we survived, didn't we?" She shot me a look. Miriel disliked the charade and resented the lies we continued to tell, no matter if we both agreed that our survival with the Duke depended on holding to our story. We could not say who might hear an indiscreet word and carry a story back to the Duke; we must pretend, always.

As we wound our way through the hallways, I pushed ahead to create space for Miriel. The Fortress was grand, but it was housing every noble family and their retinue, and a large contingent of the army. The nobles were all housed on the upper floors, crammed together, and the corridors were a nightmare. I was so relieved when the guards at the Duke's chambers flung open the doors, that it took me a moment to realize that Miriel and I were face to face with Arman and Isra Dulgurokov.

I faded hastily into the background, bowing as Miriel swept into a deep curtsy and came up. Her back was straight, her head up, but her eyes were fixed firmly on the floor. She was the very picture of demure obedience, her voice low and sweet.

"My Lord. Your Grace. Such an honor." I stole a glance at the siblings, who stared at her contemplatively. They shared the same high brow and dark hair, and the same grey eyes. There, the similarities ended. Arman might not be tall, but he had the build of a warrior, trained since childhood; Isra's petite, buxom frame and soft hands bespoke a quiet life. I had seen Isra each day at the Court as Miriel ensnared Garad, and I had learned her ways as any enemy will do. But I had known little of Arman, save that he was a man who whispered in corners, aligning Isra's interests with the Nilsons and the Torstenssons even as Garad slipped out of their control. I did not know what he might be like as a man: cruel or kind, ambitious of his own account, or only a cats-paw for his sister's hopes.

"I understand you returned to Court only today, my Lady." His voice was measured, his face open; that, I trusted little. His eyes were troubled, and I took note of it. "I hope you are recovered from your ordeal."

"Yes, thank you, my Lord." Miriel looked up to give him a smile. "By the grace of the Gods, we were not harmed."

"We?" Isra asked. Her gaze darted to me. "You and your servant?" I bowed.

"My Lady."

"This is Catwin," the Duke said smoothly. "She grew up in Voltur with Miriel, and accompanied her to Penekket."

"How interesting." Isra's tone suggested that a girl in pants would not be welcomed as a servant in the Dulgurokov retinue. "Very quaint," she added, meaningfully.

"It is well for a girl to have friends from her home," Arman placated her. He looked at Miriel. "My Lady, forgive me—I would not be so abrupt, but we have little time. Perhaps you and I could speak alone?" Miriel did not look at Isra, whose eyes had narrowed, nor at the Duke, who had gone very still. She did not look over to see if Temar was watching her, hoping to catch her in a lie. She did not look to me, to see if I might save her. I saw her draw on her courage as she met Arman Dulgurokov's eyes.

"Of course, my Lord." He held open the door to the room we shared, and she preceded him into it. As the door clicked shut, Isra looked over at the Duke coldly.

"My brother may think this is a good match," she said icily, "but he is only a man, and easily overwhelmed by female charms. I am not so sure that you can make good on your claims." Her tone was quietly venomous, but the Duke did not fear her. He smiled.

"I think you will find that you are now much diminished at Court," he remarked pleasantly, as if speaking of the weather. "An aging widow with no heirs to follow you, no hope for a husband of your own. The power in the Court is now the Warlords, and Gerald Conradine has no love for you." Isra lifted her chin.

"And you think we would so demean ourselves as to take merchant blood?" she retorted. "For I think you will find that you, also, are much diminished at Court. Has Gerald Conradine any reason to love you? Why should my brother not marry one of the Nilson clan, one of the Torstenssons? If he wishes to rise up, will he not want an army of his own?"

"He will have one. With Celys, DeVere, and Dulgurokov united in one heir, we can lay claim to the entire west of Heddred," the Duke said simply. Isra's jaw tightened and she looked away. I gaped; we had gone from marriage negotiations and insinuation to open treason in a few moments, and the speed of it dizzied me. I had thought myself accustomed to court life, but this showed me otherwise.

"You would be prepared to take care of the DeVere heirs?" Isra asked softly, her eyes narrowed. She had no such compunctions as I.

"Of course I am." The Duke bowed, smiling. "You are ambitious, Your Grace. And so am I. Our fates might rise together—or you might find your bloodline ended, and your titles passed off to another. Who would Gerald Conradine favor, I wonder? Perhaps Guy de la Marque? The most disloyal of your servants, don't you think? Quite pleased by your son's death."

Isra might have raged at him in her grief. But, as her hands clenched, she only inclined her head; the acknowledgement of one player to another. It chilled me to the bone.

"I will think on it," she said crisply. She hardly turned her head as the door opened and Miriel walked out, her hand on Arman's arm. He was pleased, unable to hide his smile, and though Miriel was very pale, she kept her head up and a half-smile on her lips, and she curtsied to Isra without a flicker of hesitation.

"I will be pleased to join such a great family, Your Grace," she said sweetly. If she hoped to gain Isra's favor by using her honorary title, she got nothing.

"Whether you will or not remains to be seen," Isra said icily. To the Duke, she said simply, "Send the contract." She looked at her brother with distaste as he kissed Miriel's hand, and then she took his arm and left the room without a backwards glance.

"She'll never allow the marriage," Miriel said flatly to her uncle, and he smiled.

"I think you will find," he said softly, "that no one wants power quite so much as those who have just lost it." He raised an eyebrow at her. "Like you, perhaps? You, who might have been Queen? Do you yet hope to supplant Marie in the King's heart? I don't think you can do it, you know. He does seem infatuated." He smiled, reveling in the open challenge, pleased to taunt Miriel with what she had once wanted most—like a predator, he remembered her moment of weakness in the aftermath of Garad's death. He got nothing for his malice, however.

"Thank you for your kind advice," Miriel said sweetly, in a fair imitation of Isra's tone. "I will see you on the morrow. Good evening, my Lord Uncle." And she swept from the room, her uncle gazing after her: the girl he utterly despised and mistrusted. The girl on whose slim shoulders, for reasons I had never understood, rested all of the Duke's dynastic hopes.

Chapter 13

"Miriel?" I asked, into the darkness. While we had undressed, we had spoken of inconsequential things: low-voiced murmurs that we were safe at last, Miriel admitting her shock at such a quick marriage, me remarking how nice it was to have my own boots once more, and being glad to have seen Roine. When the silence in the next room had become complete, I had known that Temar and the Duke, as well, had retired to bed; I had looked over to see Miriel staring at the ceiling, still wide awake.

"Yes?" She turned her head to look at me.

"What did he say? Arman, I mean." I had wanted to know all night what that man could have said, what Miriel could have responded.

"He wanted to know if I truly wished to marry him," Miriel said simply.

"Why would he ask that?" Arman was of near equal power to the Duke himself; he could order near any woman in the kingdom to his side. I did not think he would care overmuch if Miriel wanted to be his wife, as long as she was obedient. But I saw her smile, and I remembered the man's courtly demeanor and troubled eyes.

"Think about it," she said. I waited a moment, then shook my head.

"You know I'm no good at these things."

"He wants me," Miriel explained. "Do you see now?" I nodded. I did see. I understood, too, how Miriel had remained calm as we undressed, the panic sinking away. Much was forgiven an adored wife, and if Miriel and I could not escape at once, she was at least at the mercy of a man who sought her love, and not that of a man like her uncle.

"No wonder Isra hates you," I said, and Miriel nodded.

"First Garad, now..." she trailed off. Her weary amusement had fled, and I could see her sliding towards melancholy, remembering the past. I had only stood by, watching as Miriel seduced Garad, but she had been the one to smile at him and laugh with him. If I was consumed with guilt when I thought of him, I wondered how much worse it must be for her. I was struck by the urge to tell her that she could not have saved his life by failing to capture his interest, or by loving him more truly, but I did not want to draw her further along that line of thought. Instead, I propped myself up on my elbow.

"You should know what the Duke is planning, though." This was what I had been waiting to say all night. I had barely been able to keep from blurting the words out, so badly did I want to share the knowledge with someone. The casual discussion of a coup, of troops, of assassinations, had chilled me to the bone. I had always thought the Duke a hard man, but he had never displayed such contempt for life before. He prided himself on being economical, wasting nothing, winning by cunning and not by might—what did this new turn to force mean? I shook my head, to clear it. "He and Isra have a plan."

"The throne. He's always planning to take the throne," Miriel said dreamily. She had been so exhausted by the change of her fortunes—from riding through the wilderness with soldiers, trying to outrace an army, to a banquet, to marriage, in one day— that she was drifting to sleep even in her melancholy. I grimaced that even half-awake, Miriel should have guessed this, that had been such a shock to me.

"How do you always know these things first?" I asked, disgruntled. She looked over at me, trying to keep her eyes open.

"The problem with you is you don't want anything for yourself," she said simply. "If you could, you'd be able to see it better. I mean..." She shook her head and yawned. "You see it, but you don't understand it." I lay back, thinking, and when I did not respond, she struggled awake, leaning over the edge of her bed, her hair falling in a tumble of curls around her shoulders.

"What were they planning, then?"

"Oh." I shook my head. "You were right. The Duke told Isra that he could have the other DeVeres assassinated, so you could be heir. Then your child by Arman would be heir to all the west, up to the Cessor lands. They were talking about troops; I think he means to rally for the throne."

"Yes," Miriel decided, after a moment. "He can't get me onto the throne as things stand now, so he has to make another alliance." I was horrified, but she was calm. The Duke was a puzzle to her; if she could only understand him, she could face him without fear. "It makes more sense now—him telling me to trust him. Arman, I mean. He said I must trust him, and he would raise me up. That was what he meant."

"So what should we do?" I asked. It was always the point: the central point. Whatever Arman's reasons for this treason, he was nothing more than another courtier to outwit. Miriel would know how best to do that.

"Play along," Miriel said. She yawned again and lay back down; she was not worried. "We'll have the treaty signed in a week."

"You could be married by then," I said flatly. I regretted it at once, for she scrambled back up to stare at me, wide-eyed.

"What?"

"I'm sorry, I didn't mean—" I had not meant to scare her, only to show her the flaw in her reasoning. I had forgotten that she was the one who would be sacrificed if the plan went awry.

"I can't actually *marry* him," Miriel hissed, and I felt oddly reassured. The ease with which she had slipped into her mask, the glib assurances that she knew what she was doing, that she knew how to play this man and his conniving family—it had scared me. It had reminded me of what she had once been. And I had been scared, too, of how easy I had found it to watch, and listen, and catch secrets once more. Miriel's panic was unfeigned, and it gave me hope that she would not turn back into the creature of ice she had been before.

I pushed myself up to sit and rubbed at my temples, trying to think.

"You don't have to," I assured her. At her look, I threw up my hands. "Stall him! Can't you come up with something?" She glared for a moment, and then sank into repose.

"I suppose," she said. She wound her fingers together, lacing and unlacing them as she thought.

"How did you even convince him that you wanted to marry him in the first place?" I asked, skeptically, and she shot me a look. She took a breath, paused, and then her whole demeanor changed. She became frightened, vulnerable; her eyes were very wide.

"My Lord, surely you have seen that I have always admired you," she said softly. I blinked, and she looked away. "How could I not? I ask only—" She broke off, and squeezed her eyes shut, the very picture of sorrow and beauty. "To have my life shattered so suddenly, with such tragedy. I cannot even fathom it." She opened her eyes, and became Miriel once more. "That's how," she said. "And see, it worked." Distaste was thick in her tone.

"And that's how you'll stall him," I said, thinking of strategy so that I would not have to think of Arman Dulgurokov, his good sense overwhelmed by blue eyes and pretty words. Traitor that he was, I could almost feel sorry for him. "It's all so sudden—you wish to marry him in the style that his wedding deserves—you still grieve for Garad. You could work Isra around that way, I suppose."

"She'll never like me." Miriel shook her head. She saw the anger on my face and, surprisingly, laughed. "Don't be angry for me. Hasn't it occurred to you—she's the only one who's right about me?"

"What?" I frowned up at her, and she smiled her infectious smile.

"Of all the Court," Miriel explained, "Some people envied me, some people hated me. But Isra's the only one who had the sense to think that everything about me was a lie. She never trusted me."

"She was jealous that you would be Queen, and she would be pushed off the throne," I said, and Miriel shrugged.

"It doesn't matter why she was right. I think she knew, though." She smiled. "You know, it almost makes me think better of her. Don't look so grim—it's just a few days."

"And then what?" I demanded, and her smile faded away. Her smiles and her laughter had frightened me. "I'm scared already—and you should be, too, not laughing. We're only just back and we're already part of plot against the throne. I don't know if I can get us out again when we have the treaty, and where would we go now? And the war…"

I trailed off, confused by my own fear. I had never felt as if I was a part of Heddred, not really. Heddred was a nation of warm farms and rich summers, people bound together by the Warlords and nurtured by House Warden, enjoying the prosperity of their mines, singing at village festivals. Heddred was the Palace and the Court, unimaginable riches and endless schemes. I had watched both with the uncomprehending gaze of a mountain girl. Voltur had been the last outpost before Ismir, prone always to war and prey to the cold weather and the harsh, unforgiving soil of the mountains. The people of Voltur did not live, they survived, cut off from their Kingdom by treacherous passes and fierce blizzards.

even when I came to the plains and the Court, I had never felt a part of that world.

It was strange to me that I should now share in Heddred's fortunes, and know myself to be a part of this kingdom. Heddred stretched from the eastern seas, across the low plains, and into the mountains of Voltur; we were all of the same kingdom, and now we were under attack from the same foe. Miriel had always understood that, somehow; it was she who had angrily reprimanded the rebels for their lack of feeling, she who had called them to fight for Heddred. I trailed along in her wake, the tiny scale of my own existence wiped away by the glory and valor of hers, and now, at last, in the face of this fear, I understood.

Miriel could see none of this. She frowned at me in the low light.

"You truly are afraid, aren't you?" She shook her head. "I didn't think you got afraid." I could have laughed, to know just how little of my fear she had ever seen, but it did not seem amusing just now.

"I'm afraid all the time," I said shortly. "I'm a part of a world I don't understand."

"And you want to be free of it?" Miriel asked, probing for the truth. I thought on it.

"I don't know," I said, at last. "I wanted to be free of the Court, but that was because it was so dark. I wanted to do something good—and that brought us back here. I don't know what I want now." Miriel did not respond at once. She lay down and stared up at the ceiling again, and I had laid back down myself and nearly drifted off to sleep when she said,

"How did it feel to see him? When I saw Wilhelm, it was like my stomach fell out." Now I smiled, sleepily; it was strange to hear Miriel speak of such undignified feelings. When she had pined for Wilhelm after Garad's death, she had been a tragic heroine, beautiful and filled with sorrow.

Then I remembered what she had asked and my smile faded away. I could find no words for what I had felt when I had seen Temar. I had wanted to smile at him, and have him smile back. I had wanted, more than anything, for his grim expression to slip away, and to know that he was glad to see me alive and well. But he had not looked at me, even once; I closed my eyes against the pain.

"You were right," I said, and the words surprised me.

"What?" Miriel pushed the covers back and lifted her head to frown at me. She was as curious as a cat; even bone-deep exhaustion would not keep her from figuring out a puzzle.

"He is playing his own game," I explained. "I don't know what it is—but he has a plan of his own. Anyway, that's what I thought when I saw him." That, and a thousand other feelings I did not want to give voice to. If I could deny them, I thought hopelessly, then perhaps they would fade away like dreams in daylight.

"Are you afraid of him?" Miriel asked.

"Are you afraid of Wilhelm?" I countered. I could not—could not—answer her question, not even to myself.

"A little," Miriel said. "He would never hurt me, I don't think—not...with a knife, or poison. But I'm afraid, all the time, that he would say no for some reason. Not sign."

"He'll sign. You can persuade him to." I could hardly believe what I had seen at dinner; after such awestruck love, Wilhelm could not be so indifferent to Miriel. I had to believe that he still loved her, and that he was still true to the rebellion. I did not know how Miriel would bear it if he was not.

"I hope I can," Miriel said. "Because if not...then I've lost him, and the man I hoped he was. And I don't know what I could want, after that."

"You can persuade him," I assured her.

"And then what?" I saw tears glittering in her eyes. "As you said: then what? When we're of one mind and we've signed the treaty—and he's still married to *her*, and I'm to marry an old man who wants to overthrow the throne? How can we face that?"

"Then we leave again," I said quietly. "If you want. Or we stay, and you advise him on policy and the...what was it?"

"Parliament."

"That." There was a silence.

"Would you stay?" she asked, her voice very small. "If I stayed, would you stay, too—to help me? I have to know he's safe—I can't just leave, and know that my uncle is trying to overthrow him. Would you stay, if I did?"

"Always," I said honestly, and she nodded; I heard her hair brush against the pillow.

"We can do this," she whispered. "And then we'll decide."

Chapter 14

But Wilhelm refused to see Miriel.

She wrote him a simple note, saying that she must see him, that she had news of great importance, and I delivered it for her. I slipped through the unfamiliar hallways, ill at ease, and tried to remember not to incriminate myself by looking over my shoulder. Once, I had been cynically confident that the court, absorbed in its own shallow pleasures, would ignore me and never wonder at my purpose. I had known what to say, and how to move, and what corridors to take, to escape notice entirely.

When I had spent my days in the Court, I had been desensitized to the currents of tension and hunger—hunger for power, for prestige, for desire itself, hunger for more of everything—that eddied through the air. I sensed them as an old farmhand will sense a storm in the air. Now, I truly felt the country girl; I was on edge, terrified to think I might be watched, that someone would snatch at a chance for promotion by telling secrets of me. I was claustrophobic in the constant bustle of the Fortress; I missed the sunlight and the open air, and I even missed the crude speech of the rebel soldiers. The Courtiers, the servants, even the guardsmen talked with dizzying speed, loud jokes echoing in the corridors; I was overwhelmed.

The bustle faded as I approached the King's chambers, and by the time I grew close, I was trapped in an eerie silence. The hallways were lined by members of the Royal Guard, glowering at me as I passed, and at last I came close enough that they stepped into my path, lowering crossed pikes to block my way.

"What business?" one asked abruptly.

"A message for the King," I said, reaching into the little pouch at my waist and drawing out the folded scrap of paper. They moved to take it, but I snatched it back. "It's for his eyes only."

"No," one of them said, bored. "Go home, lad—lass—whatever you are."

"He must see this," I said, as strongly as I could. "It is of great importance. I must know that he has seen it."

"What could you have to say to him that he would find important?" One of them demanded. "In case you didn't notice, he's fighting a war." He and his companions laughed in my face, but I only smiled. At last, I knew what to say.

"Precisely." I held up the scrap of paper, and raised my eyebrows. "Are you sure you want to keep this from him?" Their laughter died away and they hesitated; they wavered.

"If it's so important, you can let one of us deliver it to him," the first one said, finally. His face was set, and I decided that this was the best I was likely to do. I held the note out and he grabbed it from me, his pike still raised.

"I'll wait here," I said simply, and I walked to one of the arrow slits and peered out while they muttered to each other, and one of the men hurried away, around the curve of the corridor. It was hardly five minutes before he returned. I turned at the sound of his footsteps, and saw that he was trying to hide a smile.

"He says to tell you: no," the man said.

"What?" I looked at him, dumbstruck. The other men were starting to grin, and I could feel my face turning red with embarrassment. "He said what?"

"Just that. 'No,'" the man said. I stood staring at him, and he waved a hand at me. "So go on, lad." I did not move, and his face became menacing. "His Grace isn't to be disturbed for such things, you hear?" I saw the rest of them sizing me up, flexing their hands. It was boring, being pent up here in the Fortress. They'd welcome a fight, for a moment of excitement, no matter their target. I had no choice—I backed away, my face burning, and then I turned and ran, their laughter echoing in my ears.

"He said what?" Miriel asked, only a few moments later. Even with her uncle called away to a Council meeting, she had been sitting and reading in her uncle's presence chamber, the very picture of demure obedience. But her pleasant demeanor had been wiped away by shock, and, now, rising anger. "Why would he do that?"

"He might not have known what you meant," I suggested. "Would he have known from the note that you meant...you know?" She shot me a furious glare, and I shut my mouth.

"It was very clear," she said crisply. "Very. I said, 'our greatest hope.' It could not have been more clear."

"I don't understand," I said, stupidly. I had never thought, for a moment, that Wilhelm would refuse to see Miriel. I had believed without a doubt that his indifference at dinner the other night had been feigned, and that he would be eager to see Miriel and know that she was well, and safe. If he would not even speak to her...

Miriel was pressing her fingers to her temples, either thinking, or trying to block out the worry that was coursing through her. This meeting was everything to us, there was nothing more important. This, above all else, Miriel needed. Easy enough to think that the messenger simply had not been able to reach Wilhelm before, easy enough to believe that his silence on the matter of the rebellion had been due to his sudden accession, the invasion from Ismir. Now, with the culmination of the rebellion's hopes before him, he had denied his interest, he had turned away the woman he had once seemed to love more than life itself.

Miriel raised her head, looking stricken.

"Was it all a lie?" she asked, in a broken whisper. "Was every part of it a lie?" She was shaking her head no, but I knew that she believed it, with the contrary assurance of someone who sees her worst fear, and believes that it must be true—for there could be nothing worse.

"It can't have been," I said, after a pause. "That doesn't make any sense."

"Of course it does!" Miriel said in a harsh whisper. "Trick me to find out about the rebellion, kill Garad, kill us—he knew you'd suspect him—and then crush the rebellion."

"But he hasn't crushed the rebellion," I objected.

"Not yet," Miriel said darkly, and then, wildly: "I was wrong before, about Garad. I believed I knew who he was, and that turned to nothing. Perhaps I was wrong again. Wilhelm is a murderer, he only said what he needed to say, to make us plot with him."

I shook my head, stubbornly. "No. This doesn't make sense."

"Can you think of another reason?" Miriel asked harshly. "*Any* other reason? A good reason why he would turn his back on the rebellion?"

"Perhaps he was with other people," I suggested. "He could not say anything. Perhaps he will send a message later, when he is alone."

It was something to hope for, enough to reassure me, enough to soothe Miriel. The tension fell away, and she grasped at my hand, smiling, shaking. Yes, we agreed. He would send her a message. They could find a way to meet, as she had always met

Garad. I remembered the tolerant amusement of the Royal Guard, who had always been loyal to Garad first, and his mother second. I remembered that the guardsmen had let us into the royal apartments when Garad's love of Miriel had been a great secret, and I remembered also that they had not betrayed us—and I was heartened by that.

And yet the days passed, agonizingly slow, and no word came. The Ismiri army drew ever closer; the people of Penekket barricaded themselves behind their paltry walls and cursed the nobles who had shut themselves up in the Fortress. The Duke spent his days in Council meetings, and came back looking grim. We heard reports that the King had ordered the Royal Army to make camp outside the city gates. They would wait for the Ismiri, he had ruled—to move the army away from the city was to invite some treachery, and the Ismiri would be weakened from their march when they arrived. The one advantage the Heddrians had was to choose the field of battle, and they would take that.

The Court grew more and more frantic, and Miriel shut herself away, pleading that she was overwhelmed by it all after her capture and escape. She stayed within sight of her uncle, she went nowhere and sent no messages, and as she lapsed into dull silences and, at night, despairing tears, the Duke's suspicion began to give way to bemused belief. I saw him wonder if it might not be true that Miriel had been kidnapped, that she had been in fear for her life, that her sudden freedom, the chaos of the court, and the fear of invasion were truly wearing on her.

I should have rejoiced that one of our most dangerous enemies was growing less suspicious of us, but I could take no joy in it when our plans were coming to nothing. I had learned, long ago, to push away my own panic and hide behind the mask of a servant. I could sit calmly and look as serene as a nun. But I shared Miriel's despair. If Wilhelm would send no message to her, would not accept any ray of hope from the rebellion he had claimed to support, then perhaps I had been wrong, and Miriel's fears had been correct: all of it had been a lie, and Miriel and I had wasted our escape on a failed uprising. We would be trapped at Court, Miriel married to a man she had no love for and both of us embroiled in a treasonous plot.

And then: a note. I saw it folded neatly in Miriel's laundry, and my heart leapt. Trembling, I smoothed it out—and froze. It was not from Wilhelm, not the message we had hoped for. No, it was from the High Priest. It was no more than the seal of his office, pressed into wax as black as night, but I knew a summons when I saw one.

So the High Priest wanted to speak with Miriel. I sat on the bed, staring at the scrap of paper in my hand, and bit my lip. I had not forgotten my fears, my questions. Of the few things I had brought back with me to court, one had been the dark blade that Aron had carried when he tried to kill me. When I arrived, I had slipped it away at once, secure in its wrappings of linen, and I had tried to forget it.

For a time I had kept it hidden away, superstitiously afraid to look at it, but it was not only a fear of betrayal that kept me from bringing it into the light of day—I did not want to compare it to the dagger I had seen on the night of Garad's murder. I was afraid to know the truth. But one day, unable to bear wondering any longer, I had rummaged through the trunk I had packed at the Winter Castle—carried back, without me, and dumped in Miriel's rooms—and pulled out the little parcel wrapped in linen. I had unrolled it, shaking, and had stared at the twin daggers I held, identical in every way save the ripples of steel in the blades.

I had thought on that for days, my mind churning below the tranquil mask I wore. The false royal guards could have served anyone who benefited from Garad's death: the Conradines, the Ismiri, Guy de la Marque. Perhaps it had been the disillusioned Earl of Mavol, Piter Nilson, raging at his monarch's seeming indifference to his plight. Nilson's men would have been hand-picked from his lands, chosen from amongst the citizens of the Norstrung Provinces. It was likely enough that one of them should carry a dagger made in the town of his birth.

But this was not just any dagger; I knew enough to see the interlocking circles on the haft and question if the blade had been made for the rebellion's soldiers. And that led me back to the High Priest—Garad's threat to the rebellion had been a threat not to punish the villagers, but to root out all sympathizers and kill them, and grind the rebellion to dust.

But after that, my theory broke down. If it had only been Garad, I would not have questioned it. I would have accepted the duplicity of the High Priest; I would have hated him for such a cold-blooded murder even as I saw him strive to protect the rebellion that he held so dear. But why should he call for the murder of Miriel? If the High Priest wanted a Queen who would keep Wilhelm true to the rebellion, there would have been no better choice. Any reasonable man would have doubted that a boy, thrust suddenly onto the throne, would waver in his beliefs—never mind a boy guided by Gerald Conradine. And above all—why should the High Priest call for my death? Why should he have any reason to believe that my death would necessary? I, who had served his interests?

Then again, I was forced to wonder: why should anyone think my death necessary? I was no one without Miriel, and Miriel had been broken to a nobody with Garad's death. I was the servant of a former Queen-in-waiting, practically an orphan. It did not make sense. None of it made sense. And so, even if I no longer trusted the High Priest, I told myself sternly that there was no rational, sensible reason to fear him. A man with the power of the kingdom at his fingertips, with the leadership of the rebellion in his hands, should not trouble himself with me—if we needed his help, we should seek it. This message was most lucky in its timing; whatever he wanted, we could bargain for his help in return.

I slipped the note into my pocket and, on a whim, took one of the two daggers and slid it into a hidden pocket. I could feel it dragging at the cloth, a reminder—but of what, I was not entirely certain. I took a moment to steady myself, then opened the door to Miriel's rooms and went out into the Duke's makeshift study. For once, he was there, Temar sitting calmly at his side, and so there was no opportunity to tell Miriel where I was going. I only hoisted a hamper of Miriel's sheets on my hip and slipped out the door. I took the sheets down to the laundry, and then climbed the stairs back to the floor just below the nobles' apartments, panting slightly.

Even with the impressive size of the Fortress, the chapel here was nothing to the great cathedral in the Palace proper. There, the buttresses rose to dizzying heights, and the stained glass windows spread jeweled light across the marble floors. No, this chapel was small, the ceiling low by comparison, all of the light coming from the lamps that hung from the ceiling. But it was richly appointed, with beautifully carved pews and jeweled lamps, an altar hung with silk cloth, and behind it, golden statues of the seven Gods.

I slipped past the altar with a brief, habitual bow towards the status, and found my way to the High Priest's apartments. Without giving myself time to think, I raised my hand and knocked, decisively, trying to calm the racing of my heart. The weight of the iron-hafted dagger dragged at my tunic, a constant reminder of treachery, and betrayal. I would not have thought that I would need a reminder to be careful and trust no one, but the facts spoke for themselves: four attempts on our life, and I still could not name our enemy.

When there was no answer, I tried the door, and slipped inside; I had come too far to go back empty-handed. The High Priest was alone, working at his desk. He had looked up at the sound of the door, wondering who dared to come into his presence without permission, and when he saw me, he stood, slowly. His face was utterly composed.

"Hello, Catwin."

The feeling of claustrophobia closed in. A question hovered on my lips: I had meant to ask him if he had been the one who sent the soldiers, or sent the assassin—and I could not find the courage to do so. I had been too long away from Court; I had forgotten the sense I had once possessed, that could lead me to the right question. I stared at this man, perhaps my greatest enemy, and I remembered Miriel's words, from long ago: *they're all murderers. Any one of them would have done it. What difference in allying ourselves with the one who did?*

We had no choice. I closed my eyes briefly.

"I got your message," I said. "And we need your help."

Chapter 15

"My help." The High Priest was staring at me intently; I even thought that I saw fear in his eyes. He must be afraid, I realized—Isra had been his greatest ally, even if she did not hold with his rebellion. Now, the throne was crowded with those who were no friend to him. He had always been thin, half-starving himself out of piety, but I thought he has lost even more weight.

"Why would you want my help?" he asked me now, warily. "And why would you come alone?"

"Miriel is watched closely," I explained, frowning. "I could not bring her. But anything you could tell her, you can also tell me."

"Perhaps," he said slowly. "For what I called her here to ask is what happened in Norvelt, and why she returned." So he had known. I felt my blood run cold, but kept my face straight, as best I could. His gaze was steady.

"Has your spy network not told you everything?" I was curious, even in my fear. I must find out what he hoped for, and what would enrage him. "I should think you would know everything that had happened, and why we were here." He smiled bitterly at that.

"My *network*, as you call it, is quite fragile. I heard that there was a girl who claimed to be Miriel DeVere, and a boy, perhaps her brother—no one was quite sure—who was training the men to fight the army. Then...the reports were confused." He frowned at me, and I reckoned that his lack of surety was genuine. I released the breath I had been holding, and tried not to look too relieved. We were far from safe, yet. "I heard that you had been attacked...yes?" His sharp eyes marked the pallor of my face; I had been unprepared for that question. "Ah, so that was true."

"An assassin came for me, yes," I said shortly. I looked at his face, and saw no clues there: he was watching me, intent on my expression. When I said nothing, the High Priest spread his hands and shrugged.

"And yet you are well," he observed. "And you are here. And the men of the rebellion are gone." Again I said nothing, and a look of irritation flashed across the High Priest's face, but was gone quickly. "My messenger reported to me that when he passed through Norvelt, there were no men to be seen, and the townsfolk would not tell him where they had gone—they do not know my messenger for the one who distributes the letters, you see."

"That explains a great deal," I said, with feeling. I remembered how we had found the rebellion: persecuted by Nilson's men and the army, and wholly unsheltered by the High Priest. I felt, to my surprise, an upwelling of anger. I should have held my tongue, but I could not help myself. "You realize that you've given them nothing beyond ideas," I said sharply. "They had no plan, no means for gathering resources, nothing but your letters."

"The time was not yet right for them to have such things," the High Priest said, smugly superior, stoking my anger. "The movement was not yet broad enough. Best they have no plans, in case they should be questioned by His Grace's soldiers." I frowned at his tone.

"You left them with nothing," I said. "They faced spies and soldiers for love of the rebellion, but they had no network, no way to know if there was any help for them. They were at the mercy of Nilson—and he hates them, sir, he wants the movement stamped out."

"When the movement has spread, when it occupies the hearts of all—then it will be the time to organize," the High Priest said. "But not yet; at all costs, they must not organize yet. One day, I shall reveal myself as their leader and bring them to glory." His gaze was faraway, and his smile was so self-congratulatory that I ground my teeth. He wanted to be their savior, a knight on a white horse, the triumphant leader; and his supporters would bleed for that.

Then his eyes snapped back to me. "The best we can do now is secure the support of the King. Is that why you came back?"

"Yes," I said promptly, hoping that my agreement had not been too quick. It was even true, after a fashion—and I knew at once that I should not tell this confident man, this supremely self-assured, ruthless man, that we had done just what he had refused to do. "There was no word from the city. We had thought we would hear a proclamation from Wilhelm. But there was nothing. We came to make sure that he was still true to the cause." The High Priest's face closed off at once.

"He has made a poor ally to the cause," he said darkly. "A very poor ally, indeed. If I were not assured that there was a key, a failsafe—" He bit his words off, staring at me. "Well, that is not important. To you."

"How do you mean?" I asked, and the High Priest's eyes narrowed.

"I mean that Wilhelm has taken none of my counsel," he snapped. "He once had a brilliant mind, he knew that there was *nothing* more important than this. Why, with the goodwill of all his citizens, he might not now be facing an invasion—his people would have laid down their lives for him, instead of standing in terror and being cut down like sheep. Now there is an army at his doorstep. But does he see it for what it is? Does he turn to me for advice? No! He will not even respond to my messengers."

I stared at the man in shock. He had schemed and plotted for decades, biding his time through generations of power-hungry kings, working tirelessly to raise a movement of the people, a rebellion that burned in the hearts of all citizens. If my worst fears were true, he was a ruthless man, utterly dedicated and methodical.

Only a moment ago, he had told me that the time was not right for the movement to be born of the people. And yet now, facing a setback of mere months in his attempt to persuade the King, he was breaking down. I could understand such things from Miriel, who had only her wits and her façade as her weapons, who had no power at all in the court. But the High Priest had a network of spies, the ear of the former Dowager Queen, a longstanding alliance with the King himself; him, I expected to bide his time.

"He is young, there is an army at his doorstep—as you said—and he is being advised by a Council of commanders and generals," I soothed, thinking that I was more at ease with a methodical enemy than a mad one. "It is natural for him to be fixated on the invasion. Perhaps if you were to ask him and his family to come for a private service, to pray for the country, you could steal a few moments of his time."

"And say what?" the High Priest asked bitterly. "He has told me to my face that it is not the right time to voice support of the rebellion, that his hold over the Lords is to tenuous. He delays, and the cowardice will become a habit."

"Tell him that he must sign an accord with the rebels," I said promptly. "A treaty, promising them equal rights in law. He need do no more than sign it, and then he can reveal that after the war is won and Heddred is at peace." The High Priest laughed.

"There is no such treaty—it would take months to draw up. Wilhelm must know all the provisions to be included. There is quite an extensive list." I stared at him, and my distaste deepened. I had known him to be not only intelligent, but also quite cunning, self-reliant, decisive. Now I realized that the years of isolation from the movement he had created, the years of speaking his thoughts out loud to no one, of watching Court and Church and hating the excesses of both, and yet still taking no decisive action, had begun to convince him that he could not be wrong. He alone was the leader of this movement, he was the visionary and he alone would guide King and country to accord.

He was a mirror of the Duke, I realized, with a start. He had watched and waited and plotted, and he had made a meticulous plan—and, like the Duke, his plan was being delayed and undone by what he saw as ignorant stubbornness. The High Priest was furious because Wilhelm would not take advice without questioning it. He must control everything, from the voice of the rebellion, to the careful execution of its goals—and he would determine those goals. In the Duke, who sought only power, it was understandable. But in the High Priest, who sought to give voice to the people, it was a magnificent irony.

I swallowed. I must do whatever I could to ensure that the High Priest never knew Miriel for a rival leader. He must not know that she had unified the movement of the people behind a goal and treaty of their own devising, and that she had led them in support of the Royal Army. For what would happen if he knew that he was no longer the sole architect of this movement? He would surely try to wrest back control of the movement—or he might go quite mad at the thought of his work undone.

I shrugged and smiled, spreading my hands as if to say I could not know what would be the best course. And then I saw it: the chance to have the High Priest plant the suggestion in Wilhelm's mind, the idea that could kindle Wilhelm's passion for the rebellion once more. Gods willing, the treaty would be signed and Miriel and I would be gone within the week. But if not, if the battle came before we could persuade Wilhelm to meet, if we must wait, then I must lay the groundwork.

"Now is the time to step softly," I said to the High Priest. "He is a young man, he thinks he knows best. But we—you, sir— can plant the seed in his mind. Suggest that such a treaty could be drawn up between the two of you someday. Remind him that he swore once he would support the rebellion—that might be gentle enough to call him back," I suggested. I saw the opportunity to fish for information. "After all," I said, with a wry grin, "he has just married for love. Any man may be distracted when he has a new bride. When the newness wears off, I think he may be a good sight more sensible." The High Priest was frowning off into the distance, pondering my suggestion; he hardly heard me.

"Married for love?" He snorted. "What fool told you that?" I scrambled for an answer.

"Now that you mention it...it *was* a servant in de la Marque livery."

"Yes, *he* would have everyone believe it was love," the High Priest remarked, with a sneer. I could only think he meant Guy de la Marque, the man who had stayed in power while the High Priest had been thrust down. But I could hardly think for the hope growing in my chest.

"At least we'll have the fun of watching him fight Gerald Conradine for command of the army, yes?" I said lightly, but the memory of Gerald's cold gaze sobered me. "He's a man I'd not want for my enemy." The High Priest waved a hand, dismissively.

"Gerald Conradine has no claws."

"He killed Vaclav," I retorted, and to my surprise, the High Priest laughed.

"Killed Vaclav? No. No, that was not Gerald."

"But how could you know..." My voice trailed off as I realized what he meant, and I swallowed. The fear must have shown on my face, for the High Priest laughed once more, truly amused at my naïveté.

"So even you two never guessed? Ah, wonderful."

"But..." I searched for words. "Why?"

"War, Catwin." The High Priest leaned forward. "A war to bleed the country dry, to show the people what the nobles' squabbles cost them. The court is a pit of greed, where nobles fight over the lifeblood of Heddred. With the army occupied in the West, the people could rise in the East. Of course, Garad proved singularly determined to preserve peace." His face twisted at the memory: his plans undone.

I stared at him silently. I had no words for this; it sickened me. To push a county to war, throwing thousands of lives into the balance, only to show the flaws of others? I had sat with Miriel and Jeram while they debated underhanded attacks—salting water supplies, cutting horses and oxen loose.   They had wondered at the honor of that, and now I was faced with their leader, a man who did not bat an eye at the thought of plunging a country into battle. He carried no guilt, this man; he cared only for success, and failure.

I bowed. "I must be getting back." I must get back to Miriel, tell her this new information; it was nothing to the High Priest, but everything to us.

"Wait." His voice was dry. "What did you need my help for, then?"

"Why, for the rebellion, of course. To see if you could persuade Wilhelm to stay true. Only you can bring the rebellion to fruition." I thought that I had gone too far, but he gave a truly eerie smile in response.

"Oh, no," he said absently. "I think you will do your part as well." Unsure what to say to this, I smiled and slipped out the door, thinking it better to leave quickly than give him an opportunity to trap me into telling the truth.

I decided not to go back to the Duke's rooms at once, instead making my way up to the healers' quarters. Roine had been much occupied of late, preparing bandages and medicines for the army, and preparing a small group of healers for the sights and sounds of the battlefield. It was she and her compatriots who would be some of the first to see the aftermath of this invasion, and whoever it was who won, there would be carnage and broken bodies to walk amongst, searching out the dying to offer help—or words of comfort as they died. The best she could hope for would be to see more Ismiri dead, than Heddrian, and I knew that would be of little comfort to her.

"It is necessary," she had said, white-faced, when I asked her about it. I had frowned; the Roine I knew would lecture me on the uselessness of war and conceit of war. But she was afraid, I reminded myself. We were all afraid.

I stuck my head around the door and saw the usual bustle of activity. Roine was at a table in the back, grinding herbs, and I took a basket of linen strips and made my way over to her. She looked up at me gravely.

"I thought I might help," I said, holding up the basket. "I know you're shorthanded."

"That would be good of you," she said simply, but with the same bemused look she always gave me now, as if she did not quite know me.

"What's wrong?" I asked her, and she shook her head.

"I've never understood why you came back," she said softly. I frowned as I rolled a bandage tightly and secured it with a pin. Then, as the thought sank in, I put the next bandage down and looked up at her.

"That's what you want to know? We left without a word, we ran away, and you want to know why we came *back*?"

"Yes," Roine said, after a moment's pause. She gently poured a liquid into a series of wooden bottles, and began to place stoppers in them, securing the pegs with dabs of wax. "You went to the rebellion. Why did you come back? You're not one to leave a task unfinished."

"I really can't tell you," I said miserably, and I saw a look of pain cross her face.

"What are you afraid of?" she asked quietly. "That I would think less of you?"

"What?" I frowned at her, and her brow furrowed.

"Have you not come back for revenge, then?" For the second time in a few moments, I was completely taken aback.

"Revenge?" I managed, and she tilted her head to the side.

"You were grossly mistreated," she said simply. "You were put in harm's way, and so was Miriel, you were to be used as pawns, both of you. I assumed that the only reason you would come back, would be for vengeance."

"No," I said, shaking my head, and her eyes flared.

"Then why?" she demanded fiercely, leaning over the table, her face close to mine. "Why would you ever come back here? Have I managed to convince you of *nothing*? The Court is dangerous, Catwin. It is no less full of murderers and liars than it was when you left—and more dangerous, there's a new King. Is Miriel trying to throw herself at him, too? Have you come back to watch while she makes herself a concubine?"

I sat silent in the face of her anger, trying to ignore the rise of my own. Miriel had been called worse, and had shrugged the words away; there was no sense in being offended on her behalf. And of course Roine would have hoped that we would leave, and not come back. I had been consumed with guilt for leaving her, without remembering that she had always pleaded with me to do so. I leaned forward to her, touching her hand lightly.

"It's for a good cause," I said, as softly as I could. "It's for the rebellion." I expected one of her long sighs, for her to tell me that she was proud of my courage, but her face twisted as if she were in pain.

"For the rebellion," she said flatly, and I saw that I had not eased her mind in the slightest part. To have me out of harm's way, only to come back and place myself at odds with all the Court, must be very bitter to her.

"I'm sorry," I said helplessly, but there was no changing her mind. She turned away from me and went to help a patient, her face taking on the serene patience she had when she tended to the sick. I watched her for a long time, but she did not come back, and at last I placed all of the bandages I had rolled neatly in the basket, and left without a goodbye.

When I slipped back into the Duke's rooms a few minutes with the freshly laundered sheets, Temar gave me a sharp look. I had no will to spar with him, to pretend. I only pushed my way into Miriel's rooms without a backward glance, made the bed, and then curled up on my cot and stared at the wall until I drifted off into an uneasy sleep.

Chapter 16

There was little to be done in light of my conversation with the High Priest. The most important thing, Miriel and I agreed, was that he not suspect us, and she had pointed out, bitterly, that he could hardly suspect her of being his rival when neither of them could gain an audience with the King. There was nothing for us to do but wait, and hope that Wilhelm would send for us, and so we sat in the Duke's rooms and tried not to go mad with impatience. We were studying—she, a history textbook, and me, the few drills I could reasonably practice in our cramped rooms—when the Duke returned from a Council meeting with a grim smile. I was wary at once; I never liked it when the Duke smiled. The Duke was only pleased by two things in this world: his own rise, or the fall of his enemies, and both of those meant more upheaval in a court that was already unsteady.

"Joyous news," he said, as he rounded his desk, and before I thought to stop myself, I shot a look at Temar. We rarely met each other's eyes these days, and then only with mistrust—but now, before his face went blank with his usual look of indifference, I saw a flash of pity in his eyes. My heart sinking, I looked over to Miriel, who had not noticed the look between me and Temar. She was looking elegantly interested, with a half smile and curious tilt to her head; despite her demurrals, I saw her beginning to use her pretty mannerisms once more.

"What is it, my Lord Uncle?" she asked, scrupulously polite. He gave her a curious look. He was perplexed by her lack of spirit, and mistrustful of it, but try as he might, he could find no evidence of the two of us plotting against him. Then he remembered his news, and he smiled once more.

"Oh, the very best of news," he assured her. "There is to be a special banquet in celebration." Miriel, tilting her head to watch him, had gone very still. She knew something was wrong, but she could not think what might be coming.

"Oh?" she asked, tentatively.

"Yes," he said simply, and then, to all appearances, he sat down to his ledgers and missives and forgot her entirely. I saw her clench her teeth at the rudeness, and I saw, too, Temar's small smile at the evidence of her temper. Temar had no pity for Miriel.

"My Lord Uncle," Miriel said, her tone measured. "What is the news?"

"Ah, well—it is to be announced at the banquet," he said. "But I suppose I could tell you now. The Queen, Gods protect her, is with child." Miriel went white, and her uncle's smile grew. I hated him, in that moment, more intensely than I had hated anyone. I wanted to hit him, wipe the smug smile off his face, scream at him for telling her the news this way. He had wanted to see where her heart lay, it was true—but he had wanted to hurt her, too. He reveled in her weakness, and more than that, he had turned—where before he had been careful to guard his allies, and his anger and vengeance had been sparked only by treachery, now he was no more than any other cruel man. Something in him had broken.

"Should I send for a seamstress, my Lord?" My voice was clear, and I thanked the Gods for it. The last thing either of us needed was for him to see my own weakness, as well.

"No," he said negligently. "She can wear...oh, the pink gown. Pink is the Queen's favorite color."

"I will go make ready, then," Miriel said simply. She curtsied, her gaze fixed on the floor, and left the room, and her uncle smiled after her.

"Smile, girl," he called after her. "The whole Court will be rejoicing—don't give them cause to think you aren't pleased by the Queen's condition." He made no attempt to hide his amusement. I paused at the door, standing between the Duke and my lady.

"Any news of the Ismiri, my Lord?" I was desperate to stop this torment, to give her a moment alone, away from his spite and the pity she would see in my eyes. The Duke gave me a suspicious look at the question.

"What's it to you?"

"My kingdom has been invaded, sir, and I am in the path of the army. I should think my interest would be expected."

"Careful, Catwin." His voice was dry, a memory of the calculating, cold-eyed enemy he had been before. "Your rudeness was amusing before, but I grow tired of it." I gulped.

"Yes, my Lord."

"And since you ask—the army is no more than a week out, I would guess. Perhaps less." He gave a grimace. "This will all be over shortly, one way or another. We can only hope that Kasimir is as rash on the battlefield as he is in politics."

"Or that his brother will be put in command," I murmured quietly. More and more, we heard reports that Kasimir's younger brother, Pavle, was wavering in his devotion to the invasion. But nothing would stop Kasimir's march; we heard that he had terrified Pavle into following his every order, and I had no doubt that Pavle would lead an army against Penekket if that was what Kasimir ordered. The Duke snorted, but it was in agreement.

"No one would follow Pavle," he said. "The boy's an idiot. If he were in charge, none of them would have marched against us at all." He was back at work again, examining a map, and so I only bowed and went to find Miriel.

"Are you alright?" I asked her, as I slipped into the room, and she turned to look at me, eyes red-rimmed.

"Don't *pity* me," she said sharply, as I had expected. "I can't stand to be pitied, Catwin, you know that." She turned back to the mirror, and began looking through her jewel box. "Pearls, I think," she said, in a remarkably steady voice.

"Your uncle says the army should arrive within the week." It would not comfort her, but it might distract her. She looked over at me wordlessly. "Spies are telling us that the men in the ranks think Pavle is wavering; it makes them uncertain."

"If only there weren't Kasimir to contend with," Miriel said drily. She took a slow breath, and I saw her put aside her worry for a moment. "Still no word from Dusan, then?"

"None. Kasimir may have silenced him somehow, and if not…what could he do now? He can say it wasn't his wishes, he can try to call the army back—but none of it will be in time."

"Perhaps Pavle's wavering is a sign that he *has* tried to do something," Miriel said thoughtfully. "He may have tried to call the army back. No one believes that this was his doing, after all—not even those who fought against him in the first war."

"As long as they follow Kasimir, it won't much matter," I said. I swallowed, trying to ignore my fear. In Voltur, every family, every building, bore the scars of war, but now I was learning that I had been a child of a peaceful age. The thought of an army advancing towards us, treading the ground that Miriel and I had ridden together, filled me with terror. I could hardly think for fear; it took everything I had not to show it, and I lay awake at nights, staring at the ceiling in frightened wakefulness. Many a night, I had padded out into the quiet hallways and perched on a window seat, staring out one of the arrow slits, looking west to see if I could spot the campfires of our enemy.

Miriel saw my fear, and she came to sit by me on my cot.

"Surely you aren't afraid," she said softly. "We'll be very safe here. No one has ever breached the Fortress."

"What about the people outside?" I asked, before I thought. I had nightmares of running through the streets and alleyways of the palace complex, hearing screams behind me. There would be the thunder of hooves, and fire everywhere, and every time I woke just as I rounded a corner and found myself trapped, Ismiri soldiers behind me and Kasimir himself ahead of me, lowering a spear to run me through. From Miriel's silence, I knew that she understood the fear, even if she had not had such dreams herself. She swallowed.

"We have to keep the Ismir from getting to them," she said. "Gods willing, we will stop their army in its tracks. They'll be readying themselves, they've been lying in wait. The men of the Council should ride out soon, you know—that will give them heart."

"Will they?" I asked skeptically, thinking of the Councilors: men more accustomed to comfort than valor. Those who were already war heroes might well go with the troops...but then, Gerald Conradine and Guy de la Marque would hardly want rivals for their affection amongst the troops. But Miriel nodded.

"They always do. Don't you remember the histories we read? Before the battle, the King and the Council ride through the lines and speak with the men. Like in battle, the King leads the charge." She spoke academically, but a moment later, I saw it dawn on her what she had said. She put her hand to her mouth. "Oh, Gods."

"They'll never let him fall," I said urgently, in the face of her rising fear. I rose, and pulled her with me to the far corner of the room; we had done experiments, to see where someone listening at a closed door might hear us. Miriel followed me, unseeing, and I took her by the shoulders to steady her. "Miriel, listen to me, no king has ever fallen in battle, not in Heddred. And he's a boy, they'll protect him all the more. None of the Ismiri will ever get within striking distance of him." Miriel nodded, white-faced, but I knew she could hardly hear me. She was terrified.

"Don't think of it," I advised her. Her fear turned to bitterness at once.

"Oh, shall I think of Marie being pregnant? Shall I think of her, sitting on my throne? Shall I think of the fact that Wilhelm loved me so little that he did not even care to look at me when I came back to Court?" She caught a glimpse of my face. "What?" she snapped. I drew closer, sure that I did not want Temar to hear me say any of this.

"I was not going to speak of this, yet—the High Priest said something yesterday. He said it was not a love match at all. Guy de la Marque would have people think so, but it was not."

"Why would you not tell me that yesterday?" Miriel frowned. We had spent fully an hour discussing the High Priest's motives, his ambitions, and the dangers he posed, but I had left this out. I had spoken around it, and Miriel, caught up in the emotion of speaking about the treaty, had not noticed my reticence.

"I did not wish to mention it," I said awkwardly, and at her glare, I put up my hands to fend off angry words. "Alright! I wanted to see if it was true." I drew close. "I was going to try to speak to Wilhelm myself. I thought...perhaps he might think that it was betraying Marie to speak to you. But I thought that if he knew what it was about, he might agree to see you. He would know that it was for a good cause."

"And he didn't think it would be betraying me to marry her?" Miriel asked sharply. She sighed when she saw my face. "I know. I know he must have had a reason. But to have nothing other than hope, and then to have that taken away..." She looked at me, her jaw set. "He will sign it," she said firmly. "He may have forgotten who he is, but I will remind him. And then I will go, and he will never have to see me again." I decided not to ask where she planned to go; in all my thinking, I had never come up with a place.

"I'll go to find Wilhelm tonight," I told her, barely whispering, and she nodded. "But at the ball, you must be happy—let the Duke know you are sad, but give him no reason to reproach you. He must not suspect anything." She nodded, biting her lip, and went to make herself ready.

That night, the banquet was a roar of excitement, nearly deafening in the smaller banquet hall, and so overwhelming that I was pressed up against the outer wall of the room, watching things with as much detachment as I could muster. There so many toasts that the courtiers were all half-drunk by the time the first course was finished, and I was pleased to see that Miriel raised her goblet with a smile and a cheer each time. She spoke to the companions at her table, accepting their congratulations on her betrothal gracefully, and although her uncle had watched her like a hawk at the start of the banquet, he eventually looked away to confer with another Councilor; I breathed a sigh of relief. It was one obstacle removed. A moment later, I felt a presence at my side and knew that Temar had come to stand next to me.

"Hello." I did not turn my head to look at him.

"How is she?" he asked me, to the point as he always was now. I paused.

"Dizzied," I said finally. I looked over, and found him staring quizzically at me. "To be freed, after so much isolation, only to come here. It's so...close." I could only hope that my own claustrophobia gave a ring of truth to the lie. "It's not only that, though. A year ago, she expected to be Queen," I explained. "And now the man she was betrothed to is dead. She saw the beginning of the war, at Voltur, and she was afraid to leave her mother there. Then the capture—then this. She's betrothed again, and she's afraid of the war. She doesn't know what to think, she's being charming and pretty because that's all she knows how to do. To tell the truth, I don't know what to think of it, either." To my surprise, Temar was smiling, almost sympathetically. He reached out and laid his hand on my arm, and he leaned close; I blinked, caught off guard.

"I know you're lying to me," he said, very softly, in my ear. I felt my pulse pound to have him so close to me, speaking so gently, and yet his words sent ice water down my spine.

"Why can you not believe me?" I whispered back, passionately. Once, he had told me that the secret to a successful lie was to believe the lie while you told it, and I tried to believe this now. Gods knew, there was enough truth to it all.

"You're asking the man who taught you to lie, remember," he said. He was still smiling, his touch on my arm was still light. I could smell the soap from his skin, he was so close to me; the roar of the banquet had faded away. "I know a lie when I see one, Catwin—even from you, now. I didn't once, you know. I thought you incapable of lying to me; I was wrong. You didn't know how big a mistake you made, when you deceived me for Miriel's little charade. Because until I discovered your lies, I did not know what it was that I was seeing in you. Now, I do. I know when you lie to me, and I will find out your secrets." The threat, finally, awakened the spark of anger that could free me from my spell. I shook my head.

"You don't understand any of this," I whispered back. "All you know is the Court and its lies—but there's more to life. There's honor, and love, and justice. How could you hope to know my secrets when you don't understand that?" He jerked back as if I had slapped him, a flush rising in his cheeks, and then he closed his fingers around my wrist and pulled me close.

"*Never* tell me that I do not understand that," he whispered harshly, his face inches from mine, and then he was gone, and I was rubbing my aching wrist and staring after him, pulse still racing, feeling that I had made a terrible misstep, but not knowing how.

Chapter 17

"I'll be back as soon as I can," I whispered to Miriel. I had bound my hair back once more, and patted my torso to make sure that all of my weapons were in place. "I shouldn't be long. Miriel…"

"What?" She rolled over on her side to look at me; I could see her hair glinting.

"Are you sure you don't want me to take the treaty?" I knew her answer, but I had to ask. "It would be simpler to have done with it now."

"No," Miriel said. It was the third time we had gone over this, and where she had once sounded defensive, now she only sounded weary "Let be, Catwin."

"I'll be back, then." I slipped out the door without another word, and made my way, light-footed, across the main chamber. The Duke had gone to bed only moments before, and I hoped that the sound of his undressing an making ready for bed would shield the sound of my footsteps. I opened the door as quietly as I could, and bit back a sigh when the Duke's guards looked round at me. I stifled a yawn. "Do you know if there are any healers closer than the ones all those floors up?" I asked hopefully, as I closed the door behind me. Wordless, they shook their heads, and I sighed. "Well, thank you. If the lady asks, tell her I went—and I'll be back as soon as I can." I set off, and as soon as I was out of sight, took the next stairwell down, heading for the kitchens.

"A fruit pie," I said to the lone chef who was manning the fires. "And a bottle of wine. And some cheese."

"Oh, is that all?" he asked me nastily. "Run along, boy, I've enough trouble without you asking favors of me."

"It's for the Queen," I said sharply, and he jerked into wakefulness.

"Oh. Of course. At once. Where should I send it?"

"I'm to bring it. They just said to her, isn't it the same apartments as the King?" The cook gleamed, pleased to know something I did not. He shook his head.

"No, she's got her own apartments, very fine—above his, even."

"No!" I said, as if scandalized that anyone should set themselves above the King. "Truly?" He nodded.

"Guy de la Marque said it had to be so, and a mighty fuss that caused." He was finishing up at his work, his hands busy as he scraped vegetable peelings onto the floor, to be swept up. "But her condition, you know," he said, confidentially.

"Oh, I know."

He sent a page running for a bottle of wine, and bustled into the storeroom for cheese and a pie, and I sat, kicking my heels and sneaking bites of a cold meat pie until they were back.

"Very good of you," I said graciously, and the cook bobbed a bow to me.

"Anything she needs, you send to me," he said. "She's to have everything she wants."

"I'll tell them to ask for you," I said, and slipped out, taking the stairs two at a time in my haste to be at the presence chamber before the Duke realized I was gone. I was panting by the time I arrived, and so I was pleased to see that I had been correct: this floor was nearly deserted. The Courtiers who flocked to the King's chambers by day were all abed, and even the Council was adjourned at this hour. It was child's play to avoid the lone two guards who patrolled the outer, curving corridor, and sneak into the presence chamber.

Now to see if my second guess held true. I slipped through the presence chamber, lifting the door to the Council rooms slightly so that it would not squeak as I opened it. I looked around myself, and breathed a sigh of relief that there were no guards. In the corner, as I had hoped, there was a doorway to a private staircase. Holding my breath, hardly daring to think about what I was doing, I opened the door and crept up the stairs, emerging into the King's private chambers.

When I peeked my head out of the stairwell, I saw that Wilhelm was alone, sitting at his desk and poring over a scroll, taking notes on a sheet of paper. His desk was piled with books and maps, and even from here I could see the tired slump of his shoulders. It did not look as if the crown had brought Wilhelm much joy, or much luck. I took a moment to listen for the noise of another person breathing; a groom of the bedchamber, perhaps, or Marie. When no sound came, I cleared my throat. His head jerked up, his gaze wide and frightened, and I held my hands up, showing him that I did not hold weapons.

"Wilhelm—Your Grace—it's Catwin. I am the Lady Miriel's servant." I bowed slightly, and he nodded.

"I remember you," he said, his tone even. His face had settled to stillness once more. He took a deep breath. "But you can go—I will not see Mi—the Lady." I took some small measure of hope from his use of her name. *I will remind him of what he is*, Miriel had said, but it seemed that he had not truly forgotten. It could take only the slightest nudge to tip the balance.

"I think you would see her, if you knew why she was asking," I guessed. "Begging your pardon. Your Grace." I bobbed a bow, and gave a sigh at my own incompetence. I had never been good at proper forms of address, and the months away from Court had done my small skill no favors.

"And why is that, then?" Wilhelm gave up the pretense of writing at last. He set down his quill and stared at me warily. His eyes were red-rimmed from lack of sleep, and I remembered that while the Court had been carousing until late, he had made a single, joyous toast and then slipped away from the feast early. He must have come back here, alone, to sit in fear and wonder if Heddred would destroyed within the week. I could only hope that my words would give him hope and not greater despair. F

or the first time, I hoped that Miriel was right about Wilhelm, not for her sake, but for his. One look at him showed that he desperately needed something to hope for. At long last, I felt my suspicion begin to bleed away—after the long days at court, it was a shock to see someone who seemed to have nothing on his conscience at all. Wilhelm was exhausted and fearful, nothing more; I could see no guilt in his eyes.

Still, I was cautious.

"Your Grace, it is a matter of utmost importance that no one else knows this." I cast an anxious look behind me down the stairwell. "Please tell me—are you alone? If not, can whoever else is here be trusted?"

"You have no need to worry," he said, ambiguously. Even as I cursed his phrasing, I applauded his caution. Wilhelm had seen the last King slain; he would keep any intruder on their guard. I wondered, suddenly, if he had suspected us, just as we had suspected him.

"Very well," I said. "I will speak plainly: Miriel carries with her a signed treaty from the southern leaders of the rebellion. She made a bargain with them that if they would do all in their power to turn back the invasion, she would secure them their rights in law. Even now, they should be harrying the Ismiri army. They'll be poisoning the grain stores, setting the horses free, torching wagons—they're not a large force, but they've been trained." I said a silent prayer to the Gods to protect these men. Even now, in the midst of the court, the guilt was never far away; I hoped that we had not sent every one of them to their deaths.

Wilhelm was staring at me at me, dumbstruck. "Miriel hopes that you are still true to the rebellion," I finished. "She hopes that you will sign the treaty."

"She..." He shook his head, dazed. "That is why she wanted to see me, then? Nothing else?" He forced a smile, but I saw the truth in his eyes: he had wanted Miriel to seek him out for his own sake, and so he had turned me away, sure that he could not do the same if she were to stand before him. I did not know what to say. Miriel would have some pretty phrase, but I was hopeless at these things, afraid that if I told Wilhelm of Miriel's love, he would once more retreat behind the cold mask of honor.

"She would never cause you pain," I said finally. It was the best I could do, but he grimaced at it. "She understands how things must be."

"Please tell her that I would never have married Marie, if there had been another way," he pleaded, and I looked away from the regret I saw in his eyes. "You must tell her—"

"Your Grace, why not tell her yourself?" I broke in softly.

"I cannot bear to see her," he said simply, his words confirming my guess. I wished that I might have persuaded Miriel to give me the treaty. Who could understand better than I that Miriel would wish to see Wilhelm? But it could only come to pain. Indeed, Wilhelm was shaking his head. "You must tell her—" He broke off and dropped his face into his hands.

"Just as you promised her that you would never dishonor her, so she would never dishonor you," I promised him. "She has given me her word that when the treaty is signed, and the war won, she will leave the Court so that neither of you are tormented by this."

"I think of her every day," Wilhelm said brokenly. "Her leaving will not help." I stared at him, not knowing what to say to such a broken admission of grief, and at last he squared his shoulders. "I will see her again," he said. "Once more. Please, only tell her that I would never have married another without cause."

"I will tell her that," I agreed, after a pause; I had no wish to torment Miriel with hope, but no wish, either, for her to doubt Wilhelm. "When shall I bring her here?"

"We can't meet here," he decided. "If anyone saw her, it would be..." He shook his head and his brow furrowed. "Is there any way she can accompany the Council when they ride out in two days?" he asked. "In the camp...I think we could arrange for a meeting."

"We will do what we can." I nodded. "I will send word to you from the camp. I will leave you now, your Grace. I...brought you this. I needed some excuse to be in the hallways." I gestured to the wine and pie, and he smiled absently, his mind already far away.

"Thank you," he said. He sat back down to his work, but I knew that he could see none of it. His thoughts were of Miriel, and I did not want to intrude, but as I turned to leave, I remembered one more thing.

"Also," I said, turning back. "The guards downstairs in the Council chamber."

"Yes?" He frowned at me; he had been lost in his memories.

"There are none," I explained. "Your Grace. I really think there should be." He gave me a bemused smile.

"Thank you," he said, and I slipped out.

When I was down the stairs, I took a moment to look around the Council chamber. So this, in these troubles times, was where the business of the realm was done. A long table stretched down the room, surrounded by high-backed chairs. But other than a small sideboard, the room had no adornments at all; I was impressed. I knew that the Councilors spent their hours here, and it seemed they were not reveling in luxury, after all. Perhaps these men would not stand wholly in Wilhelm's way as he strove to pass the new laws spoken of in the treaty.

I was still feeling pleased with myself when I made my way out of the room and into the presence chamber. I stopped when I saw that there was a single figure standing, waiting for me in the darkened room, and I was so confused to see that it was the Duke, that my mind went blank and I froze. That was my mistake; barely a moment later, I had been thrown to the ground, the wind knocked out of me. In the next moment, I was hauled upward again, one of Temar's hands tangled in my hair, the other pressing against my throat, and I was staring into the Duke's merciless eyes.

"Why were you going to see the King, Catwin?"

"To see—" I could hardly breathe. "—if he would agree to see Miriel."

"Truly?"

"Yes!" My shoulder was on fire where it was wrenched backwards, and Temar's thumb and index finger were pressing against the veins in my neck; there were spots dancing in front of my eyes.

"Don't think of lying to me, Catwin."

"I'm not! It's true!" I could hardly see his face, but it moved slightly; he only looked over my head at Temar, who nodded. Temar accepted my explanation. I would have been surprised, if I'd had the presence of mind for it—but reason seemed to be receding. I hardly felt my knees buckle, but gradually became aware that I was lying on the floor, my breath rasping in my throat. The Duke's face swam into view, bleached white-and-blue in the faint moonlight.

"Tell her I will tolerate no plots from her," he said softly. "If I even suspect that the two of you have more of a plan than getting her into his bed, I will kill you both outright, and find out later if it was true." He smiled. "And she's to be discreet," he warned. "None of Wilhelm's brats; if anything, have her hold off until she knows she's carrying her husband's child. Now, go. I have something to discuss with his Grace."

I did not move for a moment. The haze was still receding, the impact of his words only now penetrating into my mind. I was trying to block out the disgust when I felt the boot of his toe at my ribs, and I was flipped onto my stomach.

"I said go," he said. "Temar, escort Catwin back to the rooms—I'll not have her running off."

"I'll go alone," I said, pushing myself up and straightening my tunic. I could not even bear to look at Temar. "You don't know anything if you think I'd leave Miriel now, after everything we've been through."

"Careful, Catwin." His voice was bored. "You are trying my patience once more. I don't think you wish to suggest that your loyalties lie anywhere but with me." I made myself bow, bile rising up in my throat, but I could not make myself speak. I turned and left, and when I got into the hallway, I broke into a run, trying to draw air back into my lungs with long, sobbing breaths. I was desperate to get away, desperate to get back to Miriel before reality broke in.

There was only one thought echoing in my head: that the day had come, at last, when Temar was my enemy, open and declared—not just by words, but by action. There could be no hope for reprieve. One of us would die, soon, and their master with them—and the other would triumph. I had spent years hoping that this would never come to pass, and now I must steel myself to it. I could not let Miriel die, and her hopes with her. And so it must be Temar and the Duke who lost, who died.

Chapter 18

"Catwin!"

Footsteps pounded after me. I ran, pushing my weary muscles to a sprint, dashing through the corridors, but Temar was faster. I darted into the stairwell and ran, jumping over the railings in my descent, but he was catching up, and if I ran much farther, we would be in the stairs that led to the kitchens, with wakeful servants watching our confrontation. I needed to confront him here.

"You would have *killed* me!" I spat, choosing a landing and rounding on him, my hands in fists. I shoved away his hands when he reached out to me.

"Catwin," Temar tried to laugh, but I could see the strain in his eyes. "He never would have ordered that." He was out of breath from chasing me. He smiled, and even now, the sight was sweet to me. "Do not think I would have hurt you. Please, Catwin." I did not give a thought to his pleading, but instead I went to the heart of it at once, my words as keen-edged as a dagger.

"Would you have done it if he had ordered?"

The words dropped into silence. Far below, I could hear the clatter of pots and pans, the endless work of the cooks. Here, in this little stairwell, there was only darkness and the sound of our breathing. I looked at him, and saw—in the flickering lantern light—that he had gone grey.

"Don't ask that. Catwin, please. Don't ever ask that of me."

"I won't need to," I said coldly, and I pushed my way past him and left, climbing back towards the nobles' apartments. I felt a pain in my chest that I supposed was heartbreak, a deep aching, and an upwelling of anger. Hadn't I always known that Temar's first allegiance was to the Duke? What did I think I could have changed?

"Catwin!" I kept walking. I needed to get to Miriel; I needed to see the face of an ally, I needed the embrace of the only other person who could understand how much this hurt.

When I felt his hand on my shoulder, I did not even think. I dropped and turned, shoved my hips backwards. Temar stumbled sideways with a muffled yell, his fingertips grazing my arm, and I slid past him in the dark, letting him fall behind me on the stairs. I would have gotten away, but Temar was the one who had taught me that throw; Temar had known what I might try, and he had thrown his arm out as he hit the wall. He caught my ankle and pulled me back.

My other foot lashed out, catching him in the ribs, and I tumbled sideways, yanking on the front of his tunic, dragging him down and twisting as he fell. His arm snaked up, catching at my belt, and I fell, too, giving a gasp as I hit the left side of my body against the stone floor. We tumbled to the landing below, sprawled on the floor, his hands grabbing for mine as I tried to jab my fingers into his sternum, find the pressure points on his torso. We struggled, I desperate to hit him and drive him back, unable to rest long enough to plant my feet and throw him from here, him reaching to keep my hands back from his eyes, from his throat.

He caught my wrists, pinning me against the ground, and in the dim light I could see only the contours of his face. I yanked at my hands, but ineffectually, and then dropped my head back, onto the floor, despairing. There was nothing left but the most vicious of attacks, the most unexpected and attention-grabbing. A moment ago, I had been willing enough to use them—now, in this silence, I knew that I did not want to kill him. I could not. This very night, he had spoken of honor, of love, of justice—it was not in me to kill him without knowing, now, why he was here.

Temar's face hovered close to mine, his lips so close that I felt I could feel the warmth of his skin. I heard my instincts crying out that I had thrown away my advantage, that knowledge and honor were nothing if he killed me now, but the voice seemed very far away. We stared at one another, and I could feel my skin on fire where it touched his: his hands at my wrists, my legs tangled with his. I shaped his name silently with my lips, and I saw him shape mine, and then he bent his head and kissed me.

His lips were soft. That was my first, surprised thought. Temar was all coldness and sinew. In all my dreaming, I had never thought that his lips might be soft. Surprised, dazed, I felt myself kiss him back.

"We can't do this," he murmured, between kisses.

"I know," I agreed, but I felt my legs tangle in his and my head lift slightly, for his kiss. All of a sudden I needed to feel his skin against me and I arched my back to bring my torso along his. He gave a gasp at that.

"Catwin."

"I know," I whispered back. I could feel his hips drive against mine. "But I can't stop."

It was a dream, I thought; certainly, it did not feel like reality. His hands came away from my wrists and one cupped the back of my head where it lay against the floor, the other found my waist and tore at the sword belt. My hands were at his waist, fingers tangling in the lacing of his britches. I was burning up—

Footsteps. The one thing that could have moved us. We were up in a flash, pausing to hear whether the footsteps were above or below us, and then running, fleeing without words towards the Duke's rooms. We slowed to a walk as we approached, and the guards swung their pikes aside to let us through; I shot a glare at them for betraying me to the Duke, but as soon as we were in the room alone, I forgot their presence entirely. It was dark in the outer room; the fire had burned low and there was no sound from Miriel's chambers.

"Miriel?" I whispered. No answer, and we looked at each other in the half-light of the dying fire. He stayed a few feet away from me, uncertainly.

"Catwin, we can't do this." But he was moving towards me.

"I know," I said, but I reached for him. His lips found mine once more, and the world faded—

"Very interesting."

Temar shoved himself away from me with a curse, and I felt my head whip around to the shadows at the edge of the room. Miriel stood and stepped out of the shadows of the chair; she had waited for me, for the news I would bring back, hoping that the Duke's departure did not mean my death. I stared at her dumbly and took in every inch of her. She had tilted her head to the side as she studied Temar, cool and collected. I looked over at him, saw him breathing hard as he stared back at her. For the first time, he did not look so much furious as wary.

"You know," Miriel said, her voice like cool water, "I think you really do want Catwin." I lost my breath at her words. I had kissed him, pulled him to me, shown him without even thinking that I wanted him—I had always wanted him. I had not even thought that he might be playing me for a fool.

Temar said nothing, and Miriel smiled. It was not her uncle's smile, nor her mother's. It was the smile of a woman I hoped would never be my enemy.

"And I really think that my uncle would believe me if I told him. Don't you?" Temar shrugged, but I had seen his gaze close off. Miriel stepped closer. "And what do you think he'd do if he knew?" she asked, and I saw the first genuine fear I had ever seen in Temar's eyes. I looked away, not wanting him to know that I had seen, not wanting to watch while my ally blackmailed the man I loved.

"So you stop telling him not to trust me," Miriel ordered. "I know you've always hated me, but I swear to you, you don't know the first thing about me—and I won't be undone by you. Stay out of my business, Temar, and I'll stay out of yours." And she left. At the door, she turned and held out her hand. "Catwin."

"I'll come in a moment." I saw her face go blank; it had been an order as much as a question, and she had not allowed herself to fear that I would choose Temar over her. She turned on her heel and disappeared into her room, and the door closed behind her with a gentle click.

"Do we have to be enemies?" I asked softly. "Truly?" There was no time for dissembling; I could not make this pretty. I looked up into his eyes, and recoiled at what I saw there: darkness, and death, and pain. Over everything, pain. "Who *are* you?" I asked, before I could stop myself. *What are you?*

"I am a Shadow," he said. "We could never be allies, Catwin. Your first allegiance is to Miriel, you know that. You've proved it time and again."

"But I don't want to be your enemy," I protested.

"It's all the same thing," he said simply. "Think on it all you want, but there's no way around it." He lifted the latch, slipped out the door, and was gone.

"How could you?" Miriel asked simply, when at last I gathered the courage to open the door and face her. She was standing in the center of the room, waiting for me. She had wrapped her robe around herself, and I saw that she was shivering; even in midsummer, the stone bulk of the Fortress pulled the warmth from the air. I bowed my head in the face of her bright scrutiny.

"It was a mistake," I said shortly. I did not believe that, could not believe that; but every piece of evidence we had pointed to the fact that it had been a terrible mistake, an unforgivable lapse in judgment. Even Temar knew it.

And therein lay the greatest hurt of all. In all of my dreams and all of my longing to see Temar's face, I had not thought for a moment that he might feel the same yearning for me; it had not even occurred to me to wonder about it. I had never thought that he might love another—not he—but I would never have believed that he might want me. What there was between us was friendship and laughter—and later, forced enmity and my own unfortunate adoration. I had not once thought there might be more.

It had been heartbreaking, even that a friend might promise to kill me if I stood in his way. Had I not run from him, turned on him, lashed out at him for coming close to killing me? Temar knew me better even than Miriel, in some ways, and better than Roine; and now Temar, who had taught me to tumble and reason and spy, would kill me. I had killed, and I knew it to be the very definition of horror, but I had only killed in panic, killed men I did not know; how could one kill, deliberately, a person they had seen breathe, laugh, smile, run? Temar and I had sparred enough to know each other's very heartbeat—even if he had not loved me, how could he think of killing me? It was unfathomable.

And the fact that he might love me, and still do so, brought more pain than I had known existed in this world. Heedless of Miriel, I hunched over. It felt as if my chest was tearing itself apart, and I could not remember how to breathe.

"I wish we hadn't come back," I whispered.

"Why not?" she asked, curious despite herself. She would not reach out and touch me, and I knew that she doubted me now, but still she drew closer, and peered at me with a frown.

"In a week, we've lost every ally we had. Except Wilhelm." I looked up and saw the flash of hope in her eyes, but I was too bitter to stop there. "Roine won't speak to me, Temar nearly killed me. Jacces can't be trusted not to go mad, and I'm certain he'll try to kill us when he knows what we've done. And everything we've worked for could come to nothing in any case—what if the Ismiri win? What then?"

"We'll probably be dead," Miriel said matter-of-factly. "So I doubt we'll care very much." She looked me in the eyes, and I saw her force herself not to ask me of Wilhelm. "A question, though..."

"Yes?" I asked wearily, and she shrugged.

"If Temar just tried to kill you, why were you kissing him?" It was half a serious question and half a joke, but I would not be led, and Miriel grimaced when she saw my face. She bit her lip and looked away.

"Your uncle doesn't know anything," I said, as calmly as I could. "He thinks you sent me to see if Wilhelm would agree to a tryst. It's what he suspected in any case. He let me go, and told us he'd kill us if he thought there was anything more." There was a silence, and then Miriel finally broke.

"And what did Wilhelm say?"

"He said to find an excuse to come into the camps with the Councilors, that it would be noteworthy, but he could not risk anyone seeing you near his apartments. He will meet with you, and sign the treaty."

"Anything else?" she asked, and I tried to force away my own envy. They might be kept apart, always, but they could love each other, each without ever thinking of the other as an enemy.

"He said he would speak to you of it—but he wanted me to assure you that he would not have married Marie if he'd had any other choice." Slowly, she nodded, and she closed her eyes tightly.

"It will be over soon," she said, as much to herself as to me. "Catwin, I think I want nothing more in this world than to see him. More than the treaty, more than anything. I've been such a fool."

"No." I shook my head. "There's no logic to it." Who would know that better than I?

"Catwin, please—" Miriel's voice broke, and I saw tears in her eyes. "Please promise me you won't betray me."

"I would never betray you!" I dashed my own tears away, angry now. "Never. How could you think that?" She did not mention what she had seen in the Duke's rooms, it was too obvious to be worth discussion. She only stared at me steadily.

"Because if we stick to this plan, we'll both come out of it with nothing," she said bitterly. "Have you thought of that? I have. Anyone would think that it might be better just to cut and run. Please. Promise me."

"I promise," I said, into the darkness.

Chapter 19

We passed our days in the silence of those who wait. What else, for us, beyond the treaty? And so we did not speak of anything beyond minor pleasantries, and what little gossip we could bear. We studied and sat quietly in our rooms, and gave the Duke no reason to suspect us. And I, swearing to myself that I need only bear this for a day more, two days more, a week at most, never looked over to where Temar sat, close by the Duke's side, always at work on the business of battle: staring at maps, planning maneuvers and formulating backup plans.

As the Ismiri army drew ever closer, the mood in the Fortress descended into muted panic. When the news of the invasion had first arrived, the courtiers had been incredulous, and then angry, and then bloodthirsty. It had been nearly twenty long years since the last war, fifteen since the last skirmishes and border raids had died away, and the Court had forgotten the horror of the last war: William's death of camp fever, his brother Henry's fateful accession, and only the famed Battle of Voltur to end it all. No one remembered that it was the betrayal of one man that had tipped the scales in Heddred's favor—and after the months of border raids all through the mountains, no one would have paid any heed. It was time, they said, to end the Ismiri once and for all.

While the King and the Council had faced the horrifying reports of crops burned, towns torched, women and children put to the sword, the Court had sung ballads of bravery and written toasts to heroism and valor. It was remarkable, I thought sourly, that there was anything at all that could have lifted them from their willful ignorance, but at last, when the Ismiri army was said to be three days' march away, reality seemed to have broken through the Court, and in its wake rushed fear.

At last, the nobles began to understand that even Penekket Fortress would not save them forever. The women and children might be hidden away inside the stone walls, made ready for a long siege, but the men, trained from childhood to wield sword and spear, and lead men to battle, would be very far away from safety. Ladies and their daughters prayed endlessly, fathers and sons and brothers were called to be outfitted, and they walked as if they were dead already.

The Duke was too occupied with his forces to be frightened; where the other men seized any time they could with their families, I knew that the Duke had already ridden out several times to rally the Heddrian Army. Whatever their spats, whatever their differences, he, and Gerald Conradine, and Guy de la Marque went to the camps each day, leaving their horses behind and walking amongst the tents. They spoke to the men, smiled, clapped soldiers on the back and promised a glorious victory march. In a court filled with fear, it was one of the few stories of courage and camaraderie, and it bemused me that it was the three men I least trusted who were offering courage and support to the men.

I heard tell that the King was pressing for peace, arguing against his own Council. Wilhelm was determined to give Kasimir a chance to turn back, leave without it coming to open battle, and the Council was equally determined that they should strike fast, leaving the Ismiri army with no time to recover from its march. The Duke, above all, was determined to outmaneuver Kasimir, and Miriel and I were a captive audience to her uncle's rants on the King's stupidity.

"It's not Dusan he's dealing with," the Duke had snarled. "It's not Pavle, for the love of the Gods! Can he not see that?"

Miriel and I waited as patiently as we could, trying not to fall prey to the fear that ran rampant through the Court. The days ran long, and there was little for us to do. The maidens still had their classes in deportment, languages, music, and dancing, but Miriel, now betrothed, was no longer expected to attend, and she shut herself away gratefully. She had become quite the tragic figure of the Court—with no choice, the Duke had accepted her story of capture and escape, and Miriel's unexpected return, sad eyes, and grave demeanor only fed to the drama of the story.

Where once she might have reveled in the attention, and wound the Court to a fever pitch with pretty demurrals and fragments of the story, now Miriel did everything she could to fade into the background. The other maidens believed that she was still recovering from her kidnapping, and Miriel did nothing to dissuade them. There was no need to tell anyone that she had lost her patience with the unending, childish game of court life; now she had the perfect excuse to be absent.

I, to my great relief, also needed no excuses. There was no chance for lessons with Donnett, for he was with the Army; nor with Roine, who was too busy with preparations; nor with Temar, who accompanied the Duke on his endless errands and helped him with his battle plans. I missed Donnett's plain speech and his good humor, and was bored enough to crave a good sparring match, but I was grateful indeed that I had no need to speak to the others.

To my knowledge, the Duke had not yet noticed the new tension between his Shadows. I would have thought he would need to be blind to miss it, but between preparations, Council meetings, and marriage negotiations, he was occupied from sunup to well past sundown. He did not see that Temar and I avoided each other's eyes, or spoke little, or went to pains to keep from brushing up against each other as we moved through the small rooms.

Just as we had never mentioned our enmity, and the coming confrontation, so we did not speak of what had transpired between us. I dreamed of his mouth, his hands, the feel of his body against mine, reliving those few moments and creating, out of my own desire, a thousand others—and then, in daylight, we hardly spoke. We looked away from each other and I hoped that he could not see where my pulse beat rapidly at my throat. When we touched, by accident, I would see him tense; but neither of us spoke of it. No, it was just as well that there was no time for lessons.

Just as the Duke was too preoccupied to notice our tension, Miriel hardly seemed to notice it, either. Every once in a while, I would see here eyes flick back and forth between us, but she could not seem to summon any anger at us. She had doubted me, once—warned me away from Temar, told me to let him alone. But as Miriel became more and more fearful about her marriage, she did not waste her energy on suspecting me.

Arman Dulgurokov paid court to her with gentle gallantry. Since we had arrived back at Court, he had come to see her every day, to kiss her hand and speak a few kind words. He brought her little gifts, and his face warmed to see her smile. He left of his own accord each day, never pressing her to dance, never speaking of a date for the marriage itself. Had their marriage not been arranged for the purpose of a treasonous plot, one might have said it was very sweet, indeed.

But with Arman, often, came Isra. Isra, who watched Miriel as if she were a piece of filth, and who wasted no time with pleasantries. While Miriel and Arman spoke of pleasant nothings, Isra and the Duke spoke of the business of the marriage, and they were contentious allies at best. There might be pages of documents to be argued over yet, chilling discussions of whose troops would be moved where, and who would arrange for the assassinations of Miriel's cousins, but each day, they drew closer to an agreement, and Miriel was becoming frightened that they would marry her off before there was a chance either to escape or to secure allies to fight against the planned coup.

Sleep and knowledge were the only escape from her fear, and with nothing to do, and nowhere to go, Miriel quickly read through every book to be had in the Fortress. After that, she took to lying on her bed and staring at the walls, trying to will herself into sleep, and more than once, I mixed a careful dose of herbs into some wine or tea, and had her drink that, wishing that these days might pass quickly so that she could, at last, be free of her fear.

One afternoon, when at last her breathing grew deep and slow, I slipped out of her room quietly, gathered up my courage, and asked the Duke's permission to go see Roine. He had looked at me suspiciously, but when I offered to go in the company of one of his guards, he only sighed and waved his hand. With my own sigh that I had not tried this trick sooner, I bowed and left, wishing very much that I did have some secret errand to run. It seemed wasteful to have the Duke's permission to travel without being followed, and not scheme even a little bit.

It was the one thing that went right that day, for I arrived at the healers' ward and found that Roine refused to speak with me at all. It had taken all of my courage to come here in the first place, and so, instead of slinking away, I flatly refused to leave. At last, when I appointed myself her assistant and followed her on her rounds, she turned and snapped at me, asking what it was I wanted of her.

"What do you mean, *what do I want of you*?" I asked her, frowning bitterly. "You're my mother, and there's to be a battle—of all times, now we should not be angry with each other."

"What did you say?" She was staring at me, and I tried to remember my exact words.

"Not my mother, then—but you raised me. You're my family." She looked away at once, down, staring into her chest of medicines, and I frowned suddenly, distracted from my anger, tilting my head to the side as I studied her face. She looked up and raised her eyebrows at my expression.

"What?" she asked, warily.

"How old were you when you took me in?"

"Don't you know better than to ask a lady how old she is?" Roine asked tartly. I smiled to see her familiar humor, but she sobered again quickly enough. "I was twenty," she said, and I blinked in surprise. Roine could have been any age. She had just a few strands of grey in her dark brown hair, and her face, while world-weary, was not deeply lined. But twenty...it occurred to me that I had never thought of Roine as a young woman. She was too self-possessed, too sure in her beliefs to have been so young when I first knew her.

"Where were you born?" I asked her, pulling a stool over to sit next to her and drawing my knees up to my chin. I knew somehow she had not been raised in Voltur, but that was all I remembered, and there were no clues to be had by looking at her. The people of Heddred had mingled so much, on the plains, that there was no way of telling any of them apart. Roine might have come from anywhere.

"You know," she said, with a wry smile, "I actually don't know."

"You don't—how do you not know?"

"I was raised by the Church," she said.

"I didn't know that." My eyes were wide with surprise.

"You never asked," she said, with a faint smile. "Where did you think I learned to read? Or learned medicine?" I shrugged.

"Didn't you ever ask about your parents?"

"No. It was a closed order, many of the sisters had taken vows of silence; I was one of the only children, and all of us were orphans—I assume. It never occurred to us to ask."

"Well, how did you get to Voltur?"

Roine's hands had stilled. "I can't explain."

"What do you mean? Why can't you?"

"I don't wish to speak of it," she warned me, but I did not heed her.

"Did the Church send you?"

"Catwin, leave it." At the sound of her voice, I recoiled, and she sighed, defeated. "My past is...not a happy one."

"I'm sorry." I laid my hand on her arm. "I didn't know." To my surprise, she moved her arm away from my touch, her mouth tight as she looked down at my outstretched fingers. She had gone cold.

"I would be alone," she said simply, and I, annoyed at her sudden turn to anger, left to go without a word. But at the door, I remembered why I had come, and I turned back to her.

"Will I see you before the battle?" I asked, hopefully. She paused, and then shook her head.

"I don't think so," she said softly, and I knew somehow that she meant I would not see her after the battle, either. "Gods keep you, Catwin. I love you." There was a terrible finality about her words. In her eyes, I saw the surety of her own death, and I felt as if I could not catch a breath. I ran back to her, heedless of the servants and healers I pushed out of the way, and wound my arms tight around her. She bore it for only a moment, and then she pushed herself away from me, and I saw tears in her eyes. "Go," she said simply. "May you be safe from harm."

There was no gainsaying her; she turned away, and though I waited for long minutes, she never looked back. Finally, I walked back to the Duke's chambers in a daze. I was so preoccupied that, for a time, I hardly noticed the shouting and crying in the hallways around me. Then, as I bowed to the guards at the door, I looked around myself. There were pages running through the hallways, noblewomen in tears, men shouting. I pushed my way past the guards and into the room, raising my eyebrows at Temar, who was too preoccupied with frantic activity to pay me much heed.

Miriel, wakened from sleep, was standing groggily in the center of the room, watching as her uncle packed his ledgers and papers. Temar, who had been waiting for a stack of books, disappeared into the Duke's bedchamber, and I could hear him packing clothing into a trunk.

"Kasimir held the horsemen for the foots oldiers to catch up. Now the army is two days out, and moving fast," the Duke said brusquely to me. "The noblemen are to go to the encampment tomorrow, in preparation for the King's attempt to sue for peace. You and Miriel will stay here."

"Are we not to accompany the Queen?" I asked simply. "I had heard tell that all of the King's family would accompany him to the camp."

"That was before the Queen's pregnancy," the Duke said, distracted. "She can't be risked now—if Wilhelm falls, that child is uncontested heir. She's to be on the uppermost floor of the Fortress, and she'll have all of the Royal Guard protecting her. She's to withdraw tomorrow when the men leave." I nodded, but as I looked around the room, I saw Temar standing at the door to the Duke's bedchamber, watching his master. To my surprise, there was neither his usual blank stare, nor thinly veiled hatred on his face. He was thinking, his attention entirely caught by the Duke's commentary. When he saw me watching him, his face went blank, and when he saw me looking, his eyes narrowed slightly, and he took the closest thing to hand and disappeared, once more, into the Duke's rooms, away from my prying gaze.

Chapter 20

Tomorrow, to war.

Miriel had been white-faced and shaking, shocked into wakefulness by the sudden descent into open battle; it seemed we had been waiting forever, and her mind, slowed by the tea I had made her, could not comprehend reason, but instead only horror. I had sat with her, soothed her as she leaned her head on my shoulder and tears ran down her face. She did not sob, she only held tightly to my hand, and at last I had put my arm around her shoulders and lowered her, gently, to the bed.

"Aren't you scared?" she whispered, so softly that I had to bend my head close to hear her. I smoothed a lock of hair away from her face and tried to smile, but it was more a lopsided twitch of my lips than anything genuine. I was terrified.

"They're wearied from their march," I said reasonably. "They'll be looking into the rising sun as they fight, and we have the best generals of the generation working together. They'll have a plan. They'll win, and send the Ismiri home again." She only blinked in response, and slowly her breathing became deep and even. I was about to lever her up slightly to work my arm free when she said, sleepily,

"I should have stopped this."

"What do you mean?" I frowned at her, and her eyes fluttered; she was half asleep.

"If I was the leader I thought I was, I could have stopped this. I should have. I shouldn't have bothered with the treaty—we should have come back at once and found some way out of this."

"You did what you thought was best," I said, a weak comfort, and even so close to sleep, she frowned. Her brow wrinkled slightly.

"For Heddred," she said. "For the people." Her voice was growing fainter and fainter. "But how does this help them, if they die?" And at that, the herbs still in her blood, she had slipped into unconsciousness, leaving me awake and frightened.

I brushed my hair out and took off my suit, lined my daggers up neatly beside my bed and set out my boots, and then I put on my pajamas and slipped into bed. But I could not sleep. I could not believe that the there was an army, sitting on the plains, outside the city walls; I could not imagine that there was a second army, perhaps marching even now, through the darkness. The sheer scale of it was beyond me, so that I felt I could believe it only for a moment before my mind told me that none of it could possibly be real. For all that this invasion had been the stuff of my nightmares for weeks, I had somehow managed to believe that it was a dream. In the many nights that I had sat and peered out of the windows of the Fortress, I had never seen the invaders, and I had begun to think that they would blow away like morning mist, and never arrive at all.

I was seized by the desire to look out onto the plains. It was terrifying that I might see the armies by the light of their fires, lying in wait like predatory beasts, but now that I had wondered at it, I had to know: could I see the Ismiri army in the distance? Their thousands upon thousands of men, clustered by campfires, feeding themselves on the grain from our fields. It was like fearing an intruder in the room, or some nightmarish monster under the bed—at once mocking myself, and in terror, I knew that I must see the truth. There was nothing more important than seeing with my own eyes what Heddred faced.

I got up out of bed and put on my suit once more, brushing through my cropped hair with my fingers and slipping each of the daggers and tools into the secret pockets, and then I opened the door and left. For once, Miriel did not waken and demand to know where I was going; she was lost to the world, taking refuge in her dreams. I cast one last look at her, and then closed the door behind myself.

The guards at the door barred my way, but relaxed themselves when I pointed to a nearby window seat. It was a westward-facing wall, and there had been many a night that I had crept out and watched the plains, relaxing only as the hours ticked away and no strange lights appeared on the horizon. They might have given me up to the Duke once, but now there was nothing for them to give away; there was nowhere for me to run, no plots for me to spin. I was only a scared girl, looking into the darkness to see if an enemy waited there.

It did—this army was not the stuff of nightmares, but flesh and bone, real men with a terrible purpose. Below the shimmering beauty of the night sky, lying on the rich farmland of my nation, sprawled the Ismiri army. Staring out to the West, I saw it at once, and my heart seized. I wanted to pray, but the words stuck in my throat; praying had never brought me comfort.

There was only a day's march standing between the two armies, nothing more. Two dawns from now, the battle would join, the ranks of men shouting war cries and brandishing weapons—a fine moment that would descend at once, I knew, in chaos.

A battle was as much luck as skill, Donnett had taught me. He had been twenty at the Battle of Voltur, and he had seen the men next to him felled by arrows and swords, run through by spears, their heads split by the great war axes Ismiri generals carried. He said that he had seen men cut down by their allies, Ismiri and Heddrian both, dying before their own friends realized who it was they had killed. Battle was madness, Donnett had said, the men exhausted and filled with terror—they might go mad with fear, or with battle lust, and it was like nothing human.

The Duke had seen this, and yet he was prepared to lead an army into battle once more. He thought it rank stupidity to try for peace. A waste of a messenger, and the end of any advantage the Heddrian army might hold. The Ismiri would think us weak, telling them that their ruinous march across the plains would be forgiven, if only they went home now. It was not noble, the Duke had said, sneering, to throw away a battle and consign one's citizens to invasion—it would be nobler to cut down the army where they stood, take any means to destroy them and win peace that way. We would have no concessions from Kasimir.

If only we weren't dealing with Kasimir, Miriel had said.

I thought of Pavle, the young man following his older brother into battle. I wondered if it had been like this when they had been children: Kasimir running ahead, taunting the younger child, and Pavle tottering along behind him, unsteady on his feet but determined to follow his older brother. Even now, in such a great enterprise as this, knowing that thousands upon thousands would die, Pavle followed, determined to prove himself. The Ismiri knew of both his doubt and his devotion, and they wavered as well—but, like Pavle, they would follow Kasimir wherever he led. A man does not march thousands of miles only to abandon his fellow soldiers and march home through strange territory, cursed by his companions and his lord.

But they wanted to run; I knew that without question. Only Kasimir, with a hatred that bordered on obsession, could think this march a good plan. I thought of the Ismiri camp: hundreds of nobles and thousands of foot soldiers, weary and homesick. I wondered if they felt ill at ease, if the land looked different than their own. I wondered if they were afraid. What were they saying, in their camps at night? Did they curse the luck that had brought them Kasimir for a lord?

I tried to give up my perpetual doubt and pray. This was not the whisper of a prayer for good luck, uttered in the darkness, words uttered for convenience, with no hope of any change. This was a true wish. Feeling like a fool, and yet wondering what else I could do, I interlaced my fingers and bowed my head and I prayed, moving my lips silently so that the guards would not hear me: *Please, if you care for the people of Heddred, find some way to turn away the army before there is a battle.* It felt selfish, and I bit my lip. *It is not only for us,* I reasoned, with the invisible Gods I so scorned. *The Ismiri have families, too. Would it not be best for them to go home as well?*

Nothing. Silence.

I sighed and leaned my head against the narrow window, feeling the edges cut into my skin. What had I expected? The Gods, if they even existed, either cared very little, or would not deign to answer one such as me. There had been eight wars between our nations, and they had never once intervened—and surely many other men and women must have made much the same prayers then. We were on our own.

And, I admitted with fearful honesty, it was certain that Miriel and I were helpless. We were not soldiers, who could wield swords or even command armies. We would not be the ones who could lead the soldiers to victory, urging them on to fight for King and country. We were not wives, who could whisper in their husband's ears for courage, and we were not even healers, who might salvage something out of the ruin of battle. We were only two girls who would, if all went well, get a signature on a scrap of paper and then sit back and hope for everything to go our way.

It was sickening—it was the ruin of everything we had hoped for. And, as Miriel had pointed out, our escape and our months of work for the rebellion could both come to nothing. It was words and promises on parchment, flimsy enough to a common-born citizen, and nothing that could stand as their shield against invaders. What was it that we had worked for? Was it any nobler than the Duke, so consumed with his quest for power that he would lead an army out and face ten thousand enemies?

The thought struck me like a punch to the gut: would Temar go with him? Every general would have a standard-bearer, and a cohort to ride at his side and keep him safe from harm. A bodyguard, of all people, should be at his lord's side, but surely Temar would not be there. He had no place in a battle, he was not made for daylight and an open fight—he was a Shadow. And yet, all this was self-serving logic: the truth was, I felt all the breath leave me at the thought of him in such danger.

I could not think of it. I would go mad. I squeezed my eyes shut and opened them again. But I could see his face in my mind: the clean line of his jaw, the eyes, so deep a brown that they might be black, the skin always tanned, even when the snow and cold had faded mine to bone whiteness.

Who was he? Five years, I had known him, and what did I know now that I had not seen on sight? He had once sworn by a name I did not know—saint? Angel? God? That told me nothing, in any case. He looked like no one I had ever seen, but then, the Guards said that there were men of every color in the markets, one with skin that was truly white, and eyes that were red, and some men from the Bone Wastes with skin like cherry wood.

And yet Temar spoke Common with no accent I could discern. It was as if anything that could be erased, any sign of his life before this, had been wiped away. He had no notable scars, nor tattoos. I had seen his chambers once, and there was nothing there save his clothes—no possessions of any sort. I wondered, not for the first time, if Temar did not speak of his past because he had none at all.

But he must have a past—no man could serve the Duke, with no reasons of his own, and yet tell me that he understood love and honor and justice. There was nothing of that in Temar's service. That meant reasons of his own, and reasons meant a past.

And how could I know nothing of it? Any person, given time, would slip and tell stories. Temar knew a dozen small things about me, as I knew such things of Donnett, Miriel—even the Duke. I knew that Donnett could not stand to eat salt fish, for he had grown up in a coastal town in the north and run away in his fifteenth year. I knew that Miriel had once thought to become a knight, and dressed up in a pageboy's clothes; she had been caught, and thrashed. But I knew nothing, not one thing, about Temar, about his childhood.

Behind me, the door opened, and I jumped at the noise. I looked around to see Temar make his way out of the Duke's chambers with a brief word of thanks to the guards. His eyes swept about the corridor and came to rest on me, and he froze. There was the jolt, now, as there always was when our eyes met; I felt my lips part, and saw him swallow.

"I bid you a good night," he said, after a pause, and set off in the other direction. But I had seen his look—Temar had not wanted anyone to notice him. Temar felt guilty, and uncomfortable. And that alone was reason enough to wonder where he was going. I hastily uncurled myself from the window seat, cursing my aching muscles, and hurried after him.

Chapter 21

"Where are you going?" I demanded, when I caught up with him, and he shot me a look—annoyance quickly veiled by the sweep of his dark lashes. He was so preoccupied with his task, and I so determined to find out what it was, that for once the tension between us eased.

"Nothing," he said shortly. "Go back to your watch. Go to sleep." He was in no mood to bandy words with me. He wanted me gone. I would not have that.

"No."

"Go back, Catwin," he insisted, but I followed him as he went into the stairwell and began to climb. Normally, by himself, he would lope up the stairs quickly, taking them two at a time; he always moved quickly, even when he had no need to hurry. Now his footsteps dragged; he did not want to do this, whatever it was. We climbed and climbed, and I began to wonder where it was that we were going. When at last we approached the healers' chambers, I spoke up at last.

"You look strange," I said finally, and he jerked around; he had been so absorbed in his thoughts that he had not even noticed me following him. He had forgotten my presence entirely. I swallowed back my hurt pride and saw that he was sweating, even in the chill of the building, and his skin was an unhealthy pallor. "Are you ill?" I asked, nervously. He started to shake his head, and then said, suddenly,

"Yes." I narrowed my eyes, but there was no doubting the greyish tinge I saw, or the brightness in his eyes.

"Let me get you medicine, then," I said. I realized, with a rush of pain, that I wanted to see Roine again. I had swallowed back my tears all afternoon, and lost myself gratefully into the fear of war—for that was better than the fear of losing Roine. But I could not let her go onto the battlefield without begging her to be careful. "What is it you have?"

"A fever," he said, a little wildly. "Some men of the Council had it, even the King."

"Oh," I said neutrally, nodding, and then I saw it: the flash of relief in his eyes. "No," I said, narrowing my eyes at him. "You're not sick. No one's sick. Why would you tell me that?" I expected some glib response, but he turned me to face him, gently, and took my hands in his.

"You must go back to bed," he said softly. "Protect Miriel and the Duke. There is something I must do, and please, Catwin, if you believe nothing but this, at least trust me now—you want no part of this."

There was only one question, and I voiced it unthinking: "Who?" His face clouded, and the answer slammed into me. In a moment, I had his arm and I had dragged him over against the wall, peering into his face, wrapping my hands in the fabric of his shirt to hold him close. "No. You can't. Why would you ever do that?" He did not answer, and I felt horror rise up in me. "For the love of all Gods—she's with child!"

"I know that!" His face was anguished, but set. He was not turning back, and I could hardly find the words to speak. I was babbling, trying to keep my voice from rising.

"She's sixteen. Temar, she's only sixteen, what can she have done? What threat can she pose? She doesn't know anything."

"She stands in our way," Temar said, bleakly. "And if it is not her, then it is hundreds more on the battlefield two days hence—and that is all that matters." He spoke the words as if he had repeated them to himself a thousand times, and still did not believe them.

"It isn't all that matters! Gods above, even you're frightened by it! You've never done something like this!" It was a guess, but it hit home. He swallowed and closed his eyes, and I shook him. "Temar, wait—what do you mean, it's her or...others?" He opened his eyes and looked at me bitterly.

"The Duke seeks a way to the throne, you know this. He would take his chance to eliminate those who stand in his way—and what better time than in chaos, when a man might say he saw anything?"

I stood stock still, trying to make sense of the words. The Duke would move against his rivals in battle. But if his rivals were Heddrian lords—for I must think of this slowly, now, to make sure that I was not mistaken—then he meant to turn his forces against the rest of the army. He would cut down the lords and their men alike, heedless that he took the lives of his own countrymen. I could not believe it, but Temar's stillness told me that what I feared was true.

"That's mad," I said, finally. My voice was shaking, and I wanted nothing more than for Temar to say that I was mistaken, that such a conclusion as I had drawn was ridiculous. But he only smiled bitterly.

"Mad," he agreed. "He had the throne within his grasp, didn't he? And then it slipped away. And now he will wait no longer. I told him that, given time, Miriel might take the King's fancy—that there is no need for such a plan as his." His lip curled, as it always did when he spoke of Miriel. "But he will not wait for that; he will not see reason. He will take the chance in battle, and it will come to nothing but ruin."

"And so you would kill an innocent woman—half a child? And her with child?" I tightened my fingers around his arms. "You can't do this," I said urgently.

"I have to." He shrugged, brushing my hands away from him. "I know what I'm doing—believe me, I know. And I will pay for this. But there's no other way—his plan will fail, and I cannot let him fail. I must give him the chance to choose another path. There is more to this than you could possibly imagine."

"Try me," I whispered back, passionate, and he opened his mouth—then shook his head. He was holding me away from himself, looking down rather than meet my eyes.

"You want no part of this," he reiterated. "I would have had you ignorant of this entirely, but at least take no part in it. Go back now."

"I can't stand by and let you do this," I warned him.

"You must," he said, very seriously. "Miriel must sit on the throne, and Marie is in her way. Marie, and the baby, both of them."

"Miriel?" I frowned at him, dumbstruck. "You're doing this for Miriel?" Two thoughts occurred to me at once, the first that Miriel would not want the crown, not ever, and most certainly not at this price, and the second: "But you hate her," I said, uncomprehending.

"Of course I hate her!" His voice was harsh. At my warning look, he dropped his voice, but nothing could hide the rage I saw in his eyes. There were years behind this, years upon years of... I could not know, could not say. The more I knew, the less I could make of any of it. "She hates me, she blackmails me, she has her own games and her own plots that I must try to learn from *you*— and she has your loyalty, too, damn her! But she is the key to

152

everything. She is..." He took a deep, shuddering breath. "She will be my savior," he said finally, eerily calm. "On this one, small thing, rest thousands of lives, and my freedom."

A thought began to take shape in my head, but it was still too vague; there was nothing I could say to this admission. I stared at him, wordless and horrified, and he shook his head at me. "I should have kept you out of this," he said softly. "I should have let the Duke beat you and send you away to the village when I caught you reaching for my dagger. Forgive me."

"For what?"

"For making you what you are. There's no way back from being a Shadow, Catwin." His eyes were completely black in the low light of the stairwell. He tried to move away and I shook my head at him, holding on as he tried to unwind my fingers from the cloth of his uniform.

"No. Don't go."

"I have to." His voice was so filled with anguish that I was stopped in my tracks, and he nearly pulled away from me. I caught his arm at the last moment. "Catwin—"

"A moment, only." He paused at my assurance. "Do you swear to me that this is your own plan, of your own devising, and that there is some balance to it, so great that it could justify killing a young woman, and her with child? Do you swear?" He stared at me, frozen.

"I swear," he said, finally, his lips barely moving.

"And this ties to the first oath you swore to the Duke?" I pressed. "It is to fulfill that oath that you do this?"

"How do you know of that?" His face paled, and I shook my head.

"Not important. Do you *swear*?" I insisted, and at last, he nodded.

"I swear." I nodded and released him.

"Then I will do what must be done," I said simply.

"*What?*" He could barely force that word out, he was staring at me in horror.

"I will keep this from your soul," I said, "because I will believe you that there is a reason, and that the reason is honorable, and just, and loving. So tell me now if you've been lying. Because otherwise, I will do this for you."

"Catwin…" He gave a despairing laugh. "Do you know what I have done in my time? I am damned a hundred times over. This makes no difference."

"It does," I observed. "For even you, who say you are damned, who say you have reasons greater than my comprehension, shrink from it." He clenched his hands and looked away, then shook his head at me.

"No. I will do it."

"Then I will interfere," I said, sliding my hand to my belt, to my dagger. "I know how to avoid notice, and I know how to attract it, too. There is only one way you can do this on your own, and that is to kill me as well. So make your choice." If I was right, and he had some greater purpose than the Duke's ambition, he would shrink from killing me. If not, he would slip a dagger between my ribs, love or no, and I would be dead in a few moments. In the split-second after I spoke, I feared that I had been wrong, and that all his words to me had been no more than a clever lie. But he was shaking.

"Why would you do this?" He almost sounded pleading.

"To free you."

His brow furrowed. "I don't understand."

"I would not expect you to." I stepped closer. "My reasons are my own. I only ask you to trust them, as I am trusting you."

"I can't stop you, can I?" he asked, finally.

"No," I said, after a moment. "I don't think you can. Not without killing me." His shoulders slumped.

"I will go with you."

"No." I shook my head. "Take no part in it. Give me the poison you would have used—that was why you said there was a fever, was it not? So I would not question?" He nodded, defeated, and when I held my palm out, he reached into his doublet and pulled out a vial of poison. "Go pray for me in the chapel," I whispered. "I will come find you when I am done."

"I do not pray in chapels," he said, strangely. "But I will go and wait for you there." I nodded and turned away, but he grabbed my arm to stop me from leaving. "Please," he begged. "Don't do this. You've done nothing like this before. Let me do it."

"No." I shook my head and pointed to the stairs, swallowing back the fear that he was right, and that there was no coming back from this. "Go now. I will find you when it is done." He was defeated. His shoulders slumped and he left, hesitant, with a backwards glance over his shoulder, as if he was not quite sure what it was I had done.

I watched him go, then pulled out the vial of poison he had given me and stared at the dark liquid. I swallowed. There was only one way to do this, and that was not to think of it. I waited until Temar's footsteps had faded, and then I set off, my feet dragging as his had, my breath coming short and my skin growing cold.

I tried to clear my mind as I approached, light-footed. It was like a dream, the quiet approach, the feeling of light-headedness. I waited for the guards to stop me, seeing murder in my eyes, but I was a Shadow indeed; they did not even turn their faces as I moved past them. I paused, to look at them, but they stared straight ahead.

Rich hangings on the walls, carpet underfoot. The light-headedness was growing worse. *Gods forgive me.* Temar was right: I had never done anything like this. I approached, my footsteps silent, and I pulled the velvet bed hangings aside. Quick as thought, with no time to persuade myself otherwise, I leaned tipped the poison down. Open mouth. Lips, breath. I could see the chest rising and falling. This was life, and I had just taken it. I backed away, unsteadily.

Waiting in the darkness, I began to hope that I had failed. With each moment that passed, hope swelled. Temar had misjudged, this was no poison; or perhaps the Gods had intervened at last in the business of mortals. This must be, and yet I could not help but hope that it had come to nothing. I had killed before—with knives, solid and unbending, no slow creep of poison. I had killed attackers, a man with a weapon, not a sleeping victim. I believed, beyond all doubt, that this must be, and that it must be me who did it. And I, who had never truly believed in the Gods in my deepest heart, began to believe that I would be damned indeed, whether I succeeded or failed—if not by them, then by my own guilt.

Then I heard it: the faintest gasp, a hollow cry of pain. I squeezed my eyes shut, forcing myself to hear this, and jumped when I heard the bed curtains wrenched aside. I found myself faced to face with a monster: eyes wide, face contorted. There was the slow creep of recognition in the gaze.

"You."

"Me," I replied, my voice shaking.

"There is a special level of hell for servants who betray their masters." At that, I felt the horror lift. Just for a moment, the guilt did not press down so heavily.

"That may be," I said, watching as the skin paled and flushed, twisted in a rictus of pain. "But you were never my master." I waited through it all, watching until the last breath faded. Then I stepped over the body of the Duke, Temar's other self, the man who had truly made me a Shadow, and I left without a backward glance.

Chapter 22

Temar was waiting for me in the chapel. He was sitting cross-legged, sacrilegiously, on the altar itself, and staring at the status of the Gods. At the sound of my approach, he turned his head and his eyes were blank, uncomprehending. He looked at me as if he was not quite sure who I was. As I came to stand at his side, I saw that he cradled a dagger in his hands, unsheathed. I frowned and put my hand on his arm, peering into his eyes, and although he was staring at me, it was a moment before his eyes cleared and focused.

"I know," he said, before I could speak. "I realized—too late." He looked down at the dagger in his hands, turning it over and over. "This wasn't how it should have ended."

"I had to do it," I said softly. "Whatever bargain you had made, it had gone wrong. It was doing nobody any good." I remembered the look in the Duke's eyes, the way he had slid so quietly from ruthlessness to madness that we had not even recognized it until now, in the face of this treasonous plan. Whatever oath Temar had sworn, I thought it was to a different man than the Duke had been at the end.

"I would have got her on the throne" he said, not looking at me. "I could have."

"At what cost?" I pressed him. I shook him, slightly. "And you could never be sure. It's a terrible game to play. You'd never really win it, no one does. No one stays up forever." He smiled, genuine humor.

"I didn't plan to."

"What did you plan?" I asked, feeling my way in this strange conversation, and he looked down at the dagger in his hands. I stared at it, furrowing my brow, and then looked up at his face. It was composed, and he was calm; too calm. "Temar, no."

"I must do this," he said simply. He did not tell me that I was mistaken. He was looking towards death, and he did not even seem afraid; that, of all things, was the worst.

"Because you did not protect him? You did not fail," I protested, horrified. "I hid my purpose from you. You could not have known."

"I know you," he observed, looking over at me. "I should have seen at once that you would never offer to kill a child." In my shock at Temar's intentions, I had forgotten, momentarily, what it was that I had just done; this reminded me, and I closed my eyes against the blank horror of it. I remembered the words I had murmured to myself in the darkness after the first two times I had killed, appeals to my own mind: they came to kill you—you did no more than any beast, confronted with a predator—you saved Miriel's life—you are no monster. I would have no such comfort now.

The flash of the knife jolted me out of my haze and I reacted on instinct, dashing it away and throwing my weight sideways. The knife clattered to the floor and slid away into the shadows, and I pinned Temar with surprising ease. In the stillness and quiet of a mind prepared for death, he had not thought to put up his guard against me—he had hoped that I would be lost in my own thoughts, as he was lost in his.

"What are you doing?" I asked, shaking him. "Temar, there's no reason for this. You don't need to do this."

"I must." He struggled against me, and I scrabbled to keep him pinned. "You must let me," he insisted. He was gasping now, my forearm pressing against his throat. "It is the second half of the bargain. I took an oath."

"What oath?"

"I...can't tell you." He shook his head. "Catwin, please. This is the only thing I have wanted, for years. I have dreamed of this day."

"You've dreamed of *this*?" I demanded fiercely. My face felt hot—I had loved him, and spoken with him, he had joked with me and spent his days alongside me and I had never known that what he wanted most was to be free of all of it, and take his own life. He had known, as he kissed me, that he wanted death more than anything, but he had hidden that from me, and it felt like betrayal. He saw my anger, and his mouth twitched in a half-smile.

"Now I can be at peace." He was trying to explain, but I still could not understand.

"But you haven't gotten Miriel on the throne," I said stupidly, and he took advantage of my confusion. He struggled free and I tumbled, hard, from the altar to the floorboards, snatching for his ankle as he went for the knife once more. My fingers grazed his skin, but I could get no hold. "*Wait!*" At the appeal in my voice he stopped and turned, the knife in his hand. I could see him trembling, looking from me to the knife.

"Just tell me why," I pleaded, thinking that this was a nightmare, it could not be real. "Don't do this without at least..." I pushed myself up to sit, and dropped my head into my hands. "I did this to set you free, not kill you."

"But you did free me," he said. To my surprise, he came to kneel in front of me; he set the knife aside and reached out to take my hands. "Please, Catwin." He waited for me to look up at him, and squeezed his fingers, warm, around my own. "You did. You have done me the greatest kindness anyone could have. I never hoped for this."

"But I don't understand." My voice was high and thin, I felt like a child in the face of this darkness. He bit his lip, and then he looked up at the ceiling, considering his words carefully.

"Do you want me to tell you?"

"Of course I do." He smiled wryly at my prompt answer.

"Not all knowledge is worth knowing," he said. "And I cannot speak all of it—not even to you, Catwin. But some of it, I can tell. There were two oaths—two bargains," he said finally. "The first was with Eral—if he would swear not to harm my people, I would protect his life, and give him what he most wanted in the world."

"The power of the throne," I quoted softly," remembering the Duke's words, and Temar nodded, lost in memory.

"Just so. I tricked him, you see. I made him take the oath in our tongue, and name what he wanted. He never knew: the power of the throne—to our people, it means the lineage. I promised him that his blood would sit on the throne one day."

"Miriel," I said, softly, and he nodded. It was shifting, all of it, falling into place—his sly words to the Duke as they traveled through the hidden corridors, his insistence the Marie must die. The Duke had said *the power of the throne*, knowing that titles meant little; he would have been content to have Miriel as nothing more than the King's mistress. But Temar had changed that, for a time he and I had worked to the same ends: to get Miriel not into the King's bed, but onto the throne itself.

Temar's words called me back to reality.

"The second bargain I made was with the Gods—that if I protected their children, one day I would be absolved of all the sins I had committed in Eral's service. And at the end, I would take my life, and wipe away the evil I had done." He said the words as if they explained everything, and I saw the logic of it, terrible but undeniable. Still I shook my head at him.

"What kind of Gods would let you make that bargain? You'd use up your whole life."

"And why not? Haven't you ever wanted your life to mean something?" Temar was looking at me strangely. I only stared at him. "I've never had to ask myself if I had a purpose," he said, "because every day, in every action and thought, I was working for the safety of my people." His face twisted. "What I said earlier, that I was sorry for what I had done—it was no empty apology, Catwin. Some days, it seems the worst thing I did, to pick you. I did not want to face you when you came back, I couldn't bear to look at you. I had known for years that I was sane only because I knew that there was a deeper purpose to my actions—and I had taken you, a child, with no one to protect, no greater oath, and made you into a Shadow. I had watched you grow to hate your life, and when you left...I hoped that you would never come back. I hoped that you would leave Miriel, and I would never be forced to find you. I told the Duke that I was looking, and I never did. I never sent a single messenger." At last, a reason as to why I had never seen his spies in Norvelt. I pushed the thought aside and shook my head.

"But there is a purpose to my life now," I said. "I found it through her."

"And you can bear it, the things you have done?" He looked so hopeful that my heart ached. He could hardly believe that I would forgive him.

"I can," I said finally, and I added, "but I never thought I had a choice but to keep living." He looked down and clenched his hands, hardly seeming to notice that he was crushing his fingers around mine. He had heard the reproach in my tone.

"I know you cannot understand," he said softly. "But you trusted me enough to wonder if I was not only a Shadow. Can you not trust me enough to believe that I know what I must do?"

"You're giving up everything," I protested. "I don't see how I could ever believe that was right." He did not answer, and I shook my hands to get his attention. "You'd just end it all, then? Really? Because the Duke's dead, your life is over, as well?"

"I am already dead," he said. "Think of it that way. My life has not been my own for many years, and now that I am freed of Eral..."

"No." I shook my head violently. "I did this because…" Because the Duke had run mad in his quest for power, and we were all safer without him. Because he was dragging us all down into his mad world, and Temar could never have escaped.

"To set me free." He echoed my words. "And you have, by doing what I could not. You have saved hundreds, thousands, of lives. My last thought will be that my people are safe."

"Don't you see?" I cried, finally shouting, angrier than I had ever been. "You gave years to this bargain, to the Duke, and now you would let it take the rest of your life as well? You could finally live as your own self, not following his orders, not following anyone's orders, just…and you're throwing it away." He pulled his hands away.

"I'm not throwing it away! It is over already. I am finished."

"But you're *not!*" The words felt ripped out of me. I could feel tears hot on my cheeks, and I wiped them away angrily with the back of my hand. "You're still here, you're still breathing. You're *alive*, Temar—whether you want to be or not. You have your whole life to atone. If you die…" He only watched me, his face twisted; he would not bend. I let him see the quiver of my mouth, the tears in my eyes, and when he clenched his jaw, I knew that his mind was made up. "Fine," I said harshly. "I'll join you soon enough, anyway."

"What?" Now he did move, quickly, taking my hand in both of his. "What do you mean by that?" I stared at him, warring with myself, and his hands pressed, warm, on my own. I had not thought to tell him this—I had not even understood it to myself. Until I spoke, I had not realized that my mind had found a solution to the inevitability of battle.

"I know how to end the war," I said finally. "None of them want to be here, but they're following one man. I can get to Kasimir, I'm sure of it. If he's dead, the spell will break—they'll agree to a truce, or they'll run." Temar was pale, he was shaking his head.

"Even if you get to him, you could never get back alive."

"I know that." Now it was me who pulled away, yanking my hands back, not wanting his touch.

"Catwin, please, don't do this—" He was afraid, I knew it, and once I would have been glad to know that he cared if I went into danger. Now, I felt a rush of anger.

"Do you know a better way?" I demanded. "Can you think of any other way?" His silence told me everything.

"You're young," he told me. "You have your whole life in front of you."

"So do you!" He did not answer. "Temar, I can't stop you. I won't. If that is what you want." I could barely make out the words past the ache in my throat. "Give me the same courtesy. You know I'm the only one who can do this." There was a long pause as he looked over at the knife, gleaming in the dim light. Finally, he let out a sigh, and his shoulders slumped. He looked back to meet my eyes..

"But you're not," he said, unexpectedly. There was a hint of a smile. "There are two of us." I looked over at him, and he reached out for my hand. I let him take it, twining my fingers with his, uncomprehending. "Are you determined to do this?" he asked me softly.

"Yes," I said promptly, and he peered into my eyes for a moment.

"Then I won't argue. I know how stubborn you can be." The edges of his mouth quirked. "But let me come with you." It was a peace offering, one that I could not reject. He was giving me what no one else could. Finally, I nodded. "I will get supplies," he said. "You'll have to come down to the camp."

"We were planning to already," I admitted, and when he frowned at me, reflexively, I raised an eyebrow. "I can't tell you why. But I'll be there."

"Have you told Roine?" he asked. "Miriel?" I shook my head, and he put his hand on my arm. "Tell them," he advised. "You owe it to them. And Catwin..."

"Yes?"

"If you wanted me to go alone—if you wanted to stay, to be safe...that's what I would want most." I was almost relieved to hear the words. I had steeled myself to this task, but never had I expected him to accept it. As much as I had waited for it, his protest hurt; I shrugged my shoulders, hunching them against the feeling.

"I'm coming with you. I would have gone alone." He sighed.

"I know. But I had to offer. And I'll offer again."

"My answer will be the same."

"Even so." Gently, he pulled me close and bent his head to meet mine. Despite myself, I leaned forward and lost myself in the feel of his lips against mine. Darkness and death and fear faded away, and just for a moment, for now, I could forget tomorrow. There was only Temar's heartbeat, and my own; I wound my arms around his neck, and I could feel him smile as he kissed me.

Chapter 23

Dawn broke: dull, leaden light from the small windows crept under the double doors in the Duke's presence chamber, and from there into the bedroom. Sitting on my bed, arms around my knees, I could feel weariness dragging at me, and a strange light-headedness at the thought that I would perhaps never sleep again. I would never take off my suit and fold it, lay my head on a pillow, wake up to see the rising sun. I held no illusions about my abilities: they were precisely enough to get me into the camp, but I would never make it out alive. And that gave a strange sheen to the endless minutiae that had always so bored me: eating and sleeping, dressing and bathing.

It was beyond me, as the war was beyond me—and so I pushed it away. As many times as the thought crept back to me, I rejected it. There was only one thing to think of, and that was Kasimir. I could break it down into its parts, each of them small: moving unseen, the element of surprise, the first strike.

As Miriel began to stir, I tried to find the words to tell her that I would leave her in the camp, and not return. I knew that Temar had told me to make my goodbyes, hoping that I would not have the courage to do so, and so turn back. I smiled at that. He was wrong to think that Miriel would stop me. I did not feel guilty to leave her for this, for I did not think for a moment that she would do any differently in my place. At last, she rolled over on her side and opened her eyes. She went very still when she saw my face.

"Something's happened," she guessed, and I nodded.

"I've done a bad thing." I tried to speak clearly, but the guilt was rising up once more. She was watching me quietly, waiting, and the words spilled out "I killed the Duke." I could find no other way to say it, and Miriel paled to hear me. She pushed herself up to sit.

"Was he coming for us?" she asked, her voice small, and I shook my head.

"Not us." The shelter of sleep had fled entirely; she was horrified. She tried to nod.

"The coup, then."

"Yes," I said, shortly. "He was going to turn the troops in battle."

164

"Against—"

"Yes." At that, Miriel closed her eyes in pain.

"I see," she said finally, and I knew that she was lost—she did not know what to think, how to feel. The Duke was enemy and family, both, to her. He had threatened her with death—for all we knew, he had been the one seeking it. Now, he had plotted to overthrow his King, driven so mad that he would rather take the chance of an Ismiri victory than live one more day without the power of the throne.

"There's more," I said, feeling wretched, and wincing when I saw her wide eyes. "It's nothing I've done yet, but I think I have to. I know this war can be stopped."

"Kasimir." She was no fool, she understood my plan at once. Then her eyes narrowed. "The Duke today, Kasimir tomorrow—and who will it be the day after that?"

"It's not like that," I protested, but she glared, stubbornly.

"No? Because you've killed once—and I accept his death, he earned it. I would have told Wilhelm of his treachery tomorrow, and he'd be executed in a week. He signed his own death warrant when he plotted against the throne. But to kill once, and then again—where will it end, Catwin? How do you know that tomorrow, you won't wake up and think that only one more death will make the world better?"

"That won't happen."

"How can you know?" She leaned forward, intent, and when she saw my white face, she frowned, her anger turning to confusion. "Catwin?"

"I won't...come back." I forced the words out, but she only shook her head.

"What do you mean?" she asked, bewildered.

"Miriel." The pain I had been holding away crashed in, and I clenched my hands so that the nails bit into my palm. I could feel tears in my eyes, and such a wave of panic that I thought I might be sick. This was what Temar had hoped for; I tried to hold to my resolve. "I'm not coming back," I repeated, numbly. "I don't think I'm going to survive this."

"No! Surely you—" She broke off, shook her head. "No," she repeated, and when I said nothing, I saw panic in her eyes. "Catwin, you can't be serious about this."

"Do you think there's any other way to prevent the battle?" I asked her. There was a stricken silence and at last, slowly, she shook her head.

"But that doesn't mean that you have to be the one to do it," she said stubbornly. "Why can't Temar do it?" She broke off and her eyes widened. "Did you..."

"No," I said, unwilling to tell her of Temar's mission and our bargain. I could still smell him on my skin, and the memories of last night made me flush; I bowed my head so that Miriel could not see, and took a moment to steady myself. Then I looked up and met her eyes. "He's coming with me." She shook her head, uncomprehending.

"Then why can't you survive it?" she asked, her voice very small. "One person could fall—but with two of you..." She trailed off when she saw my face, and I saw tears in her eyes; at last I rose and went to sit at her side, taking her hand.

"We can get into the camp, and two of us makes it surer, but Kasimir's a warrior, and there'll be guards everywhere. We can't hope to—" I broke off at the look on her face.

"If you can, though, you will?" she begged me. "You'll come back if you can?" I had a sudden memory of her question to me, only a week earlier: *will you stay at court with me?* I had said yes, I had promised her that I would not betray her. And now I was going back on that promise, and she did not even reproach me for it.

"Of course I will come back if I can," I said, squeezing her hand. I tried to smile, but her mouth was trembling. She wiped her eyes, gave a deep breath, and nodded. It was what she would do, and she knew it: not only the path itself, but choice, and the action, all at once.

"When will you go?"

"Tonight, after dark. After we sign the treaty." I was trying to distract her, but even that elicited no more than a nod. "We should get dressed," I said softly, and Miriel was untying her robe when there was a scream in the other room, the hysterical shriek of a maid. The door to the presence chamber slammed open, and there was the shouting of the guards, and Temar pounding on the door.

"Catwin! Is Miriel there? Is she safe?"

"Miriel is here," I called back. I cast a quick look at Miriel to see if she was still decent, then wrenched open the door, stifling an exclamation as I looked into the main room. The Duke was slumped over his desk, his skin grey. One of the guards was frantically checking for a heartbeat, and another looked between Temar and me, his eyes narrowed.

"The two of you came and went last night—did you see anything?"

"The Duke had much to accomplish before setting out to war," Temar said smoothly. "But by the time we returned, he was in his chambers, sleeping. Catwin, you said you came back for instructions from him—did he say anything strange?" I shook my head mutely, moving aside for Miriel to make her way out of the bedchamber. She, too, gave a gasp when she saw her uncle's body, and she shot me a horrified look. It was not feigned; it was one thing to hear that he was dead, and another thing to see it. Despite her words to me, I could see her horror that I had killed, and I looked away rather than meet her eyes.

But Miriel had moved into action at once, a performance I could only admire.

"How could you let this happen?" she demanded of Temar. "How could you let an assassin in?" I saw him control the inevitable rise of his temper.

"No one came or went last night save us," he said. "Surely the Guards would have told us if that had happened. Could anyone have slipped past you?" he asked, and the guard bristled.

"No one went in," he said, his hand clenched around his sword hilt.

"Well, he was poisoned," Miriel snapped. "Tell me how that happened!" She was playing a role, but the fear was real enough. Her eyes were wild, her hands clenched.

"Begging yer pardon, my Lady," the other guard said apologetically. "But it might not be poison. There're signs, but only a healer can check for them. Sometimes men just die."

"On the eve of battle?" Temar asked him coldly. He and Miriel were glaring at the man, and I could only appreciate their skill in dissembling. I was frozen, too horrified to do any more than keep my mouth shut, afraid that I would blurt out the truth. The war, the treaty, everything had faded away and there was only this: the Duke's corpse, and the terrible realization that I had killed him. I had killed him, and he was dead, and there was no way of reversing it.

He signed his own death warrant when he plotted against the throne, Miriel had said, and I repeated the words to myself, running through them again and again in my mind. How many would have died today, tomorrow, when the Duke urged his men to strike out at their own comrades?

"Catwin." Temar shook me gently, and I came back to the present, looking at him wide-eyed. "You must get Miriel to safety. Take her to the upper floors." I was grasping for some excuse to make when Miriel spoke up.

"No," she said clearly. "I must go to the Camp."

"My Lady?" Temar and the guards stared at her as if she had gone mad, and Miriel drew herself up, her back straight, her chin lifted.

"I may not be able to lead my uncle's men in the fight," she said, "but it is a lord's duty to give courage to his soldiers on the eve of battle."

"My Lady, it is too much of a risk—"

"This is not a matter of my safety," Miriel said crispy. "I am the last Celys. It is my duty to walk among them as he would have done." She did not wait for a response, only turned and went into her chamber. "Help me dress," she called to me, over her shoulder. "I'll need to wear grey and white."

"She should not go," Temar insisted, and at last I drew myself up as well.

"She is right," I told him. I swept my gaze over the guards. "She is the last Celys. She need not ride into battle, but it is right for her to bring courage to the men." Hoping that Temar would remember my insistence that Miriel needed to go to the camp, I shot him a look and followed Miriel, closing the door to the room behind me and looking around myself.

She was not there; it was as if she had disappeared into thin air.

"Miriel?" Silence. Then, at last, the sound of a sob caught my attention, and I took a few steps into the gloom of the windowless chamber. Miriel was in the corner, hidden behind the wardrobe. She had stuffed her fist into her mouth to muffle her sobs and she was hunched over, shaking. I went to her, but hesitated. "Miriel?" I asked, tentatively, and she looked up at me, her eyes reddened with tears.

"I hated him," she said, thickly. "I told you to kill him, d'you remember?"

"I do." She had been exhausted, worn down to defiant hatred. She had ordered me to kill him, and I had agreed. Then I saw: the pain in her face was not grief, but guilt. "You can't think this is your fault," I said, aghast. I had killed him—it had been me, my hand that tipped the poison, while Temar and Miriel both had been ignorant of what I did.

"I told you to. I plotted against him—and I would have killed him!" The last words came out as a wail, and she gave a horrified look to the door, thinking of the bustle of men outside, terrified that they would hear her admission. I gave her a shake, to recall her.

"But you didn't," I said, sure of that if nothing else. "It was me, remember? I was there. You weren't. You didn't have anything to do with it."

"It was losing the throne that drove him mad," she whispered.

"It wasn't your fault," I insisted. "He plotted against the throne, didn't he? He would have been executed, wouldn't he? And you wouldn't have thought that your fault." She shook her head uncertainly, wiping away tears with her fingertips.

"No, but..."

"But nothing." I took her shoulders. "If you had never come back to court, never seen him or heard from him again, he would still have plotted treason, and he would still have been executed for it. It was always his plan to control the throne, and he would have sacrificed anything and anyone to get there." Miriel bit her lip and nodded. "And you have to get dressed in Celys colors, and go to the camp, and speak to the men." She nodded again, and tried to smile.

"And then the treaty," she whispered.

"And then the treaty," I agreed.

"And then—"

"Don't speak of it," I said, feeling the familiar rush of panic. "First, the treaty. That's all that should matter to you."

Chapter 24

In preparation for the battle, the camp was chaos. We pushed our way through it as quickly as we could, Temar trailing behind us as he was accosted by servants and soldiers alike. Rumors of the Duke's death had spread like wildfire, and enough recognized Temar's face that he could go only a few steps without another cry of, "Hoy! Voltur!" He did not waste these opportunities, instead commenting darkly that it might look natural, but he himself knew the truth—how could the Duke, one of the most feared commanders of the Heddrian army, have fallen on the eve of this battle, but by treachery?

And so, with a sly word here, and a muttered suggestion there, Temar began to drive the camp into a frenzy. Any rational person would have asked him, skeptically, how it was that an Ismiri assassin had made their way into the Fortress itself, and not killed the King, Guy de la Marque, Gerald Conradine, Efan of Lapland... But no one asked. In their fear of the battle, and their need to hate their enemy, they accepted Temar's suggestions without question, and where our little party passed, a roar for vengeance went up in our wake. If Temar and I failed tonight, on the morrow the soldiers would go into battle driven to avenge their murdered commander.

It was a lord's duty to inspire his men, and so when we reached the tents of the men from Voltur, Miriel had given a brief speech, to thank the soldiers for their courage and ask them to fight all the harder in her uncle's memory. She was only a young woman, but she was the Duke's heir, and at her insistence that they be thanked for their service, the men had sent up a cheer. To the sound of their shouts, she had withdrawn into the tent, and I had gone to pass a scrap of paper to a runner and send him off, searching for the King.

Now Miriel and I waited quietly, listening to the sounds of the men around us. The men of Voltur had set up camp with the quick efficiency of a practiced fighting force, and now they were gathered around a firepit, trading stories and sharpening weapons, while we waited, cut off from the court, horrified by the magnitude of what would happen in the coming hours.

The Duke's tent was not large, but it was richly-appointed, with carpets spread on the bare ground and oil lamps hanging precariously from the ceiling. In the corner, there was a desk for him, with ink and quills, and sealing wax. I wondered at the luxury, and then wondered—with a pang—how many noblemen were writing last letters to their loved ones, final instructions to their stewards and accountants. It had been many long years since the nobles of Heddred had seen war and death, and every nobleman I had seen in the camp had fear in his eyes. It occurred to me that we were not so different: sitting, waiting, signing a treaty that might have no purpose at all within the day.

It was late afternoon when, at last, Wilhelm ducked into the tent. I had seen him earlier in the day, always in close-headed conference with his generals, shaking the hands of his soldiers, offering encouragement. His world had narrowed to the scope of tomorrow's battle, and his face had settled into the grim expression of a man twice his age. His face showed such relief to see Miriel that I realized Wilhelm had been afraid for her.

"What did your message mean?" he asked her quietly. "My guards have been sent to track Isra's movements, and they can arrest Arman if it is necessary—but why? Was it murder, truly? Did they kill your uncle?" Miriel bit her lip, unable to voice the truth. After a moment she shook her head.

"No," she said, her voice choked. "It was I who had him killed."

"*What?*" Wilhelm and I spoke in unison, and I knew that my face echoed his look of shock. He looked over at me and I shook my head; I did not know what to say to this.

"He was planning an insurrection," Miriel said, attempting to be calm.

"Against me?" Wilhelm asked. He was holding tight to one of the tent poles, his knuckles white, his face blank. His world, already turned upside down by war, was growing less stable by the moment.

"Yes." Miriel's voice was low, and I knew she feared that her uncle's men would hear her. I could hear them outside, singing the songs I recognized from the guards in Voltur, calling out challenges to each other, betting on how many Ismiri they could kill. It would break their spirit to know that their revered commander was a traitor, and shame them in front of the other soldiers. Best they fight to avenge the man, and know nothing of his dishonor.

"Forgive me for not making it public," Miriel said, "but I did not know what to do. I could not go to speak to you, and I could trust no one else. There can be no doubt of his guilt—my marriage cemented the alliance. I feared that if the truth was known, it would sow discord. It was my uncle who would have turned the army against you tomorrow, in the battle, and I could not allow that." She folded her hands and took a deep breath. "It is death to plot treason," she said finally. "His life was forfeit." She repeated the words as she had repeated them to me, numbly.

"Who else knew of this?" Wilhelm demanded, and Miriel shook her head.

"I cannot know for certain," she said helplessly.

"A moment," Wilhelm said courteously. From the white lines at the corners of his mouth, he was holding his composure only by a thread. He ducked outside the tent and I heard him speaking, low-voiced, to one of his guards. When he came back, his face was grim. "They will be arrested," he said, "and they will stand trial. I must thank you for telling me of this."

Miriel nodded, and for a moment, neither of them spoke. In the wake of such a revelation, there was little enough they could say. They were watching each other, eyes bright, and I saw that the world had faded away for them. They could see only each other now. Miriel was staring at him as if she had forgotten how to speak; he was looking at her as I had once looked at Temar—as if he had seen her in his dreams so often that he had forgotten she was real. Then they both tried to speak at once.

"I sent for you—"

"I thought of you every day—" They broke off, and Miriel's brow furrowed.

"You sent for me?" she asked, and Wilhelm bowed his head.

"After Garad—" He clenched his hands. "I sent to your uncle, I told him that I must see you. I intended to offer for your hand, I swear it. But he told me that you had already gone, that you wanted to return to Voltur."

"I did not," Miriel protested. "He sent me back, himself."

"Later, I knew it for a lie. I knew you would not leave without—" Wilhelm broke off and shook his head. "But it did not matter. The moment they knew of Garad's death, the courtiers thought it was I who'd had him killed." His face was so anguished that even I felt my heart twist for him. "As if I ever could have done so," he whispered. "I kept thinking—if only the High Priest had come to find me sooner, we might have saved him." I choked off a gasp, and Miriel and I exchanged one swift, meaningful look.

"How do you mean?" she asked, delicately. Wilhelm had not noticed our sudden attentiveness; he was lost in memory. He shook his head as if it was hardly important.

"We had gone to speak to him about the rebellion. I would not have, after...but the High Priest came to speak to me, and said that if we had any hope of saving the rebellion, I must accompany him to plead with Garad. He told me that he would bring his own guards so that Garad would not think to set the Royal Guard on me. I wanted to go at once, but he delayed, and later I realized— Garad was dead only by minutes. Every day now, I think: if only we had not taken a side hallway, if only he had come to me earlier or I could have persuaded him to go sooner...."

I looked down, biting my lip. If only, indeed; Wilhelm had no way of knowing what he had just revealed to us. If only the High Priest, with his brace of twenty men, had arrived moments earlier, Garad would yet live. I thought it incredible that Wilhelm had never wondered at the High Priest's tale. It would be a hanging offense to bring armed guards into the King's presence, blatant treason to attempt to cow the King into making peace with the rebellion by force.

If Wilhelm thought of it for a moment, he would have known that the High Priest had no legitimate right to bring his own men against the King. But Wilhelm, wracked with guilt, had never thought of it. And so Wilhelm had never thought to wonder if the timing might not have been just wrong—but instead precisely correct. Who was it that had benefitted from Garad's death? Wilhelm, who gained the throne so unexpectedly? Or had it been the High Priest, who at last had a monarch he could trust to support the populist movement?

And at last, as the pieces fell into place: not Conradine guards, not Nilson's forces, but instead forces loyal to the High Priest, to Jacces. I had doubted it, even as I held the proof in my own hands, but there was no denying it now. The commander had known that he was committing high treason, but he had acted without hesitation, secure in the knowledge that his work would bring the ascendancy of the rebellion. And that was how he had led his men into a massacre, for he had not realized that he, too, would be sacrificed. A force of twenty men, used to kill a King, could only be a liability: twenty men to be seen, recognized, caught—and tortured until at last, broken, they revealed the knowledge that it had been the High Priest who sent them to kill Garad. No, Jacces was far too cautious for that. He would let Kasimir take the blame. It would even serve him to have Wilhelm suspected, for as he defended the young King against rumor, he would gain Wilhelm's trust.

And that last realization showed me, finally, why the men had also been told to kill us: a knowing ally was not an asset, but a liability. The High Priest had seen the danger at once when I came to him. He knew that he had a choice: to trust in Miriel's abilities to turn the King back to her, and to the rebellion—or to wipe the slate clean and install a King who would himself support the movement. And then what was Miriel? She was a useless ally, a woman whose marriage to Wilhelm would be incredibly suspect, undermining the legitimacy of the King Jacces had worked so hard to enthrone. More, she was an intelligent woman who might, at some point, wonder just why it was that Garad had died so conveniently. She, like the men who had carried out the treasonous mission, must be eliminated.

I saw from Miriel's face that she suspected the same, but she only shook her head slightly and forged on. This was no more than the unveiling of an enemy we had always suspected; had it been Guy de la Marque, or Gerald Conradine, she would only have nodded, pleased to have an answer at last. She would not let herself think on the fact that the High Priest, after promising to aid her, had instead sought her death. She would find him later, and demand the truth; but now, she had only a few moments with the man she loved, the man who could sign the treaty to change the world—and she would put the High Priest's treachery from her mind.

"And the courtiers doubted you?" she asked. I could see that she was offended on Wilhelm's behalf. "Did they not know that you were his closest friend?"

"What should they have thought?" he asked, wretchedly. "A King dies by murder, and who is the first suspect? Who stood to benefit? And worst—" He swallowed and closed his eyes. "Some of the men remembered that I had spoken of you, once. And then to marry you would only have been to fan the flames. Some believed it was Kasimir, but it was such scandal to suspect me..."

"And so you married your rival," Miriel said softly. While I followed Wilhelm's words, her mind had skipped ahead, as it always did. Wilhelm lifted his head, his eyes wide and hopeful.

"Do you see now? She was the one they would have murdered me for—already there were whispers that men were pledging forces to her father, to put her on the throne. Her own mother had told the lords that she would step aside, and cede the throne to Marie; it was moving too quickly. The only way to end the uprising without bloodshed was to bind de la Marque to me. And he was happy enough to get what he wanted without a battle." Miriel nodded, looking down at her clasped hands. She was pale, but composed; I could even see relief in the set of her shoulders. Bitter as it was, this was the man she knew, a man who would put duty over all else. It was no more than Miriel herself had done, when she pledged that her marriage to Garad would bring safety to the rebellion.

"Please believe me," Wilhelm pleaded. "I would never have done this save in direst need."

"I know," Miriel said, and Wilhelm held out his hands to her.

"There is not a day that I do not regret—"

"Don't." Miriel looked up at once, her face white. Her lips barely moved.

"What?" He frowned.

"Do not speak of regrets," Miriel said simply. "I cannot bear it." Wilhelm nodded, looking away from her. Marie's presence seemed almost tangible, and with a pang of unexpected pity, I remembered her stricken look when she had seen Miriel. She might never have loved Wilhelm herself, but it would be bitter, nonetheless, to know that her husband loved another.

And then, my mind wandering, I remembered Miriel's fear when at last her betrothal to Garad had been signed and sealed. She had faced the prospect of ruling with little enough joy. Now, as I looked at Wilhelm's tired face, I wondered if he and Miriel could ever have been happy, ruling together. I wondered if I had not been wrong to curse the Gods for keeping Miriel and Wilhelm apart; I wondered if fate had, instead, been kind to keep Miriel from the throne.

Miriel broke the silence by reaching by holding out the leather case. "The treaty," she said, as if she had forgotten for a time, and only now remembered why Wilhelm was here, meeting with her secretly. Wilhelm took it from her, looking awed. I waited as he went to the chair and began to read, lost to the world. He held the treaty as if it were a precious artifact—the bones of a saint, the first crown of the Heddrian kings. He sat and he read, in silence, and, to my shock, he wept. At that, at last, Miriel's reserve broke. She went to stand at his side, and she held to his hand as the tears ran down his face.

At last, his hands shaking, he dipped the waiting quill in ink and put his name to the treaty, dropping wax by his name and pressing his signet ring down. The Conradine crest, crown and sword, shone in the dim light. It was done; I let out a breath that I did not know I had been holding.

"If we survive, we will build a new world," he told her, and she smiled despite the fear. If I did not succeed, then death awaited us all tomorrow. And after that, treachery.

"You think you can hold the Council to this?"

"I am their King," he said simply, and his mouth twitched in a smile. "And if there were one thing to decree, this would be that one thing."

"They will not deny you?" she asked, and he shook his head.

"When Catwin came to speak to me—" he nodded his head at me, I raised my eyebrows, impressed that he remembered my name "—I wrote a proclamation, to be sent as soon as the battle is won." His jaw tightened, but he did not admit the possibility of defeat.

"Whether I live or die, it will be sent out, saying that I have signed this document, and that it is my will that the people of Heddred live as equals. The lords can argue with me if they wish, but it is done—and all their people will know it." He looked up at her, and there was hope in his eyes. "Will you stay, to advise me?"

My eyes went to Miriel's face, and I found that I was holding my breath. It was no longer any choice of mine— tomorrow, by dawn, I would be dead, and she would be alone in the world. If she wished to stay in the court, it was not mine to deny her that; but I was terribly afraid. If she remained, she would be faced every day with the nobles who hated her passionately, with the Queen who feared her, with the three most ruthless men I knew who had wanted her dead and gone. I felt my heart ease as she shook her head.

"I cannot stay," she told him, and she tried to smile at his look of despair.

"Do not leave me," he begged her, and she knelt at his side, taking his hand in hers.

"Your Grace," she said, "your reign will be glorious. You will bring a new age, an enlightened age. I would be at your side if I could; but the throne must be unified, above the shadow of rumor. I have given you what I could by bringing you this treaty. But when the battle is done, I must go."

"Where will you go?" he asked her, and Miriel's brow furrowed.

"Voltur, perhaps. In truth, I do not know." She closed her eyes briefly. "But I do know that I must go. And you must go now, your Grace, before anyone notices that you have gone." She stood, moving away as he also stood. He held out his arms to her, but she shook her head, her jaw clenched. "Please," she said simply, and he bowed his head and left without a word. Miriel looked over at me and her eyes were bright.

"May I be alone, please?" she asked, her voice small, and after a moment's thought, I decided that she would be safe enough with her uncle's soldiers to guard her.

"I'll be back soon," I said softly, and I left her, and went to find Roine to say my goodbyes.

Chapter 25

I searched the healers' quarters at the back of the camp, but Roine was not there, and none of the other healers were able to tell me where she had gone. I made a round of the great camp, hastening after each white robe that I saw, but as the sky began to darken, I knew that I had missed her. For a moment, I thought I might burst into tears, out in the open as I was. I did not think that I could face this night without saying goodbye to Roine. Then I thought of her face, thought of what she would say when I told her where I was going, and I thought that perhaps it was better this way. She had told me that she would not live to see the end of the battle, and if tomorrow dawned without a fight, and it was I who had died and she who had lived—then she would, at least, have made her peace with not seeing me again.

But it was very bitter, indeed, to know that we had parted in anger. I would never again feel her arms around me, and at that thought, I felt the tears spill over, down my cheeks. I ducked my head as I returned to the campsite, pushing past the soldiers who were hurrying to and fro, setting up their camps and making ready for the morrow.

At our camp, surrounded by her uncle's men, Miriel had at last emerged from her tent and was—to raucous cheers—singing a rendition of "The Western Mountains." As she sang of winter nights and the women of Voltur, the men hummed along, wiped tears from their eyes, and hoisted their tankards to her. I smiled to see it: with her grief put aside, she was glowing. The uncertainty of the past weeks had fled, and even Wilhelm's marriage could not dull her pure happiness that he had signed the treaty, that he loved her still and had not betrayed her.

When she saw me, however, her face sobered, and as soon as she had finished the song, she came to sit with me, bringing me a mug of beer. There were no words left to speak; I smiled my thanks and we sat for a time, enjoying the simple camaraderie. But abruptly, the closeness of the people, the roar of the cheers and the heat of the fire became too much. I stood, gulping down the rest of my mug of ale, and slipped away into the tent, hoping that Miriel would have seen that I must be alone, and that she would not follow.

In the tent, I leaned against the desk and gasped for air. I wondered what it was like to be a soldier of the army, praying that they would live to see the end of tomorrow. Knowing that I would not was more than I could fathom. I thought I might be sick, and as I stared at the pattern of the rug, willing myself not to vomit, I realized that I did not want to die.

I nearly laughed at that. No one wanted to die, I knew that. But I had told myself that my wish and my purpose were one, and that I truly wanted to do this. By this act, I would turn every moment spent learning to sneak, and spy, and murder, into something worthwhile. I could not deny that I wanted that—but I could not deny, either, that I did not want to go. I could feel panic in my frantic heartbeat, a rising urge to run away, be a coward and live.

I had just decided to go to Temar, and beg him to go with me now, so that I did not need to wait any longer, when I froze, considering. At last, in the quiet of the tent, I could recognize a feeling that had been nagging at me all day—the call of the mountains, the sense of the chill air, the lonely whistle of the wind. I thought I could hear the echo of my mother's voice, calling across the years. Hardly knowing what I was doing, I knelt on the carpets, my back to the doorway. I laid my hands on my knees to still the trembling, and then I bowed my head and I waited, stilling my mind, trying to listen.

I did not know how much time had passed before I heard the footsteps approach, slipping around the back of the tent, a shadow out of the corner of my vision, cast along the canvas wall. There was a pause before the tent flap was pulled aside, long enough for me to doubt everything, to think that I had indeed gone mad, and this was nothing more than idle fancy. But at last the fabric moved, and I felt, rather than saw, the figure move to stand behind me. I gave one last breath out, trying to empty my mind, and then I whirled, driving my shoulder up and knocking my attacker backwards as their knife flashed down. I grabbed their wrist, twisting, and I heard a cry of pain, hastily bitten off. As we stumbled and fell, my hands seeking their throat, the hood fell back.

Roine.

I froze, dumbstruck, and she rolled, pushing me so that I sprawled onto the hard-packed ground. She lunged for the knife, and as her fingers curled around the haft and she swept the blade back. It was only instinct that saved me. A hundred, a thousand drills moved my muscles into a block, even as my mind went blank. My foot lashed out and caught Roine in the stomach, and she doubled over; it was quick enough work to strike out, pressing the tips of my fingers into a pressure point until she gasped and the knife fell from her fingers. I shoved her back, snatching up the knife myself, and the two of us settled into a wary fighter's crouch, her at the back of the tent and me blocking her egress.

For a moment, I could not speak. At this vital moment, I found that I had no words to ask what I must. I only stared at her, and she stared back; her jaw was clenched, her eyes bright, but there was no uncertainty in her gaze, and no remorse.

"You?" I whispered finally, and her jaw clenched even as her mouth trembled.

"Who else?" she asked bitterly, and the breath fled from my lungs and left me gasping. There was a terrible truth in her words—there was no one else, there had never been anyone else. How many could I say that I had trusted without question, never doubting, never wondering? One. There was only one. I had doubted Temar, I had doubted even Miriel; only Roine had never earned my suspicion.

"But why?" I could make no sense of any of it, and I shrank away when I saw the rush of utter hatred in her eyes.

"Do you not know what you are?" she spat. "Did you heed none of the prophecy, do you not understand that this had to happen?"

"*Why?*" The word burst out of me, I could form none other. At last, Roine drew herself up, the pain falling away from her.

"For the rebellion," she said, as if it were self-evident. "What else? You were the key, the last piece of it all." I gaped. I had grown up listening to her passionate speeches on nobles and common people, on the rights of the few and the many. She had been the staunchest supporter of Miriel's interest in the rebellion. And yet it had never occurred to me that Roine might truly be a part of the uprising, sheltered as she had been in Voltur, isolated as she seemed to be even at the palace.

Unbidden, the connections began to form in my mind: her hours of prayer in the chapel, the way the High Priest had known my name—known anything about me, known about Miriel, and that he should not oppose her as a match for the King. It was coming together with awful clarity. How many times had she warned me of undercurrents, of movements larger than myself and larger than the Court? She had taught me the principles of the rebellion almost from the cradle, muttering about the excesses of nobles, derisive of the courts. And she had been placed, always, to strike: because it had been I, always, who had told her where her targets would be.

"How could you not *know*?" she cried, suddenly, and at last I understood the hatred in her eyes. Her pleas for me to go, her endless insistence that I run away from court, her tears in the wake of the first murder attempt—it had not been a clever pretense, an exquisitely-made trap. She had loved me, and she had warned me to run away, out of her reach. She had pleaded with me, I remembered. She had begged me to go, and I had never understood.

"How could I?" I flung the words back in her face. "I should have guessed that it would be you who would poison me? The woman who raised me?"

"There was no one else it could be!" she cried back. "You should have run!"

"I should have?" I fought the urge to hurl the knife at her— not the precise throw Donnett had drilled into me, only the simple, childish urge to lash out. "How could you?" I asked, my voice cracking. "How could you—"

"Do you think there was any way out of this?" Her eyes were wild. "This is what you were born to be, Catwin—there is no cheating fate!"

"Fate? You think this was fate?" I did not think I had ever felt anger like this; my vision seemed to cloud. I could hardly feel my feet on the ground or the knife in my grip. "You took the words of a village woman and you thought it meant you had to kill me?"

"Oh? And you have not dreamed of it?" she challenged me. "You have not heard your mother's words and believed them?"

"It's different! I saw the prophecy—and I have not—" I broke off. Roine had tried, time and again, to kill me; but where she had failed in her missions, I had succeeded. She had sought my death, but of the two of us, I was the murderer. It was I who had taken a vial of poison and tipped it into the Duke's mouth, knowing full well what I did.

"And I saw the prophecy as well," Roine said strangely. Her face had been drained of all color; she was far away in memory, hardly moving. "I was twelve when I dreamed of it, and they told me my fate—when they turned me out. I had a soul condemned to hell, they said. I would never be redeemed. I was cast out of the monastery, to wander, and I heard a voice call me to Voltur. I arrived at the castle barefoot, alone. I begged a post, and I waited—" She broke off, her eyes closing in pain, and when she spoke again, her voice was so soft that I could hardly hear it.

"I waited so long that I began to think it had been nothing but a lie. And then…there was you. They gave you into my keeping." Her eyes focused on my stricken face, and, horribly, she smiled. "And so now you see. You have to die, and it has to be me who kills you. But you are here for the rebellion. You understand—you know that there can be nothing more worthy than this. The Heddred you know will fall, and another will rise in its place. It will be built on our ashes, yours and mine."

"No," I said. I could not have said if it was a true prophecy, or only a reflex, the simple will of a beast to avoid its own slaughter.

"Catwin, you cannot fight this any longer." She held out her hand to me, still smiling her terrible smile. I knew that smile—it was the gentle smile she had used as she cleaned my skinned knees, taught me to grind herbs, first watched me run. She had smiled so when she kissed my forehead and wished me a good night's sleep. "Give me the knife," she said.

"How will my death give you what you wish?" I asked, genuinely fearful. The confidence in her voice terrified me—I wanted to reach out and put the knife in her hand. I wanted to believe her.

"Do you not wish it, too? It is not for me to question the Gods, Catwin. You and I will pay for the world that must be created, but can you not see that it is necessary? Have you never wanted your life to mean something?" At that fatal question, the echo of Temar's words, I felt myself come alive.

"It will," I said, my voice shaking. "There is more that I must do, and through it you shall have my death, if that is what you want. But not now, not here."

"No," she said, at last. She was incredulous. "You cannot deny this, Catwin. This must be. You and I both, all of us—through our deaths, the rebellion will be born. And it must be me who takes your life." She stepped forward and I pulled the knife out of her reach, behind my back.

"Leave now," I told her, my voice growing stronger. "Leave me and run, because I swear, if I survive this night, I will find you." It was a lie; I could never have brought myself to seek her out and kill her. But neither could I face her again. More than anything, I wanted her to go. If I survived, I could never forgive her; I could not bear to see her again.

"You will not," she said, finally beginning to grow angry once more. "I must do this, and you will not stop me."

"I will not?" I actually laughed. "You cannot win." I thought of the hours of practice, drills of blocks and strikes, tumbling and grappling, throws. I was quicker, stronger. I was better trained. I was incredulous, but Roine only smiled.

"The Gods will guide me." And she lunged for me, stumbling as I circled away. With terror, I realized that my muscles were sluggish, horror slowing my reflexes. I knew what I must do. She had no armor, no defense; one quick strike and I could end this—if not with her dagger, then with my own. But I could not bring myself to do it.

"What have you done to me?" I asked, horrified, still trying to move, and she smiled.

"This is the Gods' will, Catwin."

I barely saw the movement behind her before her face changed, shock and pain twisting her expression away from its awful certainty.

"It is not the Gods' will," Miriel said simply, as she jerked a dagger free from Roine's falling body. She looked down at the woman on the ground, and her face was like ice. "And if you wanted Catwin's death, then you should have known that you would need to reckon with me." She watched, impartial as an executioner, as Roine died, wordless, at her feet, and then Miriel dropped her knife, stepped over my mother's body and hurried to my side

"Are you hurt?" she asked, urgently. "There's blood on the knife, did she harm you?"

"No," I said, surprised into response. I looked down, and saw, as Miriel had said, dried blood on the blade. "This isn't mine."

"Whose, then?" Miriel wondered aloud. She took my hand and pried my fingers, gently, from the hilt of the knife, dropping it aside. "Catwin. Are you okay?" She looked up at me, and whatever she saw on my face, she bit her lip. "I'm so sorry," she whispered, and she wrapped her arms around me. At that, I finally dragged my gaze away from Roine's body, and reality slammed down, crushing the air from my lungs. I closed my eyes, buried my face in Miriel's shoulder, and began to cry.

I should have known, I thought. It had been right in front of my eyes, and I had never guessed—all of these years, it had been there for me to see, and I had been willfully blind. Who had known that Miriel could betray the rebellion to her uncle's troops? Only Roine. Who had warned Jacces of who I was, and told him that Miriel and I might be with the King on the night of his murder? Temar might have guessed, but only Roine had known, for a fact, where I would be. Who had known where I was, to send an assassin while Miriel and I worked with the rebels? Not one of our enemies had known where we were—only Roine.

There were no words for the depth of this betrayal. I could have accepted the hatred of Isra, of the Conradines, of the High Priest. I had known, always, that Temar might one day be my enemy, and I had prayed that he would be the one to betray me. But it could not have been him, for I knew to watch him, I knew not to trust him. It was only Roine who had been with me, for so long, that I could never have suspected her. My first memories were of her smile. It was she who had taught me the hymns of the church. She had watched me grow up, from an infant, and all the time she had known that she would one day strike at me, to take my life.

I wanted to scream, I wanted to throw something, tear down the tent, curse the Gods for whatever twisted trap we had been caught in, all of us. But I only wrapped my arms tighter around Miriel, bit my lip until I tasted blood, and cried silently, feeling the sobs shake my body. It was not fair, I thought, and I felt like a child, wailing about being denied sweets—it not fair, not fair. Why did I have to know? Why could I not have gone to my death tonight, never knowing that it had been Roine? Of all the moments in my life, the betrayal had to come now, and of all the things I wanted, I realized that I had wanted to go to my death with the love of those I held dear.

And I could not even have that. I choked back a sob and straightened up, trying to calm myself enough to breathe evenly. Miriel was looking up at me, her gaze searching my face for clues.

"Catwin?" she asked tentatively.

"I have to go," I said softly. Tears came to my eyes, and I blinked them back. I tried to smile at her, but my mouth was trembling.

"You don't have to do this," she whispered, pleading, but I shook my head.

"I do. What would you do in my place?" At that, she looked down and nodded.

"The same. But I hope you come back," she said, in a rush, and I could hear a sob in her voice. "I don't know what to do without you."

"You'll survive," I said, trying not to break down. "I promise you, you can survive anything. You've got Voltur now. You can go be a philosopher in the mountains if you want." She gave a sound that was half laugh, half sob.

"I could do that," she agreed, and she stood up on tip-toe to hug me. "Be safe, Catwin. Don't give up. Come back if you can."

"I will if I can," I agreed. Easy to say so; there was no way I would have that chance; it would take all my skill even to make it to Kasimir's tent. "Be safe, yourself." I slipped out of the tent without meeting her eyes; determined as I was, I knew that I could not leave her if I saw her cry. I pushed my way through the crowd of men at the fire and made my way to the edge of the camp, edging my way between tents and ducking out of the way of messengers and patrols.

There, facing into the darkness, was the tent Temar had described to me, a single blue ribbon on one of the tent poles. I squared my shoulders and walked towards it. There was only one test left, and that would be not to waver as Temar pleaded with me to stay.

"I'm here," I said, as I pushed aside the tent flap. "Are you ready—"

The tent was dark and empty. Temar had already gone.

For several long moments, I stood, frozen, in the darkness. I knew without question that Temar had gone hours ago, as the sun set; he had set out for the Ismiri camp as soon as we had parted. Perhaps he had watched, to make sure that I was truly setting out to find Roine—to make sure that I was not going to try the same ploy. Then he had slipped away, a shadow disappearing into the dusk, and by now, Gods willing, Kasimir was dead.

Temar had known that I would understand what he had done—where he had erred was in believing that I would not follow, both to assure that the mission was completed, and to give him even the merest chance of escaping. It was wishful thinking to believe that I would accept defeat so easily.

Grimly, I checked each of the tiny pockets in my shirt, the sheathes in my boots, and began to run through the series of stretches, trying to bring my mind to stillness. I had no poison for my daggers, no wire, no ether-soaked rag to silence any guards who might see me. But that did not matter; I had accepted this mission as my purpose, and the elegance with which I accomplished it was nothing to me. All I needed was to get close enough for one of my knives to find its target.

All of the pain of Roine's betrayal, all of the fear that was coursing through my veins, all of the hurt of losing Miriel and Temar—all of it would be gone soon. I would sleep, knowing that my life and my death, both, had been given to defend thousands of lives. Jeram would go home to his wife and children, Donnett would see his sister and her babies once more—I could smile for that, at least.

I was straightening up to set out at last when I heard, faintly, the shout go up from a patrol and dashed outside, the cry ready on my lips as I recognized Temar, sprinting towards me out of the darkness.

Chapter 26

"Hold!" The patrol reached me a moment after Temar collapsed into my arms. I could see his eyelids fluttering. "Hold," I repeated, my heart pounding. "He's Heddrian, he's one of us. Temar?"

"It's done," he whispered. Blood ran from the corner of his mouth, seeped through his shirt to soak my fingers; my hand was moving, searching, trying to find the injury, but all my fingers found was a mess of blood.

"You," I said to one of the men. "Go to the King, speak only to him, and tell him to summon Miriel DeVere, and to tell her that Catwin's mission is done. She will be able to tell him what that means. Do you have that?"

"Miriel DeVere—Catwin's mission," he repeated blankly.

"Go now, all of you!" They ran, and I stumbled into the tent, barely getting Temar to the bedroll before my own legs gave out. "I need to get a healer," I told him urgently, and he smiled sadly, reaching out to take my arm as I stood to go.

"It is too late," he said softly.

"Where is the wound?"

"All...over." He gave a gasp of pain, and his face twisted. "Please...stay with me."

"I should get a surgeon—" I broke off as he moved his hand, and I saw the wound in his side. The fabric had torn, and I could hardly see the flesh for the mess of it; bone glinted against the blood.

"My stomach," he whispered. "The poison is in my blood now. I don't have much time left." Silently, slowly, not knowing what to say, I dropped back to kneel at his side.

"It's done," he said again, trying to smile.

"You went without me," I whispered, staring down at him with tears in my eyes, and he smiled at me.

"I couldn't let you go," he said softly. "You know that." One of his hands closed around mine, and I squeezed my fingers, feeling my face crumple; there were tears running down my cheeks. The events of the night rushed back to me, overwhelming.

"Roine tried to kill me," I said, hearing my voice crack. "All the time, it was her. All of the times they came for us." I shook my head. "I don't know how to live with that," I confessed. "I thought I'd die tonight. But now…"

"Is she dead?" His voice was urgent, his fingers gripping mine tightly.

"Yes. Miriel killed her." I shook my head as Temar gave a laugh that trailed away into a cough. He was smiling wryly, to think that the girl he so despised had done what he would have, in her place.

"Miriel? Thank her for me. She…freed you. As you freed me." I shook my head and wiped tears away, trying to find words to say, trying not to think of the fact that he was dying, his blood soaking into the ground. I closed my eyes against the pain, and heard his voice, as if from very far away.

"Mihail did not betray Dragan at the Battle of Voltur."

"What?" I opened my eyes and frowned at him. "What do you mean?

"He did not mean to." Temar's dark eyes were full of pain. "I snuck into their camp and I pretended …told him I'd put poison in his wine, and I'd only give him the antidote if he told me their battle plans. All…" He grimaced in pain. "…a lie. His family was executed," he added. "I've never told anyone. Only Eral knew."

"You're the one who won the Battle of Voltur," I said, awestruck, and he shook his head. He was pale, sweat beading on his skin.

"They were planning something, anyone could see. No time to go for help. Eral was…he was a good commander. But we had nothing. We needed luck. I had sworn that I would lift him up."

"But why?" When he did not answer, I felt my heart seize. "Temar?"

"My name is Necthan," he murmured.

"What?" His eyelids fluttered slightly. He looked up at me, trying to breathe through the pain.

"Necthan." He gave a grimace. "I wanted…someone to know." He gasped, and gripped my hand, and I saw fear in his eyes at last; panic rose up in me. "Please—do one last thing for me."

"Anything." I was shaking, my fingers wrapped tight around his, leaning close to hear the thread of his voice.

"Bring my ashes home," he whispered, in my ear. "Tell my sister, we are free. Tell her what you did, and how I died." His eyes began to close.

"Where is your home?" I whispered. He did not answer, and I squeezed his hand. "Temar? Necthan? Where can I find your sister?" I thought he was gone, but his eyes opened once more and he smiled truly, a smile of remembrance.

"The Shifting Isles." His gaze was faraway. "I should like to know that my body came home." I could barely see for the tears, but I nodded.

"I'll do it," I promised him, nodding, and he reached up to touch my face. I leaned my head against his hand, and tried not to sob, and he smiled at me.

"It's okay," he said. "I'm not afraid."

"I don't want you to die," I whispered. I could hear sobs and knew they were my own, and he brushed the tears from my cheek with his thumb.

"I thought that I would die alone," he said softly, "and my family would never know my fate. But you are here, to guard my passing, and one day, my people will know that I kept my promise. This is a good death." I could feel the life leaving him, but he smiled at me. His hand slipped away from my face. "I love you, Catwin. Be safe."

"I love you," I whispered, but he did not hear me. His eyes were open, but he did not see me anymore. He had died with a smile on his face, and I was left in the darkness, holding his hand, stifling my sobs into my palm. I sat in the tent, holding his hand, and the sounds of the camp faded away. There was only me, and Temar lying at my side. I did not know how much time had passed when the sound of voices, and pounding feet jolted me from my haze. I looked around as the voices grew closer.

"Catwin?" Miriel flung herself through the entryway of the tent and stopped as she saw me sitting by Temar's body. Behind her, Wilhelm and Gerald Conradine pushed their way into the tent, and I saw Guy de la Marque slip in, quietly, behind them.

"What is this?" Gerald Conradine demanded. His eyes swept around the tent, looking into the corners, where danger might lurk in the shadows. Miriel bristled at his tone, but I could hardly find the energy to care.

"This man killed Kasimir," I said, and Gerald's eyes narrowed at me.

"How do you know? Who is he?"

"That's the Duke of Voltur's servant," Guy de la Marque said. His eyes were fixed on Temar's face. "I remember seeing him in Council meetings. So he was an assassin, then. I always wondered." I saw a flash of humor, unexpected, in his eyes. "You know, I *had* always suspected that Eral meant to kill us all." He fell silent when Wilhelm looked over at him.

"We heard the commotion in their camp, but we did not know what it was," Wilhelm said to me, gently. He came to kneel by my side in the mud, heedless of his fine clothes. "Is he dead?"

"Yes," I said shortly, and the King looked over at me, noting my grief. He reached out and put his hand over mine.

"This man will be given a hero's funeral," he assured me, and I saw genuine kindness in his eyes; for the first time, I felt hope that perhaps Heddred might truly change for the better under Wilhelm's rule.

"Thank you." Somewhere, distantly, a shout went up in the camp, and I heard the clamor grow. The men looked around, nervously, to the tent flap.

"Your Grace," Miriel said softly. She cast an apologetic look at me. "That is surely the envoy. You should go, to accept their surrender." She looked, as ever, only in the direction of her hopes; she was like a beacon, I saw Wilhelm's tension ease in the face of her steady belief.

"Indeed." He nodded to me, courteously, and stood.

"We should stay on our guard," his father warned, and Wilhelm gave a placatory smile.

"And we will," he said simply. "Will you come, my Lady?" He held his hand out to Miriel, but she shook her head. She stepped back, managing to look as if she had not noticed Guy de la Marque's narrow-eyed look; his good humor had fled entirely.

"I will stay with Catwin," Miriel said softly, "and keep vigil." The men filed out silently, and Miriel knelt at my side in the darkness, her gown pooling around her.

"He said to thank you," I said, into the silence.

"For?"

"Roine." Miriel smiled a little.

"And I would have thanked him if I'd had the chance—he went without you, didn't he?" I nodded, unable to speak for grief, and she reached out to touch my hand. We sat for a while in silence, and then, tentatively, she asked: "Who was he, then? Did you ever know?" I shook my head, my eyes fixed on Temar's face.

"I don't know." It hurt to admit that, to know that I would never truly understood Temar; Necthan, I told myself. I had a sudden memory of him, dark-eyed and secretive, telling my twelve-year-old self that the Shifting Isles were nothing more than legend. He had hidden all of it, a-purpose, and even at the last, confessing his sins to me, he would not give up his secrets.

I wanted to do nothing more than sleep, lay my head down and lose myself before I could think. I could feel my mind working, thoughts spinning, a jumble of memories. *Those whom fate has touched...well, let us say that they are drawn to one another.* And, so sharp a pain I could hardly breathe: *It is the Gods' will.*

"Breathe," I heard Miriel's voice. "You have to breathe. Here, move my hand." She reached out, tentatively, as she must have seen Roine do; the memory hurt. "In. Wait. Out. Wait. Keep breathing, Catwin."

Weariness dragged at me, bone deep. Exhaustion, understandable, began to leech the strength from the grief, and I felt my eyes begin to slip closed. How long had it been since I had slept? I leaned against Miriel, feeling the comfort of her warmth.

"I promised him that I would bring his ashes home," I told her softly, and she nodded.

"I won't let them take his body. Sleep now, Catwin."

"Wake me if..." If there was a battle. If she was in danger. But I could hardly finish the sentence. "Stay near Wilhelm."

"I'll be okay," Miriel promised me. She lay me down on the ground and swung the cloak from her own shoulders, draping it over me. Her smile was the last thing I saw before exhaustion claimed me.

Chapter 27

When I awoke, it was daylight, and the camp had descended into chaos. As I slept, I had been moved; now, I lay on the Duke's cot, in his tent, surrounded by the full-throated roar of a victorious army. I pushed myself up, panicked, and then saw that Temar's body had been brought here as well. A workbench had been brought in, and his body laid out. The blood had been washed from his face and his hands, and his hair combed and re-braided. With a new tunic, to cover his wounds, he might only have been sleeping peacefully.

I walked to his side and knelt on the ground, looking at his face. The other memories, fresh in my mind, were trying to surface, and I thought that if I could only think of Temar and his death in my arms, I could feel a clean grief, a pure grief. His death had been honorable; at the last, it had been peaceful. If I could only weep for that—

Then I would not have to remember Roine.

Alone in the tent, the sound of my tears sheltered by the raucous celebrations outside, I broke down at last. There was no need, now, to push away the sobs, to save my strength, and I gave way entirely. I curled over and pressed my forehead onto the cool earth, wrapping my arms around myself, squeezing my eyes shut; the sobs came anyway, wracking my whole body. My throat was raw. I ached with it, pressing my hand flat over my heart as if to stop a wound, and I rocked back and forth, lost to the world in my grief, wanting only to scream my anger out—and that scream was lost in tears, drowned out by the shouts of the men.

I was curled on my side when I came back to myself. My arms were still wrapped around my sides, my knees up to my chest. My breathing was deep and slow, my body drained of its rage and its anger. For a time, I only lay and felt the steady rise and fall of my ribs, only stared ahead at the canvas wall of the tent, feeling the discomfort of bones against the ground, the pain seeming very far away.

There was nothing to do but get up. Some long-lost vestige of instinct, perhaps, the same plain pragmatism that forced soldiers through the pain of lost limbs; the very earth itself might seem changed, everything immaterial, but there was nowhere to go other than onward. I was still breathing, my heart was still beating, and my body had a will of its own.

I got up and dusted myself off—clean clothes, minutiae, the right thing to do, and, because I could not think of where to go or what else to do, I went to the desk and pulled out the chair, and I sat in the darkness and waited. I knew that I could not go out into the camp; the canvas walls and the solitude of the tent were my only shield against the world. I could not face the jubilation of the army.

It might have been morning, when Miriel came to find me, or midday, or afternoon. I had lost track of time, it did not mean much to me. I knew that I was hungry, but I could not leave Temar's body. I could not even be bothered to search the trunks and packs in the tent for food. I was sitting quietly, staring at Temar's still face, when the canvas rustled and Miriel made her way into the tent. She stopped when she saw me, and I saw her eyes take in my red-rimmed eyes, the tangle of my hair, my white face.

"You're awake," she said quietly. Behind her, Wilhelm stooped and made his way into the tent. He nodded, as courteously as ever, to see me. He was trying to be grave, I knew, and he was exhausted in the wake of the past days—but nothing could have dulled his joy. The years were stripped away and he was a young man once more, confident and happy. I thought it over in the strange stillness of my mind, and decided that I could not blame him. His happiness was rational. I nodded back at him.

"They surrendered," Miriel said quietly. "As you had said they would. With Kasimir gone, none had the heart to go to battle; Pavle confessed that Dusan had tried to recall them." She came to stand beside me, leaning down to look into my face. "They're going home now. They laid down their weapons and they'll be given free passage to the border."

"We kept Pavle here," Wilhelm interjected. "All the commanders. We could not just let them go after—" He broke off when Miriel shot him a look.

"The war is over," she said to me, her smile encouraging. "Because of you, Catwin."

"Because of Temar," I corrected her. There was a noise at the door, a crisp command to halt. "Wait here," Miriel said urgently, and she darted out the door, motioning the Wilhelm to stay where he was. I could hear her low-voiced conversation with the guards, and the sound of a voice I knew well, but in my haze, could not place.

A moment later, she stepped back into the gloom, and to my surprise, I saw Jeram duck into the tent. He raised his eyebrows to see me, and a body beside me, and then he looked over to Wilhelm. I saw him frown as he saw the blond hair, the rich clothing, the cloak pins with the crests of Warden and Conradine.

"Are you the Warlord?" he asked bluntly. Wilhelm smiled.

"After today, I think not," he said. "But I am the King, yes." He inclined his head, and his smile did not flicker when Jeram only nodded in return, unwilling to bend the knee.

"And you signed the treaty?" Jeram's skeptical look took in Wilhelm, Miriel, and even me, sitting beyond their small circle.

"I did." Wilhelm drew out the leather case and beckoned Jeram over to the table, spreading out the scroll to show his seal. "As I told the Lady, a proclamation will be sent tomorrow— before, Gods willing, my Council knows of this." I saw irritation in his eyes, the look I had seen so often as Garad spoke of the Council.

"And why tell me?" Jeram asked Miriel, pointedly. "Should you not have told... Jacces?" Wilhelm looked up and around, his gaze fixing on Miriel's face.

"You know who Jacces is?" he demanded. "Why did you not tell me?"

"It was not important anymore," Miriel said to him, gently. To Jeram, she said, "Jacces is dead."

"What?" The conversation had flowed around me like the babble of a stream, but at that last sentence, I felt my curiosity begin to return. "How do you know? How did he die?" Miriel looked down at once, but I had seen the pity in her eyes.

"I think it was Roine. He was found dead this morning— stabbed." *All of us*, Roine had said. *Through our deaths, the rebellion will be born.*

"The High Priest?" Wilhelm demanded, incredulous. "He was Jacces?"

"Yes," Miriel admitted. "He had planned this for decades— he tried to sway Isra, and Garad, and when he could not, he chose you for his King." She spoke plainly, and her gaze did not waver when Wilhelm dropped his head into his hands. I could see her fighting the urge to go to him; her fists were clenched. But she would not spare him the truth.

"What are you talking about?" Jeram asked, finally. He had been looking back and forth between the two of them, his eyes narrowed. Wilhelm raised his head, his eyes dull.

"The High Priest had my cousin murdered to make way for me, because he knew that I would support the rebellion." He cast a bitter look down at the scroll on the table. "And see, it worked."

"Not how he had planned it." It was little consolation, and Miriel knew it, but at her words, the final pieces of the puzzle fell into place. I had known all of it: the High Priest, Roine. But none of it had made sense until this moment.

"Me," I said, and all three of them turned to look at me. My gaze locked with Miriel's. "When the soldiers were looking for us after the murder, they were looking for *me*. The food sent to our rooms that night was for *me*, in case we escaped the soldiers. When Aron came for us, that's what he meant—he wasn't trying to kill you at all."

"But that was Roine," Miriel said, shaking her head.

"I told you, he said there was a key—it did not hinge on people or Kings, but that there was one key. He meant me. You were right." I could feel a sob building, the urge to laugh despairingly—or scream, I did not know which. "The balance that would tip, and the ending, you said it was the rebellion. They thought so, too. Roine was the one who convinced him of it." Miriel looked at me, her lips parted, her eyes wide. Behind her, the men exchanged a quick glance, Wilhelm frowning, Jeram staring at us as if we had gone mad. And then Miriel said the worst thing of all:

"She was right."

"What?" Roine had not been right, none of it had been right. I was not dead, but the treaty to cement the rebellion lay on the table only a few feet from me, signed. She had been wrong, the betrayals had been meaningless—and that made it all the worse. It had all been for nothing, and still, the pain of that fact was as nothing to the possibility that she might have been correct. I fought the urge to lash out, reach for something and throw it.

"What happened the first time someone came against us?" Miriel asked. "That was when I found the rebellion. And the second time, that was when we became allies, you and I. Every time they tried to kill us…" I swallowed, closing my eyes. It did not help; the pattern was burning in my vision. Each betrayal had brought us closer, propelled us further towards the rebellion.

"But she didn't succeed," I said softly, and Miriel shook her head.

"It was like Jacces' plans. She succeeded—she just never knew it. She did not know what the prophecy meant, but she was right to trust it."

"She *wasn't!*" My voice broke on the shout. "It didn't need to happen this way!"

"But it did happen this way," Miriel said. I shrank away, but I could not block out her voice.

"And they have paid for their treachery," Wilhelm said. His voice was gentle; he meant to calm me, but the grief rose up so strongly that I thought I would choke. They had not paid, either of them—Jacces would not have regretted anything, I knew that well enough, and when Roine had died, it had not been guilt that I saw in her eyes, but fear. She thought that she had failed. Her only regret was that she had not killed me.

"Get out," I said, my voice ugly.

"Catwin—" Miriel came to me, but I put out my hand to stop her from touching me.

"Go. All of you." They left, Jeram rolling the scroll gently, handling the leather case as carefully as he would hold a baby. I saw Miriel cast a look over her shoulder as she left, but I turned my face away; I could not meet her eyes. When they were gone, I grabbed the ink pot from the desk and hurled it at the wall of the tent. A small chest of books went the same way, and the tent lurched, but the shadows at the door stayed constant. Wilhelm must have asked his guards to stay.

I dashed the hanging lamp down onto the ground, watching the flames spread across the Duke's carpet for a long moment before finally beating them away, smothering them in a blanket, burning my hands and coughing at the fumes, heedless of the tears that ran down my face. When the fire, at last, was out, I slumped to the floor by Temar's body, stifling my gasps into my shirt. After a few moments, I crawled to the edge of the tent and pulled up the edge of the canvas, leaning down to breathe the pure air, clenching my teeth against the stinging on my hands.

I sat there for a long time, my arms around my knees, and gradually the sunlight faded. The camp began to grow quiet as the men streamed into the city. I could hear music carrying faintly on the wind, and when at last I heard nothing outside the tent, I got up and pushed aside the door flap.

The camp was deserted, and the fire had burned low. I looked around myself in the moonlight, and at last turned back to the Royal Guards, who were watching me silently. They nodded their heads to me; if the King had said to guard me, their manner implied, then surely he knew best.

"I need to build a pyre," I told them. "Guard the tent." They nodded and I set off, taking brush and makeshift weapons racks, piling them over the fire pit at the center of the Voltur camp. At long last, I beckoned the guards inside the tent with me, and between us, we carried Temar's body out and laid it, carefully, on the pyre.

I stood and watched as smoke began to curl from the edges, as the crackle grew and flames began to lick at the wood, the light flickering faintly, and finally, as the pile itself was consumed. The flames leapt skyward and the heat from the fire made me wince, but I kept my gaze fixed on Temar until the last, as the blaze began to die. I stood and cried, my only companions the two silent guards, and I felt the anger begin to bleed away.

I was alive—that had been Temar's gift. I was alive, and there was no prophecy left to govern the rest of my days. For the first time in six long years, I could face the next day without fear of betrayal, without distrust. It was over; I was free.

Chapter 28

Barely a week later, when the business of the surrender had been concluded, and Pavle had put his name to the treaty, the trial of Isra Dulgurokov and her brother began. The two had been arrested as the festivities reached their peak, when the news of the King's startling proclamation had been running rampant throughout the city. The nobles had been so preoccupied that few had known of the charges until Wilhelm called his Council away from their roistering in order to sit as a jury for the two. They were charged, the crier read, with high treason: the attempted seizure of the throne, and murder of the DeVere heirs.

The trial, conducted near in secret in the recesses of the Fortress, was nonetheless a shock to a court drunk on celebration, all the more so as it became clear that Isra and her brother were guilty—guiltier even than Miriel and I had known. Afraid of her uncle's growing madness, we had believed without question that the plan to turn the troops on each other was his, and his alone. But a young soldier gave testimony that the Dulgurokov men had been ordered to break the planned charge, falling back behind the DeVere men and cutting them down from behind as they led their troops against the Ismiri, and a maid of Isra's was called to give evidence that she had found a dozen little vials of poison in her mistress's jewel case.

In fear for her life, Isra turned on her nephew, snarling that it had been he who killed her son. She accused Gerald Conradine, before all the Court, of disguising his men as the Royal Guard, and she accused Guy de la Marque of aiding the murder, having been assured that his daughter would be Queen when Wilhelm came to the throne. As Isra raged, her eyes red with tears, I began to wonder if she did not believe what she said—if this had not been revenge for Garad's death. She rejected, absolutely, the dying confession of the High Priest's head servant, a man who had killed himself in the Great Cathedral when he heard of Jacces' death. Lies, Isra proclaimed. Wilhelm's story was lies, his rise to the throne had been treason—and she would gladly admit to plotting against the man who had murdered her son.

Wilhelm sat quietly, his hands clenched on the arms of his throne as he listened to the accusations against him. Marie sat beside him, a circlet of gold over her veil, the crest of House Warden embroidered on her gown. When Isra spat that Wilhelm's sons, too, must die, Marie went white, her hand pressed over her stomach as if to shield her child from the malice of the words, and her blue eyes went cold and hard. Any pity she might have felt this woman, whom she had once expected to be her mother-in-law, was lost in Isra's uncompromising hatred.

Arman listened to the charges laid against him with his head bowed. He offered no defense but a whispered plea that he was innocent. He had no hope of reprieve, and his grim face said that he knew it well; but still his head jerked up, his face incredulous, when Miriel was called to give evidence against him.

Miriel, veiled, dressed in stark black for the loss of her uncle, gave a final performance to put Isra's to shame. To the horrified men of the Court, she admitted without a shred of remorse that it had been she who killed her uncle. Her voice low and mesmerizing, she spoke of overhearing his treacherous plans on the eve of the battle, and of giving him the vial of poison and swearing that she would expose him to the Court if he would not end his life himself. It was she who named Isra and Arman as his accomplices, her gaze not wavering from the peers; she did not see Isra's fury, nor did she see as Arman dropped his head into his hands, accused by the very woman he had hoped to make Queen.

Isra had admitted her guilt openly, and there was no defense Arman could make—and with the men of the DeVere line sitting judgment, there was no hope for leniency for the two of them. The court ruled, to a man, for execution, and the King and Queen, sitting silently on their thrones, only nodded—had I not known Wilhelm for a populist sympathizer, had I not seen him sign the treaty, I would have thought him a Warlord of the old line. There was no pity in his eyes as he watched Isra walk to her cell.

When he turned back, his face was no less determined; in the rise of his chin, I saw that he was dreading his next words. Before I could stop myself, I shot a quick glance over to Miriel. To my surprise, I saw the faintest hint of a smile, hastily wiped away as the courtiers followed his gaze and looked to her.

"Miriel DeVere," he said clearly, "come forward." As his side, Marie looked down, unwilling to face her rival. "You have averted the massacre of our troops and the murder of your King, your Queen, and the heir of House Warden," Wilhelm proclaimed.

"For this, you are to be commended. But we cannot, and will not, condone the murder of the peers of our realm. You are to be stripped of your titles and banished, henceforth, from Court." Marie looked up and around, her eyes wide with shock, and the murmurs rose of the peers began to rise. It was only when I saw Miriel look down to hide her smile that I understood.

"I accept your judgment," she said, after a moment. "I wish your Grace a peaceful and prosperous rule." She sank into a beautiful curtsy, and then removed the heavy signet ring of Voltur from her finger and held it out. As it was taken from her hands, it was if a great weight had been lifted from her shoulders; she closed her eyes and took a deep breath, and then nodded once more and left without another word, a faint smile on her lips.

"You could have warned me," I muttered to her as we walked through the crowded corridors, Palace Guards clearing the way around us, servants and minor nobles pressing forward to look at Miriel, now a famed murderess.

"I didn't know how it would be done," Miriel said simply. "But he asked what thanks I would have for what I had done, and this was what I chose."

"So you chose banishment? Nobles are crazy, I've always said so."

"Oh, did you want to stay at Court?" Miriel laughed at the look on my face. "I thought not. You can thank me now."

"Thank you," I said grudgingly. "But where *are* we going to go?"

"I really don't know," Miriel admitted, her face grave at the thought. "I suppose we could—"

Both of us stopped, confused, as we emerged into a side courtyard, and I saw the grooms waiting. A detachment of the Royal Guard was waiting for us, mounted, the Warden and Conradine pennants flying above their heads, their horses outfitted in the royal colors, but all the men in most somber black. Two horses stood riderless, and, secured to the pommel of one was an urn carved of jet.

"An honor guard," said Wilhelm's voice, and the two of us turned to see him emerge from a hidden door, pushing aside a wall of ivy, guards trailing in his wake. "The Lady—" he broke off. "*Miriel* told me that you had promised this man you would bring his ashes home. I hope you will accept that his body be escorted by my men. He has done us a great service, and we wish to honor him."

I only nodded and bowed. My throat was tight, and I stepped up to the horses to run my fingers lightly over the urn.

"Are you sure about this?" I heard Wilhelm ask Miriel.

"You know there is no place for me here," Miriel said to him, and I looked back to see her standing, determinedly, apart from him. She had wept over this in the past nights. She had left the celebratory banquets as soon as she could, not because she was in mourning, but because she could not bear to see another woman sitting at Wilhelm's side. But there was no sign of it now, save the weariness in her face. She tried to smile. "Thank you for sending me away." Wilhelm did not smile in return; his face fell.

"I wish I could have you for an ally," he said, his voice very low. "The Council is against me, to a man. I do not know how I can hold to this treaty without you."

"You will," Miriel said, with quiet confidence. "I know you can. And you have thousands of allies. I am you ally, always. But there should be no court with two Queens. And so I will leave. I must."

"Where will you go?" Wilhelm looked at her, and she looked at me.

"North," I said shortly. Even Miriel did not know yet where we were going; I would not tell the King, and half the Royal Guard besides. At the pleading look on Wilhelm's face, however, I felt my heart ache for him. As much as I might disapprove of this prolonged goodbye, I had to admit that it was one thing for Miriel to leave her love and go into the wilderness, and quite another for Wilhelm to return to his wife, a furious council, and a resentful court. "I'll keep her safe," I promised him, and he nodded.

"I bid you farewell, then." He watched as we were thrown up into our saddles, and raised his hand in farewell. As we trotted out of the courtyard, Miriel and I both turned back. Wilhelm still stood alone, his hand raised, a small figure against the bulk of the Fortress. Miriel took one last look at him, her own hand raised, tears in her eyes, and then she turned and spurred her horse to a canter.

I looked around myself as we made our way through the winding streets of Penekket, soaking in the sight of the philosophers on the steps of the academies, the brightly-colored tents of the vendors. Children dashed underfoot, and men and woman cried out their wares, holding up ripe fruit and fresh bread to try to tempt us. Groups of priestesses made their way through the streets, offering prayers. Everyone looked up to see the Royal Guard go past, marking the fluttering pennants and Miriel, dressed in black and looking ahead, unseeing, biting her lip to keep the tears back. Few enough thought to look at me, with my ragged, honey-colored hair and my own somber black suit, and not one paid attention to where my hand cupped, protectively, over the jet urn.

I thought about it, and decided that Temar would like that: to move through these streets, even at the last, as a Shadow. He would not want to be celebrated for what he had done, and I thought I could understand that, a little—I would never wish to have ballads sung about the Duke's murder, either. But beyond that, even, Temar was not of this land. He had confessed his origins to me in his last moments. He would not want to be a legend here, in Heddred. So I held my hand over the urn, protectively, as we rode through the city, and only took it away as we emerged onto the broad highway, an avenue of white stone stretching northwards to the sea.

We rode until sundown, cantering through the heavy summer air, and we did not speak amongst ourselves. The men cast sidelong glances at the two of us, and I wondered how many of them had watched us through the years, seeing Miriel when she was only a girl, wide-eyed and clever, catching Garad's heart. Then, I realized, I had half hated her—I had been sullen in her service, a country girl who despised the palace. Now, only a few years later, we were a puzzle indeed: two young women who had left the court, twice, of our own volition, without husbands or families or fortune.

They did not know what to make of us now, and I thought, when I looked over at Miriel, that we did not even know what to make of each other. Who could say what life held in store for Miriel? She had the wit of an academic and the manner of a Queen; where could such a woman go? And what use could I be, a girl who was trained only for intrigue, if we were leaving the seat of power to wander, homeless, across the world?

I looked over at her, my ally, and saw that she rode with her head bowed. The pride that had propped her as we left the city had now bled away, and she slumped, exhausted, in the saddle. She had been crying, I could see, and I remembered that

Miriel had left behind not only those who hated her, but a man she had loved for years, who she had sworn never to see again. Instead of being a Councilor, setting her talents to use in implementing the philosophies she held so dear, she was instead riding away, north, to an uncertain future.

I had expected to share her fear, leaving the city behind, but instead I felt, unmistakable, a rush of joy in my veins. We were free. Our lives were not to be determined by another's schemes, by the whims of a court that was mad for scandal and intrigue. We could live as we wished, watching the changes of Miriel's devising, knowing that we were not bound to any one place, any one goal. I swallowed down a laugh of pure joy, and clenched my hands tightly around the reins, promising myself that I would rejoice— but only when Miriel shared in my happiness.

When we made camp that night, I did my tasks as quickly as I could and then went to seek out Miriel. She had wandered away from the bustle, and for the first time in my life, I had let her go without a backwards glance, unafraid that there would be an assassin lurking in the shadows. I found her sitting, alone, at the edge of the camp, holding a folded scrap of paper. She was gazing up at the sky, where the stars were beginning to glimmer. I walked towards her, trying to think of something to say that would make her smile, but as I joined her, she looked over at me sadly.

"I'm afraid," she said bluntly, but I knew that she embraced her fear; it was easier to bear than her grief. "Where do we go, after...?"

"We'll find a place," I assured her, and she looked down at her hands.

"I've been praying for them," she confessed. I knew without asking that she meant Arman Dulgurokov, and Isra. "I watched them go to their deaths and I thought they deserved it. I still do—I think. But I've been thinking, today...Isra truly thought that Wilhelm had killed Garad. I believe that. And Arman would have been kind to me. He didn't mean to hurt me."

"He meant to hurt a great many other people," I pointed out, and she nodded, biting her lip. "If he was truly kind, he would not have plotted to kill his own allies. If she had truly sought justice, she would not have sought to kill the DeVeres as well as the Conradines. He signed his own death warrant, and she signed hers. Wouldn't it have been worse to pretend it never happened, and leave him there to plot against the throne again?"

Miriel nodded again. Then she held out the letter to me.

"This is for you," she said quietly, and she put it into my outstretched palm. "Jeram gave it to me. It was found on Aron's body, and the Merchant didn't have the courage to read it until after we were gone. But it was for you. I wasn't going to give it to you..."

I closed my eyes and felt my fingers close around the paper. "It's from Roine," I guessed, and Miriel nodded.

"I wanted to burn it," she said. "I wasn't going to tell you about it at all. But that didn't seem fair." She stood, awkwardly, brushing pieces of bark from her skirt. "I'll leave you alone." She trailed away, looking back over her shoulder, but I hardly saw her. I sat for a time, fighting the urge to open the letter, willing myself to walk back to the camp and toss it into the fire. Better never to know, I told myself. Better to let whatever mad words die with Roine, and be forgotten.

She had intended me to read this after killing Aron, after all—she had suspected that he might fail in his task, as each of her other plans had also failed. Whatever words awaited me here, they were her thoughts after I had run, when she thought that I had gone from her forever. Even without looking, I knew that this must be her confession to me, and at last, holding the little scrap of paper, I knew why she had been so fearful when I returned. I should throw it into the fire. I should destroy it, and never know the depth of the betrayal.

But I could not. In all the nights that I had lain awake, trying not to think of Roine, trying not to remember what she had done, I had told myself that I would never understand, that it would never make sense. I told myself that to try to comprehend madness was to seek it myself. I told myself that all of this was beyond my comprehension. And yet now I held the key to it, Roine's own words, and I found that I could not simply cast that away.

Fingers shaking, I unfolded the paper.

Chapter 29

Catwin—

My greatest hope is that you never see this letter, for if you are reading it now, then I will have failed at my only calling in this world, and you will know me for a false friend and an enemy. And yet, as I write this, I find that my hope is also that you have survived to see this. Although I know I will spend eternity in torment for my sins, I feel that if I could only know that you had forgiven me, I could be content.

But how could such a thing be? You have run from the Court, but that will not help. You cannot survive. It is your fate to die by my hand, betrayed, just as it was foretold to me that I would one day betray the one I loved most in this world. I knew, for many years before I met you, that I would be your murderer, and that I would pass out of this world with sins on my conscience that could never be wiped away. It was a bitter fate, but I had made my peace with it—until I met you.

On the day you were born, the winds called out my name in summoning, and I went to take you from your mother's arms and bring you back to the castle. Catwin, when your father told me what little he knew of the prophecy, I could not believe him. You were so small, and so perfect; you seemed to know me from the first, and yet you trusted me absolutely. When you slept in my arms, my heart broke. I held you and I wept, and I prayed that you were another child, unmarked by the gods.

I tried to believe that your mother had been mistaken. I tried to cast away my faith. I had not doubted the Gods, even when the priestesses had turned me out, but I doubted them as I saw you grow from an infant to a child. How could I see you, so young, so full of life, and believe that you would ever die? How could I embrace you and kiss you goodnight, and believe that I would ever lift a hand against you?

When Temar named you a Shadow, I fought him. I wanted to turn your fate to something smaller, leave you in Voltur forever, where you might be safe—but you told me that you had dreamed of your mother, Catwin, and I knew in that moment that my fate had come for me. The words she spoke laid my path bare for me, for at last I knew why I would betray you: for no lesser purpose than to bring about a better world and an enlightened age. I had watched Heddred as it was marred by the pride and greed of the nobles, and I saw that you would be the key to free us all.

I did not go willingly into the darkness; I hope you can believe the truth of it, even in the face of my betrayal. Do you remember that I begged you to run away, not once, but many times? Even if it caused me to fail in my purpose, I could not help but offer you a way out. I had not known how it come to pass that I would betray you, but it was clear to me when the moment had come at last—you were determined that you would help Miriel as she crushed the rebellion, and I could not allow that.

When you survived, I did not know what to think. I had steeled myself to betray you only once. How could I know that I would fail? I hoped that it was finished, that you would never learn what it was that I had done to you. But you were grown, beyond me now—you saw the world clear-eyed, you and Miriel had your own plots and your own schemes. And when fate called me once more, I answered it: it was I who told Jacces where you would be, it was I who agreed with him that, if anyone could name Garad's killer and bring our plans to nothing, it would be you. You had been forged into our enemy, Catwin, and you did not even know it.

When you ran from me at last, I could only think that you knew I was your enemy. There was a relief in that—I cannot describe it but to say that, when you told me where you had run, when it became clear that you trusted me still, I felt the greatest despair I had ever known. My task was not yet finished; I must, once more, lift a hand against you.

Bitterly, to the last I do not know why it is that the Gods require your death. I do not know why it must be I who betrays you. I will never know, and I hope that you, also, will die ignorant of these things. I will pray that you may one day see that your death was the key to a greater, more enlightened world. I pray, also, but with no hope, that you will one day forgive me.

With love,
Roine

I sat in the dark, tears streaming down my face. I felt as if I had been bled dry; I had no more rage left in me, to throw things, to beat my fists against the ground. The grief was no longer sharp, but wrapped about me like a blanket, so overwhelming that it was all I could do to sit, and breathe. I sat until at last Miriel came back to find me. She took the letter from my hands and folded it, the gentleness of her fingers and the tightness at her mouth suggesting that she would rather tear it into tiny pieces, and then she handed me a bowl of soup and a piece of bread. She sat with me, patiently, until I realized what I was holding, and ate. The soup was cold, but I could taste none of it; I had to remind myself how to chew.

"Are you alright?" she asked me, finally. I wiped the last of the soup from the bowl as I considered. I did not know if I was alright. Everything seemed to have gone dark, narrowed in scope, and I could find nothing of myself—I did not know how I felt, or what I thought. Finally, I shook my head.

"No. It's useless—meaningless. She didn't have to do it." I thought of her words, and clenched my hands. "She didn't even know why, just that it was *fate*, just that the *Gods* wanted it. And so she tried to kill me—and she was wrong! The rebellion succeeded. I didn't need to die."

"But it was your betrayal that brought us to be allies," Miriel observed. Even in the face of my anger, as she had left me before, she had not let go of her belief. Once, it had been I who understood that we walked a piece of a great pattern; now it was I who was fearful, and Miriel who saw the path. "Maybe she had to believe that, and we had to fear for our very lives. Every betrayal brought us closer, and together, we brought the rebellion to fruition."

"It didn't have to happen like this," I said, stubbornly, and Miriel only smiled.

"You're the Shadow," she said. "I'd think you would be the one who believed in omens and portents and prophecies." I only shrugged, finding it less amusing, and she sobered at once. "Catwin..." I looked over at her, and whatever she saw in my eyes, she shook her head. "Never mind. We should rest." She took my bowl and spoon and we walked, together, back to the camp, undressing in silence in the privacy of our tent and stretching out on the bedrolls.

"Catwin?" she asked uncertainly, into the darkness.

"Yes?" I hoped she was not going to ask about fate again, or prophecies. But she did not.

"Where are we going?" I rolled over on my side and propped my head up on my hand, and she leaned close when I beckoned to her.

"The Shifting Isles," I said quietly, and she drew back to stare at me, her eyes wide.

"Really? But I thought..."

"I thought so, too. He always agreed that they were a myth when people said so." I took a deep breath and rolled onto my back, staring at the ceiling of the tent. It did not seem real that Temar was dead, and yet I never forgot it; always, at the back of my mind, was the ache that he was gone, and that I would never see him smile, or hear him laugh, ever again.

But I forgot about Roine, I always forgot what she had done, and how she had died. My mind cast it all away, time and again, and with each realization, it seemed to hurt just as deeply. It was not only guilt, as I felt for the Duke's death, not only grief, as I felt for Temar's, but grief, and guilt, and anger, and helplessness, all rolled together so that I could make no sense of it. I could forget everything else, but her one, hateful question: *How could you not know?* The words haunted my dreams, so that I woke gasping, soaked with sweat. How could I have been so ignorant? It had been there, before my eyes, every day.

It did not seem real to me that I could not go to her now, to have her embrace me as I cried for the loss of Temar, wipe away my tears and say something wise to make me smile and face the world with my chin held high. I did not know how to face this pain without her—the loss of Temar, the guilt at what I had done, and above all, the tangled grief of losing her. She should be the one to comfort me now; instead, she was gone, and I did not even know where her body had been buried.

In the darkness and quiet of the tent, Miriel reached out to take my hand, and we fell asleep with our fingers laced together. It was a simple comfort to hear her breathing as I woke in the morning, to know that she was still alive: not unscarred by the war, but whole, and safe. I had protected her life, at least. And when we had walked away from the Court, neither of us had had to go alone.

Indeed, we were very far from alone, for we rode with the Guard for three weeks. Gradually, as the fortress dwindled to a speck on the horizon, the rigid etiquette of the Court eased, and the guardsmen grew less stoic. They joked with us now, taught us their marching songs and laughed when we blushed, and shared a campfire with us at night. Miriel told them of Jeram's exploits: the men slipping into Ismiri camps and setting the horses free, setting fire to the tents and the battle plans, and one time setting a herd of goats loose in a camp to spook the horses and chew up the tents. Whatever they thought of the rebellion, the guardsmen laughed at the thought, and I smiled to hear that my tactics had worked.

Miriel learned to put up tents and feed horses, and I learned the finer points of cooking over an open fire, she and I laughing at the thought of the terrible cooking I had done as we made our way south, in our escape. After the sheer magnitude of the events at the Court, after the constant noise and crush, there was a solace in open sky and quiet companionship, and if we did not find an end to our grief, either of us, we had at least remembered how to smile by the time we drew close to the northern coast.

The plains of Heddred were rich land, rolling hills carpeted in thick grass and stands of trees, the fields fragrant in the summer heat. As we traveled north, it all gave way to leaden skies and rocky hills. Twenty miles from the coast, we could already smell the tang of the salt air, and the birds pecking at the fields and eying our dinner were not pigeons or hawks, but sea gulls, and they cried constantly as they wheeled overhead.

We parted from the Guard a few days out from the coast, sending them back against their insistence that they would stay with us as long as we wished. Miriel had been calm, almost content, as we said our goodbyes, but her chin trembled as she watched them go, the Conradine standard fluttering proudly in the sea breeze. She had chosen her path willingly, her eyes open, but it was one thing to choose, and another to see the guards ride away from her, the last link to her former life.

We rode for the coast in silence, making our way past fishing towns and farmsteads alike, little outposts in this harsh land, so different from our home. The people coming out of their houses to watch us, curiously: a woman in the finely-made gown of a noble, but without jewelry, without a train or a standard; a young man, or a young lass, lanky, looking around with the sharp eyes of a soldier. At their wide-eyed stares, I wrapped my hand once more over the urn, the only thing of value we seemed to carry with us. As we rode away, down the sandy outcropping at the edge of the beach, I could see them watching us, wondering who we might be, and as we faded into the mist that rolled off the ocean, I began to wonder if we would ever see them again. It felt as if we had passed out of Heddred entirely, and we were alone in some other world now.

"They'd never believe us if we told them any of it," Miriel said, and I laughed to hear that she had been thinking the same thing.

"Who you are? Where we're going? No," I agreed, and she turned to me, her little pointed chin held high, a few curls straggling loose from her braid.

"So?" she asked. "What now?" I looked to the ocean.

"We wait," I said. "Wait and see."

Epilogue

We waited for three long days, in near total silence. The beach was a windswept spit of land, smooth pebbles slick and treacherous underfoot; waves lapped at the shore, hidden by the thick mist, their sound carrying strangely. The sea seemed to be all around me, the smells of salt and seaweed heavy in the air. When the mists parted, the Isles shone in the sunlight, shimmering green and grey, a mirage that seemed to flicker in and out. When the fog rolled in, the world itself disappeared, and there was only the ocean, and the lonely crying of the gulls.

It was a good place to mourn, and Miriel and I sat together without speaking, both of us lost to memory. I thought of Roine's smile, the reddish sheen of her hair, the warmth of her arms around me. It was all I could do to remember her last words and the hatred in her eyes, but I could not leave that memory alone. I found that I grieved for Garad, who had died too young, and without the love he had sought. I grieved for Donnett, whose face I would never see again, and I even grieved, curiously, for the Duke—such a figure of legend could not be gone, surely.

What Miriel thought of, I did not know. Sometimes she cried, and sometimes she walked slowly along the beach, stooping to look at the smooth pebbles or looking up at the sky. Even in her grief, she was at ease here; she liked to walk barefoot with the waves lapping at her feet, and she slept outside, looking up at the stars.

When, on the fourth morning. we heard the scrape of a boat grounding, I motioned Miriel to stay where she was, silently, and I began to pick my way over the slick ground, peering into the mist. I stopped when the figure emerged ahead of me—a young man, perhaps twenty years old, with his dark hair drawn back from his face. He looked at me strangely, and I found myself frowning at him. He looked so familiar that I was certain I must have met him before, but I could not think where.

"Where is your companion?" he asked me, startling me with the sound of common. "In my dream, there were two of you—you, and a girl with hair as black as night."

"Who are you?" I asked, rather than answer, and he smiled, white teeth flashing in a grin. He held out his hand to me.

"I am Fidach. Come—you are to meet the Queen, both of you."

"Queen?" I asked, and he smiled once more.

"She knows you have come," he said seriously. "And she knows why, although she has not told me. Will you come with me, you and your sister?" I looked him over, unsettled. Familiar as he was, he was standing easily, no hint of a fighters' crouch, no sign of weapons concealed beneath his clothing. His gaze was open and honest, and at last I called over my shoulder, into the mist,

"Miriel." She appeared like a little ghost. In her grey gown, with her pale skin and black hair, she seemed almost a creature of the mist herself until she looked up; then the deep blue of her eyes was piercing. She, too, frowned to see Fidach, although she curtsied prettily enough to him.

"We're to meet the Queen," I told her simply, and she accepted this without comment, handing me my pack and stepping, daintily, into the little boat Fidach had drawn up on the beach. I followed her and we sat together, both staring covertly at Fidach as he shoved the boat into the water and leapt in gracefully. He cast us a curious smile, his gaze lingering on Miriel, and then he took up an oar.

The boat cut through the water almost silently, only the faintest splash coming from the paddle. Spires of rock appeared suddenly out of the mist and faded away in our wake, and more than once we saw broken masts standing forlornly, the wood rotting with age, the ship lost to the currents. On clear days, I had seen rough waves, white-capped, but where our little boat passed, the water was eerily calm. We passed a few gulls, floating contentedly on the waves, and once, a shoal of fish broke the surface in a ripple of silver. In the near silence, colors drained and muted, it was like a dream world.

We leaned against each other, lulled by the rocking of the boat, and I gave myself up to sleep. When I woke, stretching lazily, Fidach was still in the prow of the boat, his oar cutting through the water quietly, his back unbowed. I was wondering how long we had slept when I saw an island looming before us, and I shook Miriel awake at once. We watched, wide-eyed, as the shape of it grew and changed. Even cloaked in mist as it was, we could see hills and cliffs, dark stone and verdant green. As we drew closer still, we saw that our arrival was expected: there were two figures standing on the rocky beach before us.

They were not warriors, as I had expected, or even a party of dignitaries, but instead a woman and a child, standing alone on a beach quite as desolate as the one we had left. The boat ran aground with a groan, wooden timbers scraping across stone, and Fidach and I leapt out together, grabbing the prow to pull the boat clear of the waves. Miriel took my hand to steady herself as she stepped out of the boat, and then we stared uncertainly at the woman and child.

She wore a grey gown and a green cloak, a heavy necklace of gold at her throat. Her dark hair was tinted with red, I saw, and it fell past her shoulders in waves. There were lines at her eyes and the corners of her mouth, but for all that, I could not have guessed her age. She held the child by the hand, a young boy with her high brow and—my heart seized—Temar's dark, slanting eyes and high cheekbones. I cast another look at the woman and thought I saw a resemblance to the man I had loved: the shape of her mouth, the set of her jaw. She nodded at me, self-possessed, and I saw that this was the queen Fidach had spoken of.

None of them spoke, and at last I knelt on the rocks and unrolled the tiny bundle I carried with me, at last uncovering the jet urn, unmarked, stopped with wax. For a moment, I curled my fingers around it, my eyes closed, saying goodbye—then I held it out to the woman, and she let go of the child's hand and came to take it from me. Her eyes were dark with grief, and I knew that Fidach had been correct: this woman knew why we had come.

"These are the ashes of Necthan," I said, shaping my mouth around the unfamiliar name, and the woman bent her head in acknowledgement. "He wanted you to know that he kept his promise," I said simply, my throat tight with grief. "And to tell you that he died keeping my country from war." Something eased in the woman's face, a fear I had not known to look for.

"And Eral?" she asked me at length, her accent twisting the name strangely. Her gaze was fixed on the jar she held, as if she did not dare meet my eyes; the words would have been cold but for the yearning in her voice.

"Eral Celys is dead," I said, and at last she looked up at me, her brown eyes wide and stricken. I swallowed at the pain I saw there.

"You know this for certain?" she asked me, her voice low, and I nodded.

"It was I who killed him," I admitted. I did not want to say it, not to this Queen who had spoken of him with such fearful hope, but I could not let her think that it was Temar who had killed the Duke. I darted a glance at the man, at the boy, and they stared back at me wordlessly. At last, I looked back to the woman, who was gazing at with an expression I could not fathom. She looked as if she would strike me down where I stood, and yet as if there were no words she had wanted to hear more than those I had spoken.

"I did it to set Temar free," I said wretchedly. The excuse sounded feeble to my ears, but all three of them stirred at the sound of the name. "Necthan," I corrected myself. "But I knew him as Temar." The woman smiled at that, and a tear rolled down her cheek.

"He was both," she said. "Though I had not known he took that name." She saw the incomprehension on my face, and the look of anger faded. "Did he not tell you who he was?" I shook my head, wordless, and she handed the urn to the young man and came forward, drawing me away from the others. "Come with me," she said, and there was no anger in her voice.

For a time, we walked along the shore in silence, until our companions were lost in the mist. I had no words to speak—it was Miriel who should be called away, to walk with Queens and Kings, not I. But the woman seemed content in her silence, sure of her purpose. The cold water lapped up onto shore and soaked into her gown, but the woman did not seem to notice. She was tall, taller than me, and she walked not as if she owned the land, but instead as if she were a part of it.

"The people of the mainland say that these isles are legend," the Queen remarked finally. "The waters are perilous, and many who seek our shores are lost to the Gods. It is rare that any man finds his way through the rocks, but it has been known to happen." She shot me a look, her brown eyes veiled with thick lashes. "Eral was one of those men. He washed up on our shores of Priteni half-dead, and half-mad from his ordeal."

We walked, her face serene but her hand clutching at my arm. She was struggling to find words, and at last I spoke, a guess:

"You loved him."

"I did." She stopped and looked over at me, her lips pressed together. "He was...like no one I had known." She smiled faintly at the memory, and I tried to keep my face blank; I could not imagine the Duke, dour and grim, as the object of any woman's desire, but there was no denying the longing on the Queen's face. I tried to think of the intelligence in his eyes, and wondered if, once, it had been paired with wit and charm, instead of grim ambition. At my side, the Queen took a deep breath, as one steeling herself to speak an unpleasant truth.

"I found him on the beach, and we could understand enough of each other's words to speak of our lives, and our dreams. He...shone. I was young and foolish, and although my mother the Queen warned me against him, I married him in secret. Her health was failing, and I did not think I could bear to rule alone." Her eyes closed briefly. "I wanted a companion, but Eral wanted, more than anything, to prove himself. He wanted to be King—but it was not enough for him to be the King of Priteni, of our tribe. He must show us to the world, make Priteni a power to contend with your..." She searched for the name.

"Heddred," I supplied quietly, and she nodded.

"So. It is the Queen's right, to ask any one of her husband—anything he can grant her, he must. And it is his right, as well, to ask any one thing of her."

"Heddred." My mouth was dry. "He wanted you to invade." She nodded, and her eyes were bright with tears.

"I begged him not to ask it of me—we have been our own nation, sheltered from the world. We did not want to rule your country, and I did not want to send my warriors to die in a strange land, never again to see their families. But he would not bend."

"And so Temar—Necthan—" I broke off, and she nodded, white-faced.

"There is an old myth," she said, her voice barely a whisper. "Of a King who was trapped into a bargain with the Faerie Queen: she had sent him a gift, a cup of gold, and by accepting it, he had given her the power to ask somewhat of him in return. She wished to rule the mortal realms, and he would not have been able to refuse her—but for one of his warriors, a man named Temar, who swore his life to the service of the Faerie Queen if she would go back once more to her realm, and set his people free of her spells." Her mouth was trembling at the memory.

"Necthan was only a boy," she said softly, and she looked back down the beach to where the child waited. "Connor is the very image of him. So young, so proud." She blinked back tears.

"He was my little brother, and I would not have let him make the bargain if I had known—but he hid it from me. It was the priestesses who told me what he had done when he had already gone, he and Eral both. I never saw them again—and Eral never saw his son."

She smiled at my surprise, and I looked into the mist as if I could see Fidach standing there: Fidach, with his blue eyes and his wide mouth. The resemblance was unmistakable now that I knew to look for it, but with his carefree smile, Fidach hardly seemed his father's son. As if she knew what I was thinking, the Queen smiled sadly.

"I don't think I could bear to know what you knew of Eral. Fidach is much like his father, when I knew him—but he has little taste for the throne. It is Connor who will take my place when I am gone. He is my sister's son. I could never bear to take another lover, not knowing if Eral was alive or dead. I had made an oath."

I bit my lip. In those last words, at last, I had the key to Miriel. As the Queen turned and beckoned me back along the beach, I tried to find words to tell her this one fact. The Duke, ruthless, had sought power above all else—I thought. I had thought that his search for advantage knew no bounds. And yet now I saw that the Duke had shown more loyalty, in this one way, than anyone I knew.

"He was true to you," I said simply. She looked back at me, hardly believing what I had said. "He never married, even though he had a dukedom," I said awkwardly. "Miriel—my companion— she was his heir. She is his sister's daughter."

"Thank you." It was quietly spoken, and her face had gone still; she had withdrawn behind the mask of Queenship. I saw her look up at her son as we approached, taking solace in the sight of him, and then her gaze slid past him to Miriel, standing quietly at his side. As I went to Miriel, the Queen spoke.

"Where will you go now, travellers?" We looked back at her, and then at each other.

"We hadn't decided," I said, thinking of Voltur, of the eerie whistle of the wind; there was nothing for us there, any longer. There was so much of Heddred we had never seen: there were the Bone Wastes, and the Eastern mountains. We would be welcome in Mavlon, surely, or in the Norstrung Provinces, amongst the common people. But, having passed through the mists, and traveled across this stretch of sea, I could almost think that we had passed out of that world, entirely.

"Stay here." It was Connor who spoke, his voice clear and light. At his side, the Queen smiled and inclined her head. "You have done our people a great service. You would be welcome to live among us, if you wished, or to travel our land." I waited for Miriel's polite demurral, but saw her looking about herself, at the glimpses of rolling hills and clear blue sky, and saw that she, too, had realized that we had no home, no place to call our own.

She looked over at me, a question in her eyes, and I caught my breath. In all my days spent waiting, and grieving, I had not been able to touch the memories of Temar. But now the breath of the wind, the green of the land, seemed an invitation. It was a last gift. *Bring my ashes home*, he had asked me, and I thought now that he had meant for me to find a haven here. I swallowed, and nodded to Miriel.

"We would like that," she answered softly, for both of us and for the first time in days, I saw her smile, the color coming back to her face, her eyes bright. She reached out for my hand, and our fingers twined together.

"Yes," I agreed.

####

Thank you for reading the conclusion of the Light & Shadow trilogy! If you enjoyed the series, you can find more of my works online! Whether you liked the book or not, I encourage you to take a few moments to leave a review—not only will your feedback help other readers to make an informed choice, but it will help me to improve my storytelling! You can find more information about my books, including upcoming works, at my website:

http://moirakatson.com

Made in the USA
San Bernardino, CA
27 July 2016